Praise for the Freak Scene Dream Trilogy, including True Love Scars

"Michael Goldberg is comparable to Kerouac in a 21st century way, someone trying to use that language and energy and find a new way of doing it."
 MARK MORDUE, author of "Dastgah: Diary of a Head Trip"

"*True Love Scars* reads like a fever dream from the dying days of the Summer of Love. Keyed to a soundtrack of love and apocalypse, Writerman pitches headlong into a haze of drugs, sex and confusion in search of what no high can bring: his own redemption. Read it and be transformed."
 ALINA SIMONE, musician, author of "Note to Self" and "You Must Go and Win"

"So who is this protagonist anyway? Holden Caulfield meets Lord Buckley? Speaking in a crazy-assed, hell-fucked jargon, yet choosing his words so carefully it seems like his words are choosing him? And exactly what's happening here? Coming of age in the era between the Beats and the Punks? Licking the combination plate of sex, drugs and rock 'n' roll? Balancing on the tightrope between horniness and empathy? Carrying a torch along the route of Teenage Heartbreak Olympics? Revealing a threesome among guilt, blame and accountability? Tripping on the power of shared musical obsession? Naïveté serving as a gradual learning experience morphing into sophistication, layer by layer. Caught between Dylan's suggestion, 'Take what you have gathered from coincidence,' and Freud's observation, 'Being entirely honest with oneself is a good exercise.' Excuse me, what was the question again?"
 PAUL KRASSNER, author of "Confessions of a Raving, Unconfined Nut: Misadventures in the Counterculture"

"There never was a Seventies. They never existed. You could, however, construct a reasonably functional Seventies love-doll, inflating it (you guessed right) with canned or frozen Sixties sexual effluvium. Fill it fat, saggy or shapeless—your call. CAREFUL: there will be some broken glass and flammable scum. Shards of chthonic Romance—whew—as radioactive as Godzilla. Only the BOLD need apply. Whoops—beware!—Mr. Goldberg has been there first, and 'had' her first. Reader-side litrachoor is often a matter of 2nd in line. Bon appétit!"
  RICHARD MELTZER, author of "Tropic of Nipples" and "17 Insects Can Die in Your Heart"

"Michael's written quite a series of novels about the early Seventies and the death of the Sixties and the rock 'n' roll dream. I think they're very good. I've never seen a novel talk about Feminism and the Seventies like his Freak Scene Dream Trilogy does. Plus he's a total rock 'n' roll geek. He knows everything about everybody. Believe me, every detail from Captain Beefheart to the New York Dolls. Bob Dylan is God. And a straight guy with a raging sexual agenda searching for his 'Visions of Johanna chick.' It's a terrific read."
  TOM SPANBAUER, author of "Faraway Places," "Now Is the Hour" and "I Loved You More"

"Michael Goldberg reminds us of the difficulties of remaining true to our own visions amidst the powerful exigencies of young adulthood. He paints crazy intimate portraits of the excesses and eccentricities of the sexual revolution. And he speaks to us in the voice and language of the brave microculture of his youth. In this, he opens a door to the rough adolescence of our own 'grown up' disillusioned macroculture. All the dreams and wishes and bright energy buried therein is still brawling for a release. Our inner teenager still wonders what the fuck we think we are doing. To hear a voice from this realm is a blessing. Goldberg makes of himself a channel from that forbidden country. Through his recounting, we remember how we learned to love, how we learned to listen, and how we learned to do whatever it is we do best."
  JOLIE HOLLAND, recording artist, whose albums include *Catalpa*, *Escondida* and *The Living and the Dead*

TRUE LOVE SCARS

The First of the
Freak Scene Dream Trilogy

a novel by
Michael Goldberg

Neumu Press
P.O. Box 6740
Albany, CA 94706
insider1@neumu.net
www.truelovescars.com

ISBN: 978-0-9903983-0-1

To my beautiful wife Leslie,
who makes every day a
Days of the Crazy-Wild.

TRUE LOVE
SCARS

How can I explain?
Oh, it's so hard to get on,
And these visions of Johanna,
they kept me up past the dawn.
   — BOB DYLAN, "Visions of Johanna"

ONE

1. LORD JIM

THE DAY I MEET Lord Jim is the day I begin to remember who I am. The who-I-am I was before Sweet Sarah told me it was over. Writerman and Sweet Sarah, over, then and forever.

That day I meet Lord Jim, that was the day.

Crazy-beautiful perfect, that day. Crazy-beautiful perfect, sun overhead, bright yellow fireball floats in the sky. Crisp pale turquoise sky, crisp white cloud wisps float across pale turquoise sky, and I walk, and I walk, and I walk.

I walk down the dirt path, the meadow spreading out to my right turned a luminous dark green from first fall rains, crunch of dirt and pine needles and tree leaves beneath my Keith Richards snakeskin boots, and rising up, rising on my left, rising, between the path and the road, crazy-beautiful coast redwoods and Douglas firs and coast live oaks, all the crazy-beautiful wild nature, the glory, the glory, almost enough to make me believe in a crazy-beautiful wild nature God, all the glory, only I'm absolute-positive-almost-for-certain there isn't. God. No God. No God stand by while a freakster bro crash and burn how I did. How I would.

Across the meadow two deer trot fast and gone baby gone, gone lost in the trees. And that's the crazy-wild nature brought me here, and the innocence, the innocence, man, try to get some of it back, the innocence I lost when I betrayed my Visions of Johanna chick, you know, Sweet Sarah. Study amidst the forest, beneath the sky, on the soft dirt and flat needles, my back against the tree trunk, one of those towering sky high redwoods, read Faulkner or Hemingway or Joyce. Fuck yeah, read the Big Men. And try to remember who I am.

A wind comes up off the Pacific. I can't see the ocean as I walk but I know it's there in the distance, down the hill, University-built-on hill, down past Liquor King and down some more, past the Raven's Woods Mansion, past the far side of downtown, what everyone calls Loserville, the pawn shops and pay-by-the-hour hotels and the porn theater, and further out, past the Boardwalk and Giant Dipper and the Great Ferris Wheel. On a day like this I know it's shimmering beneath the bright bright sun. Forever Infinite Pacific.

Yeah, baby.

Sometimes I figure that wind comes down the coast from far as Canada, down past Point Reyes and San Francisco and Half Moon Bay on down to our scene. Other times I figure maybe it blows up from L.A., up past Big Sur and Esalen with the spirit of Kerouac and Ferlinghetti and Henry Miller. Probably isn't true, but it's what I thought. You know, when all this gone down.

Walk onto the Arts College quad, faint wind in my hair, smell of salt water and the redwoods, and stop at one side of the cobblestone courtyard, my dorm towering behind me. Stand there, look around, not a soul. No one. Don't matter, 'cause if there been a one. A someone. I don't know 'em.

I'm back at The University. Nineteen, yeah. Supposed to be my chance to start over. After Sweet Sarah, and the total bust of freshman year. Well forget about it. Not so easy to get a new life going. Me, I drove the gotaway car. Gotaway from home, and Sweet Sarah, and my friends. Left my past for the promise of a new life. The New Trip.

And as I stand there, out in front of me stretches my future, and if my future is gonna amount to anything, I gotta recover the elusive of who-I-am. 'Cause the sad-ass truth of it, when I lost Sweet Sarah, I didn't only lose my Visions of Johanna chick. I lost the sense of self I had when she was my old lady. So easy to misunderstand. I thought the last freakster bro standing, guns a-blaze, crazy-wild freakster bro, was me. Well it was a reflection. And when Sweet Sarah was gone, the mirror was gone.

So lost, man, so lost.

Let me stop a minute, we'll pause from the scene I'm laying down so I can speak to you. That year, 1972, I was starting over at The University. This was to be a new beginning, and first and foremost I had to find my Visions of Johanna – and fall in love all over again. So let me explain.

Ahab got the whale, which is a huge symbol for some unreachable mammoth goal we yearn for, and Columbus gotta prove the world's not flat, which is mammoth too, and he runs right into America, and if that's not mammoth, nothing is. And Gatsby got Daisy, who's pretty much the same deal as the whale and America. No disrespect to Daisy, but she's a symbol too. Well daunting as any of those three might be are my trials regards my Visions of Johanna. I needed a chick bad that fall day. And I'm not talking about getting laid. This was way deeper. I was searching for the key to the rest of my life. If only I could find my Visions of Johanna chick, she'd do for me what Sweet Sarah once did, mirror back to me who I am, and once again I would stand tall. Once again I would be the last freakster bro standing, guns a-blaze.

Yeah, I was so starry-eyes back then.

The quad's empty. Huge expanse of cobblestones. New old cobblestones. As if you could throw money at new construction and make an old campus. Two dorm buildings. Well nothing old regards *them*. Sheer flat cement walls broken up by rows of glass windows. Three stories high. Each dorm shaped same as the letter "u." One behind me, with some of the meadow behind it, my new home.

Well I can't go back to that dorm room. Lie on my bed alone. Feel the ache of my scars. My two scars. Goddamn sophomore year. Gonna be the same lonesome deal. How it was before Sweet Sarah, and how it been ever since. And right then, as I'm about to write off the New Trip as No Trip, I hear him.

And everything changes.

Lord Jim, and he makes his grand entrance. Lord Jim being Lord Jim. Man, *Thee* Freakster Bro lets you know he arrived. Don't go gentle into that good night, or however Dylan Thomas wrote it.

Thee Freakster Bro.

Me and my buddy back home, Rock 'n' Roll Frankie, and even my loser friend Big Man Bobby, we're all freakster bros, but Lord Jim, he's *Thee* Freakster Bro. Just the way it is, and nothing more to say about it. Only when I hear that voice in the quad I haven't met him yet. He isn't *Thee* Freakster Bro. Isn't Lord Jim either. He don't get that name until after he falls for Jaded, and neither of us have met that chick. Yet.

Too loud too too loud voice. Crazy-ass freakster bro walks fast across the quad, yells more than sings. Out of tune missing the melody, but still.

And from his mouth comes a line from "Honky Tonk Women," the one about screwing a divorcée in New York.

Thee Freakster Bro having himself the best of times total overwhelming oblivious, he's maybe halfway between one side of the quad and the other, bunch of smoke from his mouth, hand holding the cigarette drops to his side, and I can't keep away a smile. Hear the Yo-ho-ho-and-a-bottle-of-rum exuberance in his voice, and yeah, I want some.

I want some too.

And I shout, "Why'd you have to go all the way to New Yawk? Haven't you heard of 'California Girls,' man?"

He stops, looks around. Oh man, now what?

He's one scruffed-out freak, tall as me but his body a pudge. Sees me, and he's walkin' this way, my way, aiming for where I stand. His bird's nest hair outta control, mirrored shades set on a bulbous-wide nose, ragged cut-offs, and grody leather sandals long past done. His stained orange t-shirt—*Black Sabbath* in jagged lightning bolts.

Black Sabbath!? Oh come on, man. Dylan, sure. Lennon, of course. Jagger, yeah. But hellfuck Black Sabbath?

Mid-day, and no one but us two in the quad. Up above

somewhere, someone shuts their window. Not everyone digs a freakster bro shouting out "Honky Tonk Women" loud as they can shout it. Closer he gets, and funky he is, same as those hairy cats in The Mothers of Invention.

Ghost of 'lectricity. Yeah, that's what I call it. When I'm gone baby gone. My body still standing there but the present vanishes. A memory. Or a vision. What could happen or would happen or never happen. Ghost of 'lectricity.

    This time a memory, 1967, Summer of Love summer, my shitty suburban bedroom. Black and purple album cover; The Mothers' *Freak Out!* And the ugly men on that cover sure aren't pretty freaks. Black vinyl spins on my crappy Zenith stereo. "Hungry Freaks, Daddy" and "Who Are the Brain Police?" and the hard sarcasm of Zappa's Watts riot blues, "Trouble Every Day," and I haven't heard of the Watts riot. Still a kid trying to figure it out, what the ugly men on that *Freak Out!* album got to say. *Trouble. Every. Day.*

    I got that one nailed. I know trouble.

Another memory, 1971, my dark bedroom, another day I play The Mothers. I'm 17, stoned and skinny-ass naked and losing my mind. Mattress on the floor, dirty clothes and unsleeved records and too many magazines and the books. Goddamn obstacle course to get from the door to my mattress. Sweet Sarah so young lies there. So young pink tits, so young and fresh and perfect and no one's touched her except me. I was her first and she was mine. A beginning, and an end. Fuck her as that crude "Mud Shark" song plays. And no joy. No Forever Infinite Ecstatic. Just wham-bam-thank-you-ma'am. Oh God-who-don't-exist, what have I done. *What have I done.* And my conscience gonna explode.

I stand there in the quad shaking, man. Try to shake away the ghost of 'lectricity. I don't want nothing to do with the darkness. Only it won't. Shake away. Some things you can't never shake away.

Lord Jim takes a slow drag, head back, smoke rings float, and the faint breeze stretches them same as a Dali clock, melting into the pale turquoise.

"Got something to say to me, old sport?"

Old sport? What's that about? Understand it's one of Lord Jim's affectations. Same as how he sometimes speaks in an affected formal manner and the deal with his cigarette, holds it between his thumb and index so it juts out, and the smoke rings, and there's the cane, only I don't know any of it, not that day.

And he don't have the cane. Yet.

We exchange first words, and I let it pass. Freakster bro wants to cop language off Gatsby, let the freakster bro cop away. Nothing to do with me, and anyway, that's when I get a clue. Under his right arm he's carrying a mess of albums.

"What are you into, man?" I say.

"Got the new Sabbath," he says. "I'm reviewing it."

There's two freakster bros at The University who write record reviews for *The Paper*. There's me, and a guy I haven't met. Only I guess I have. *Old sport*. Yeah, let's see how hip to shit *Thee* Freakster Bro is.

"Yair," I say.

"Faulkner," Lord Jim says. "Right on, brother," and maybe we're tuned to the same station. We'll see. So I lay some language from Kerouac on him, something Dean Moriarty said.

"Well now—ah—ahem—yes, of course," I say.

Lord Jim takes off his shades, sticks 'em in the bird's nest so they sit on his head, and his bloodshot reefer eyes got the freakster bro dotted-lines to my eyes.

The freakster bro dotted-lines eyes.

From then on it's a way of him looking at me and me looking at him. I mean there were ways I used to look into Sweet Sarah's eyes, ways I'd look into Rock 'n' Roll Frankie's eyes, and later, Beat-Chick Elise's eyes, but nothing same as that freakster bro dotted-lines eyes look. It's a look where me and him stone cold connect. The look says we're on the same page. Although not always. Sometimes it says, *hold on bro, even if you don't get it, soon enough you will. Hear me out, and dig the authentic real of what I say.* Dotted-lines eyes, flexible to the extreme. And yeah, he knew Kerouac, didn't say a word, but yeah, *yeah.*

"Costello, man," I say. "James Costello, right?"

His weight on his left leg, then his right, back and forth, left, right, left, right.

"It's Jim," he says. "How'd you know?"

Gets his mirrored shades back on, and looking into 'em I see me twice reflected. Gaunt angular face, Dad's big boney Jewish nose, high forehead and my own crazy-wild curly hair, only mine's parted in the middle, Lennon-style, and I got the round wire-frame Lennon specs. Wanted so bad to look same as Dylan, *Highway 61 Revisited,* which I don't, but I'll take Lennon, how he looks in that Avedon photo, *The White Album,* and if you squint, I kinda do.

Something about me, let me pull you aside. That September day, first day sophomore year, skinny-ass freakster bro, 6 feet tall weigh 146 pounds. Black cowboy shirt with the white pearl snap buttons, and the threadbare bellbottom jeans, and the *Keith Richards snakeskin boots.* Righteous, those boots. Same kinda boots Keith wore during the '69 tour, and Altamont, and at Muscle Shoals recording "Wild Horses."

But all that's the surface of the surface. You could see the truth in my face if you looked close, when I didn't have that phony-ass grin going, the one I flashed at a freakster bro or chick in hopes they'd tell me everything was OK. When my lips were closed and I was the serious deal, and the way I held myself, stood tall, head up, yeah even at 19 I'd experienced the heavy shit.

A few things might help. Kid years I did the competitive swimmer deal, won a lot of races, and if you don't believe, well my mom still got the trophies. She could show you. Has my Eagle Scout medal too, framed, on her dresser. So she'd remember. Before. When things were groovy and I was her do-no-wrong golden boy. Before I go weird on her. Before my freak-out. Just trying to clue you in.

Teenage years I was cool. Me and Sweet Sarah. Fifteen with a chick same as that. Crazy-beautiful virgin chick. And she let me touch her. My hand on her tit, my mouth on her lipstick-free lips.

Just trying to clue you in.

Jerry Garcia.

Now I got your attention. Me and Big Man Bobby, we're 16, walking along the side of the road toward Polanski's dad's mansion in Tiburon. OK, Polanski is really Rodney. I call Rodney Polanski 'cause he's so into the young chicks. But anyway. Jerry Garcia at the top of the driveway, and it was me, not Bobby, who talked him into it. An interview. For our fanzine.

Yeah, I know. Jerry Garcia.

And more. Maybe you wonder about how I speak. Middle-class freakster bro same as me. Starts the day I go to Village Music and ask John Goddard, he's the owner, why "Hi Di Ho" is printed on his Village Music bags. He tells me about the hipster slang of the jazzbos, and the way blues men talk. I mean already I hear Jagger sing how he can't get *no* satisfaction, and that's not what they teach in school. And Jagger's a rock star, and those English teachers are loser chumps. And what about Dylan? He's a middle-class Jew no different than me and he talks like an Okie. And I read Salinger, and Holden sure don't talk same as Mom and Dad, read Kerouac, and that blows it wide open.

Well Lord Jim looks kinda same as William Blake, if Blake were 19 and had crazy bird's nest hair and a thick brown mustache and a wild-ass matted beard and dressed same as a beach bum into Black Sabbath.

"You write for *The Paper*," I say.

Smells of weed, Lord Jim, barely 1 p.m., already he smells of weed.

"Me too," I say.

Heard me, Lord Jim did. Me, a freakster bro who takes him serious as a writer, and he stops the back forth, stands tall.

That's what happens when you acknowledge a person for who they are. Give them respect. If we all did that, this world would be a total different deal.

"You read my shit?"

"Dug the Bowie review," I say. "You write kinda same as Meltzer."

Yeah we're on the same page. The Stones. Faulkner. Kerouac.

"Beautiful," Lord Jim says.

And Meltzer.

You know Meltzer, right? R. Meltzer, who wrote "The Aesthetics of Rock." Everyone says it's brilliant and the best, but no one can get through it. I mean anyone writing music reviews got it lying around with a bookmark at page 6. Lester copped his whole trip off the cat. Meltzer wrote the hippest reviews in *Creem*, and in the early days he wrote for *Crawdaddy* and *Fusion* and *Rock*, all the music mags, but the far-out grooviest trip of his scene, he writes lyrics for the Blue Öyster Cult. "Harvester of Eyes," which has to be the best song title ever, right?, and "Stairway to the Stars" and there's others.

Meltzer's not same as all the other wannabe rock stars doing the rock critic deal as a poor substitute. No man, what the Blue Öyster Cult put on record, Meltzer's part of the trip. His lyrics speak in tongues. "Stairway to the Stars," written from the point of view of a rock star, and still to this day I dig it the most.

You can drive my motorcar, it's insured to thirty thou, kill them all if you wish.

You know when someone tells you something, and it's not funny or meaningful or any of that, and they say, well, I guess you had to be there. That Blue Öyster Cult lyric, yeah, well, I guess you had to be there.

Lord Jim takes a hit of his Pall Mall, and that's the first time cigarette smoke smells groovy.

"I'm gonna write an opus on *Black Sabbath Vol. 4*," he says.

"I'm not into Sabbath," I say. "But I'll dig to read it."

"Maybe you'll get to. If it gets past that bastard Roth's dreaded red pen."

"You mean King Editor?" I say, and we get a laugh outta that one.

Larry Roth, editor of *The Paper*. Already I left a review of *Clear Spot* at his office, you know, the Beefheart album. You're hip to Captain Beefheart, right? Well if not, I'll clue you in. Later.

"I'm Michael, Michael Stein," I say. "But people call me Writerman. I reviewed the *Pet Sounds* reissue."

Pet Sounds. Brian Wilson's "Les Demoiselles d'Avignon," his "Tender Is the Night," his "Citizen Kane." That record was The End. The Beach Boys never made another album can touch *Pet Sounds*. All that acid put Brian out of commission. If the Beach Boys is a person, that person is brain dead.

All the heaviest critics reviewed *Pet Sounds* in '66. Everything that can be said been said when I was 13. Greil Marcus finds all that's romantic and lost in *Pet Sounds*, an America that might have been. Robert Christgau, New York tough guy, compares it to *Aftermath*, grudgingly gives *Pet Sounds* the one up. Ellen Willis with her post-Feminist deconstruction of *Pet Sounds'* pre-Feminist sensibility. Cosmic tripster Paul Williams gone off on it as "a metaphor for the rise and fall of a youth culture in flux." The Sausalito Cowboy, man, such an innovator back then, wrote a short story about Brian's secret life. For his review. *A short story*. And Meltzer, contrary as ever, dismisses it as "the unholy cluster fuck of sentimentality, melodrama and the 101 Strings Orchestra, in other words, a total piece of shit." He said anyone with a brain would get more out of letting the needle grind away on the turntable platter sans rubber mat, volume jacked full-bore to 10. I dig Meltzer the most.

Lord Jim sings a line from "Caroline, No," my favorite song on *Pet Sounds*. His voice soft, tries to hit a high octave, mimics Brian. Sings that heartbreaking line where he wonders what happened to her long hair, and to the girl he used to know.

And that song captures so perfect when it was over, when me and Sweet Sarah can't make it no more. Could have cried, only I never cry—that's something you oughta know about me —well, pretty much never. You know the scene in "Breakfast at Tiffany's," when it's raining and Holly leaves Cat in the alley? Every time that movie plays late night on the TV, and it gets to that scene, I'm bawling, man.

Lord Jim tells me he read my review. "Beautiful," he says, and sings another melancholy line.

Yeah well back then so many songs remind me. Of her.

Ghost of 'lectricity. Spring, 1971, Sweet Sarah in my room buttoning her white cotton blouse, turning away, gone. Her luminous auburn hair hanging slightly past her shoulders, the soft silky hair I would never run my fingers through again. It was after she'd cut my hair, my crazy-wild freakster bro brown hair, that I betrayed her, and she lost faith. In me. In life. Everything gone wrong. Black. The crushed souls.

Lord Jim sings Brian Wilson's sad words, and my stained memory of Sweet Sarah, my guilt and regret, all that in seconds, and it's over, and me and him standing in the Arts College quad, bright bright fireball sun up high.

"Fuckin' *chicks*," I say.

"*Fuckin'* chicks," Lord Jim says.

We give each other the dotted-lines eyes, and we laugh, in on the joke, not even sure what the joke is, and we're two freakster bros, bros-in-arms, man, even if we don't know that either.

Snap of the fingers, Lord Jim. Cool cat speaking hipster rhythm. Like "Hey," pause, big emphasis, "bartender." Now *he's* testing *me*, and I don't get it. Freakster bro grins, shifts his weight again. Man, I don't know. *Hey, bartender?* I give him the sage nod. Of course I understand. Yeah, sure.

"Got this collection of jump blues," Lord Jim says. "Beautiful thing, old sport."

Snaps his fingers again, and his whole body snaps to the rhythm.

"Gotta hear that song!" freakster bro says. "It'll TRIP. YOU.

OUT."

And he looks over, quizzical, and what's that look like? The look of mixed-up confusion, look of uncertainty, look of what's-going-on-here? He tenses his forehead, head tilted to one side and his face kinda weird and fucked-up, his nose wrinkled, or one eye partial closed, and the mouth open, awkward. Some of those facial quirks, maybe all of them, or maybe others too. Quizzical, how Lord Jim looks at me.

"Or you heard it already?"

"Heard what?"

"The *song*, old sport," he says. "The *song*."

"What song?"

"'Hey, Bartender.'"

"Oh, yeah, well, no."

Hesitation, and Lord Jim don't look same as a freakster bro at all. And that was it.

Un moment decisif.

There's always a decisive moment. Always. First I hear of it is when I read about Henri Cartier-Bresson. The photographer. You know him, right? Yeah, same as you know Meltzer. And Beefheart. What Cartier-Bresson said was photography gets down to one thing. Click the shutter at the right moment. *Un moment decisif.* When everything comes together in the frame. I figured it was Cartier-Bresson's idea for the longest time, and his language: *un moment decisif.* I mean it's his trademark. Only it's not his idea. Yeah, every artist is a thief, what Picasso said. Trust me. Cartier-Bresson got his *big* idea from Cardinal de Retz.

Rien dans ce monde n'a son instant décisif, de Retz wrote about 300 years before Cartier-Bresson shows up on the scene. Yeah well, if you don't speak French, too bad. You're out of luck. Go buy a French-English dictionary. Just kidding. I mean I don't even know French. Anyway, what Cardinal de Retz wrote: *There is nothing in this world that does not have a decisive moment.*

For me and Lord Jim, the moment has arrived. When time waits for no one, and you gotta make a choice. Take the first drink, or leave the bottle on the shelf. Pull her to you, or say goodnight. In, or out. Same as Lord Jim. What he said. That he wants to play "Hey, Bartender." For me. Yeah, Lord Jim's made his decision. He's *in*. Same as Lord Jim, man. *Un moment decisif.* And what happens in the moment?

"Uh, I could play it for you," Lord Jim says. "That is, if you were interested."

The moment. Friends for life, or we both walk away. And then, 'cause Lord Jim can't help himself. "You *got* to hear it!"

I'm not sure, and he knows. That melancholy deal again, as if my hesitation triggers in him memories being the odd guy out. And how desperate am I? How bad do I need a freakster bro? Act out of desperation, and be doomed. The moment. It has arrived. In, or out? I have to make a decision.

Un moment decisif.

Fuck it. And if I'm deciding when to click the shutter, waiting to get Lord Jim just right in the frame, well I click it. I'm *in*.

"Yeah, sure man," I say. "Let's go."

"Beautiful," he says, and the moment begins to stretch, 'cause that's what happens. When you say yeah. And now we're both in the moment, me and Lord Jim, and we'll find out if we're right, if there is something here, some kinda connection. And I hear the blue melody of "Caroline, No." Again.

Ghost of 'lectricity. Early spring, 1970. Me and Sweet Sarah going too far in her upstairs bedroom, and the wind, wild-ass wild, shaking the leaves of the huge oak outside her windows, and one limb cracks, and it dangles above the backyard same as some tree creature's broken arm, and I should've known. The wild-ass wild wind. The crack of the branch. The tree creature's broken arm. That was the day Sweet Sarah got pregnant, and we didn't even fuck.

I stand there jerking my head back forth as if I can shake that shit away, and has Lord Jim noticed? No man, he's sucked into his own internal. He adjusts his shades tries to be the cool scene.

"You know my serious writing, old sport?" he says. "Well, I'm a *poet*."

I laugh 'cause in those days everyone was a poet. I mean there was a time I thought I was a poet, and I'm not no poet. Turns out Lord Jim is an authentic real poet, only he don't know it that day. He says he's a poet, but in his heart he don't know. And what do I know, man, freakster bro I meet in the quad says he's a poet. Yeah, right.

"You mean same as Ferlinghetti?" I say. "And Ginsberg and e. e. cummings?"

We walk toward the north entrance of the West dorm, me and him, dig on the scene of no longer being alone.

"Post-Beat," Lord Jim says.

"Stream of conscious?" I say.

Man, those days, sometimes we don't know what the fuck we're talking about.

I live in the West dorm too, on the third floor, Penthouse West they call it. Lord Jim's room is on the second floor, Middle Earth, and whereas I'm on the south wing of Penthouse West, Lord Jim is on the north wing of Middle Earth. He bounces up the stairs giddy. Gotta hustle to keep up.

"You shootin' to make a living as a rock critic?" I say. "When you graduate?"

"You're pulling my leg, right?" he says. "Writing reviews is a pastime. Like Updike. A lark. Something to keep the muscles in shape between books. Face up to the truth, old sport. Rock critics are parasites living on the backs of the musicians. Sucking their blood and writing about how it tastes. To be a writer you have to create something new. Something of your own. Bleed your own truth."

Well that was the wake-up, the Buddhist deal, *Bodhi*, 'cause I'd never thought about it that way before but soon as he says it I know it's the authentic real.

"I got a novel going," I say. "I toss King Editor the occasional review but it's not *my* main trip either. Yeah, a lark."

Well that's a lie. I don't got no novel. And I never thought of my reviews as any lark. But that's gonna change. If I'm gonna be a real writer, I gotta take it serious. A novel. The New Trip.

"So, old sport, Mike or Michael?"

"Michael! Goddamn parents call me Mike. I hate it."

"Well, OK then, Michael it is."

"Or call me Writerman."

Ghost of 'lectricity. Fall, 1967. I'd been up all night reading "The Great Gatsby," and next day at the break, this is freshman year at Tam High, I see my good buddy Big Man Bobby, we were real tight back then, sitting on the steps of the amphitheater, back of the school where we always hung out. Where everyone went to get stoned or cop a smoke. Tell him I got my destiny all figured.

"Gonna be a writer, man," I say.

"Writerman?" Big Man Bobby says, and he laughs that truncated smirk laugh he does, almost a cough but it's a laugh. "Is that like Batman or Superman? Writerman can speed-write a book in a single day? Leap tall pencil sharpeners in a single bound?"

"No, man, I'm gonna be a *writer*. This is important."

After that it stuck, so I'm Writerman. Then and forever.

Lord Jim pauses on the outside dorm stairs, and will he cede that to me? It's heavy if you're the freakster bro everyone calls Writerman, 'cause, well, they start to think of you as The Writer. Maybe Lord Jim don't wanna think of me as The Writer. Well it don't matter if he does or he don't.

"Writerman," Lord Jim says. "Well, OK then."

2. HEY BARTENDER

I MIGHT AS WELL tell you right now, it's a Days of the Crazy-Wild day for sure, that day I meet Lord Jim. A day when something happens. A day you point to later and say, *that was the day*. A day you see or feel or do the alive of being alive. Bob Dylan's life, every day. It got to be that way. And Jean-Luc Godard. Every day, man. I made a pledge when me and Sweet Sarah got together. Every day on out gonna be a Days of the Crazy-Wild. Yeah, well, I didn't know some would be the days I betrayed her. Or the day she closed the door on me for the last time. But that's supposed to be behind me now, and I'm trying to focus on my new scene, you know, the New Trip.

Heavy glass ashtray full of Pall Mall butts and roaches and ash on Lord Jim's desk next to the *Magical Mystery Tour* double-fold folded open, seeds and stems along the spine. And a cardboard shoebox. Doper's room. Chaotic mess of rock mags on the rug between the end of the bed and the desk. Open *Penthouse* face down on the bed, black sheet partial off the mattress, and a wool blanket balled up.

Lord Jim only been here couple days same as me. Said his mom drove him up from L. A. Saturday. Today it's Monday, and how many cigarettes and doobies can a freakster bro smoke in three days? Must be lot of shit this freakster bro wants to forget.

Where to sit? He already got his butt seated, man he's hyped, rolls his chair up to his desk across a copy of *Creem*, an old one, Black Sabbath on the cover. Picks it up, Lord Jim does, cover torn some, stares down at it as if staring can undo the tear.

So what if he digs Sabbath. Plenty sounds we both dig. Both dig *Pet Sounds*. Both into Bowie. And didn't he review *Electric Warrior*? So both into T. Rex. Probably digs Mott the Hoople if he digs Bowie. If he digs T. Rex.

Tosses the mag at the bed, misses, and it's back on the rug. There's a folding chair folded open, pile of books on it. Where am I to sit? Lord Jim reaches for the shoebox. *Thee* Freakster Bro flyin' high and high flyin'. See it, smell it, know it.

"Let's get stoned, Writerman."

Un moment decisif.

Freakster bro removes the lid; the shoebox is the doper box. He gets Zig-Zags out, and a baggie. "First Aid Kit," he says.

Shoebox. Doper box. First Aid Kit. He's always got a baggie of weed, a metal cough drop box with hits of blotter, and usually some hash wrapped in tin foil. Got Zig-Zags and a roach clip and a hash pipe too. And a red plastic Cricket lighter.

"*First* thing you do," he says, "if you need *aid* to get high, get hold of the *kit*."

I haven't smoked weed since my freak-out, over a year ago, and if weed was a person, weed was the fall guy. For me betraying Sweet Sarah. For my freak-out. For all the troubles I cause my folks, and the three weeks in the loony bin. Yeah, it was the weed. Sure it was. Me, and Mom and Dad, and the shrink—we can all agree on that. The lie is a story we tell again and again.

Un moment decisif.

In, or out. Yeah, and my choice gonna determine if me and Lord Jim are on our way to solid freakster bro-hood, or already spinning off the track.

Nowhere for me to sit, nowhere.

"This weed," Lord Jim says. "Beautiful."

He's got Meltzer's "The Aesthetics of Rock" on the desk, and has he made it past page 6? Another thing on his desk. Most important object in his room. A Royal Quiet Deluxe. Fuck, told him I'm gonna write a novel, and he got the same typewriter Hemingway used to write "The Sun Also Rises." The shit Smith Corona I got sucks.

None of the Big Men used a goddamn Smith Corona.

In, or out? Freakster bro shifts the pile of books, top volume a collection of e. e. cummings poems, off the chair to the floor.

"OK, here you go."

I sit, and pick up that ripped-cover copy of *Creem*. Sausalito Cowboy got a review in there. I know the Sausalito Cowboy. Can almost call him a friend. I've got the mag folded back so Lord Jim can see the Sausalito Cowboy's review of *Hot Licks, Cold Steel & Truckers' Favorites*, and soon as he sees it, he sings a line from Cody's send-up of a loser's lament, "Down to Seeds and Stems Again Blues." He pours the weed from the baggie onto the *Magical Mystery Tour* cover.

"You ever read the Sausalito Cowboy, man?" I say. "'Cause I know him."

Soon as I said it, wish I hadn't. That's what Polanski always does, Polanski whose dad is the movie biz big shot, I mean I never did find out what exactly he did, but he knew everyone. Movie stars, artists, writers, rock stars. He knows Jerry, knows Grace, fuck, I think Jagger's at their place when the Stones play Oakland in '69, the tour that ends with Altamont. Polanski brags about all the stars he's met. As if him meeting 'em 'cause of his dad makes him special. Well it's different, what I said. I got to know the Sausalito Cowboy on my own, no help from my dad, but then the Sausalito Cowboy isn't a rock star, he's a rock critic. There's a difference. I don't understand that back then.

"Buckaroo, too," I say. "You know, his byline is Brandon Williams. Hang with those guys all the time. Buy promos off 'em. They're cool."

Lord Jim separates out the seeds and stems, he's got the intense focus on the folded out double-fold. I'm talkin' nervous talk kinda talk. Freakster bro has a rolling paper between his thumb and index. "You know the Sausalito Cowboy?"

"What I told you, man," I say. "They ask me what I think of

bands. They're getting old, want my opinion."

Freakster bro gets the rolling paper flat on the album jacket, a pinch of weed, sprinkles it on the paper, another pinch and another 'til he got enough for a righteous number. Rolls it tight, holds it to his lips, licks along the paper edge and smooths it against the joint.

Sticks an end in his mouth to wet it, twists that end and a repeat for the other one, and that number sticks out of his mouth ready for blast off. Red plastic Cricket lighter, blue-gold flame, that gasoline kinda smell of lighter fluid, and he takes a toke, fills his mouth, lets it fuck him up, keeps it in 'til he gotta breathe. He gulps for air, and holds out the number. I haven't been stoned for two years. The shit makes me crazy. The story we all agree on.

Ghost of 'lectricity. Early summer of 1971, bootleg of Dylan's Royal Albert Hall concert blasts through the crap suburban house I live in my whole fucked-up life. All 17 years. No shirt, bare-chest and so skinny you woulda seen my ribs if you been there. No one there. Just me, black top hat, hair cut short. I've already done that John and Yoko trip, cut off all my hair. And betrayed Sweet Sarah. She's gone baby gone. No shirt, black top hat, and the black Levi bellbottoms. Chaos in my brain overwhelming. Smoke that shitty weed Polanski sells me, cheap electric guitar hangs from my neck. I wanna be Dylan so bad and my mind exploding, shards of electricity falling around me. Flash and burn. I try to jam along but I don't know the chords. Scream with Dylan, *for I know that you know that I know that you know, something is tearing up your mind.* I wanna break free so bad. From this house. From my parents. From my high school. *Something is tearing up your mind.* And I'm screaming, man, screaming for the truth. Wanna be Dylan so so bad but I'm not him. And I'm never gonna be him. And there's Mom in the doorway, face tired same as she gives up, and Dad, yelling at me my whole fucked-up life, yells at me one more time. Same as he always does, same as he always gonna do. "Can't you see what you're doing to your mother, Mike? Why? Why do you have to do this to us?!" Yeah, and why? Hell if I know.

There in Lord Jim's room I squeeze my eyes, shake my head.
Whole body shivers same as a junkie shake, only I'm not a
junkie. Not that day. Not that year. Guys with nail guns going at
my skull from the inside.
     "You OK, old sport? Bad trip?"
     "Yeah, yeah," I say. "No, I mean it's nothin'. Play the song,
man."

Ghost of 'lectricity. December of 1967, Tam High. First time I
get stoned, it's because of a girl. We're in the back row, Social
Studies, and it's the last day before Christmas vacation. I'm 14,
high school freshman.
"Give me your hand," Jenny says.
     "Why?"
     "Come on, Michael!"
     Jenny looks kinda Pattie Boyd, you know, George Harrison's
wife. Jenny wears flowered dresses and oval wire-rim specs with
lavender-tint lenses. Jenny don't really look same as Pattie Boyd,
Jenny being 14, Pattie Boyd being 24. It'd be so groovy to have a
chick same as George Harrison's chick. All that year I had a
crush on Jenny. I'm not Jenny's type; I'm too square for her. My
hair taking forever to grow, and those four-eyes glasses with
thick black rectangular plastic frames. For squares for sure those
glasses. Jenny sits on the lawn in front of the school with her
girlfriends at lunch, except when she hangs in the back parking
lot with the greasers. Black leather motorcycle jackets and black
engineer boots, and hot black asphalt. I see her in this one old
guy's black hot-rodded '58 Chevy burn rubber out of there,
going places I've never even read about.
     Jenny takes my hand and places a doobie in it, and a book
of matches too.
     "This'll get you crazy-wild," she says. "It's gonna
psychedelicize you."
     I put the number and the matches in my shirt pocket.
     "What's that mean?"

"You know," she says. "Like that button you wear, 'Escalate the Mind.' It'll change you."

Since school started I let Jenny copy my answers, and the doobie is my consolation prize. When class is over, we go outside, and I figure she'll go off with her girlfriends same as she always does.

"Come with me, Michael," Jenny says.

Don't look back, just look forward, Jenny's little ass sways, and I follow. The power chicks got, man. Follow her around the corner of the building and soon as I get back there where she is, she spins quick-like to face me. Jenny's bright bright face, and her freckles, oh man, and she got super straight blond hair coming down to her chest, and the lavender-tint granny glasses. She steps forward against me bra pressing through her dress into my chest and kisses me on the lips. Cold lips hard against mine. My first kiss, close my eyes, spinning, spinning.

I thought I was gonna fall over. Her lips, and pushing between mine, her slippery wet tongue, spinning, man, about to lose my balance, off the edge and into the rocks below.

That was a Days of the Crazy-Wild day for sure, man. The first one.

Next thing I knew we were standing there looking at each other. I never seen Jenny any way but the cool scene, only right then her face got a pink blush 'cause of what she done. I should say something to make this into more than it is but already she's stepping past me.

"See ya 'round, Michael," Jenny said.

Un moment decisif.

Only I don't know it, not back then, not when I'm in high school. Always, a choice. Always. Already she's back to the corner of the building and I gotta say something. Time waits for no one. Regret, and a sadness and she's around that corner, my opportunity gone baby gone, and I'll never have a girlfriend. Touch the front of my pocket and feel the crunch of the weed. Don't got Jenny, but I got a number.

At the back of the school is a hill slopes up to a 6-foot chain-link fence. Get up there, crouch behind some shrubs and get out the number. Put an end 'tween my lips, light the other, suck a mouthful of the harsh, and I'm full-bore into a coughing jag. Exhale, cough some more, calm, calm—my heart, my heart. Another drag, and this time I'm ready, hold the harsh in long as I can. Wait to get psychedelicized. Wait for the crazy-wild. Don't feel nothing.

That day, what I think: Maybe it's not really pot and maybe Jenny's putting me on. Well it was really pot, and no put-on, none of it.

Lord Jim's got his hand out. Still. Fat bulbous number. Sweet musky smoke. And this is the day.

Un moment decisif.

In or out? In, my life goes one way, out, it goes another. The moment has arrived. And I can handle it. Really, I can. Weed makes me crazy. That's a story we could all agree on. Me, and my folks, and the shrink. A lie of convenience. A lie all the same.

Click the shutter. Yeah, yeah, and *oh yeah*. He got big hands, stumpy fingers, brown tobacco stains on the half inch back from the tips, and I got my thumb and index next to his fingers, feel the warm live human, and it's too intimate. I want him to let go, and I got big hands too, my fingers are long and thin, got a grip on the number, and he lets go. I suck a mouthful of the harsh. Been a long time. Hold it. Over a year. Hold it. And my mind melts, no more guys with nail guns.

"Potent shit," I say.

"I got a solid connection, Writerman," Lord Jim says. "Hook you up, old sport," and yeah, sounds good. I'll need a connection. Already I know. On the wall above his bed, the Rolling Stones' poster of the red tongue logo, and I'm floating.

"Cool boots," he says.

Thee Freakster Bro notices my Keith Richards snakeskin boots. Lucky boots, only they haven't brought any good luck.

"Hey man," I say. "Saw the Stones at Altamont, man."

Ghost of 'lectricity. December 6, 1969. We'd been there all day,

and when the sun gone down that idiot wind, the one Dylan
sang about years later, came outta nowhere deadly deathly cold,
so cold our hands and feet hardly got no feeling and our ears
hurt. Yeah and we're so creeped-out. Me and Sweet Sarah and
Rock 'n' Roll Frankie and the rest of us. Creeped-out in our
cotton shirts and jeans, stand in the trampled bone dry burnt
brown grass on the side of that sloped hill. We'd gotten
ourselves far enough from the Hells Angels and the crowd
where trouble and death and bad vibes coagulate. Should feel
safe on the hillside. Only we don't. Stand there, man, things
total outta control, and it's not only the free concert.

Spotlights on Mick, black tights and a black top hat, does his
"I'm the Devil" routine, Keith by his side a junkie ghoul with a
shag haircut grinding out snaky rhythms on a clear Dan
Armstrong guitar. Ominous heroin-infected Jack Daniels-laced
rhythm guitar. Sound of death swoops in. Yeah, soon the Hells
Angels gonna call the Stones' bluff. The music too too loud for
the amplification system, funhouse mirror distortion.

So fucked-up, man, yeah, so fucked-up.

We gotta leave. Sweet Sarah's through with this ugly scene.

"Such a mistake," she says. "You always talk me into these
things."

And me, torn, torn and frayed. Devil's jukebox tempting
me, pulling at me, the Rolling Stones, man, the *fucking* Rolling
Stones.

Un moment decisif.

Fires burn further up on the hill from where we stand. Hells
Angels sit on top of their bus, and one of 'em, he got on a jean
vest and no shirt, tosses an empty into the fire. Flames shoot
high, naked chicks dance, their silhouettes against the flames. A
voice shouts loud, *Shake it, baby,* and someone grabs this blonde
chick's tit and she's screaming.

"You were at Altamont!" and Lord Jim loses his cool. Fan boy,
only right then it's same as he's dropped down an elevator shaft
—the paranoia trip. "Did you, uh, see the Angels whack that
spade?" and he passes me the number, stained fingers, half

gone up in smoke.

We didn't know about it 'til the next day. Meredith Hunter. He was 18. Holding a long-barreled black .22 caliber revolver, but still. An Angel did it with a knife. Right in front of God-who-for-sure-don't-exist and everyone. Right in front of the Stones bashing out "Under My Thumb." I say to Sweet Sarah, "They're playing 'Under My Thumb.' Don't you wanna stay for that?" A lot of chicks woulda stayed.

I should have known, man, take Sweet Sarah to Altamont and that shit gone down. Shoulda known something else, it being December 1969, that Altamont was a symbol. The End. The media and the squares called the Sixties scene the counter-culture or Woodstock Nation, but to me and my friends it was the Freak Scene Dream, 'cause we were freaks, different from the squares, and how groovy the scene in Marin and San Francisco seemed—'66 and '67 and even '68—groovy enough to be a dream. 'Course you had your choice of symbols. There was the Manson deal, that was in '69 too. Or how about Jim Morrison? July 3, 1971. Heroin overdose in a Paris bathtub. Each the perfect symbol for The End. Or maybe there never was a Sixties, so it don't need a symbolic end, maybe it was only a dream. A dream we tried to live as if it *was* real. And maybe Sweet Sarah wanting to split Altamont don't mean nothing more than she was tired and cold.

Lord Jim don't know the hellfuck of that Altamont scene. Read about it in *Rolling Stone*. Saw "Gimme Shelter." A false memory. Funny how something you read about, or see on TV gets mixed up with memory. You forget. What's your life, and what isn't. His voice a whisper, his face contorted. Reefer, man, take you to fucked up places.

"That was a bummer," he says. "That guy getting whacked."

Nothing I can say that won't sound stupid. *A bummer.* Well *yeah.*

Lord Jim reaches out, holds the roach clip, and I go for

another toke. Speak too fast same as I used to when I was stonered and spent too much time with Polanski and his chick Faithfull.

"Well-it-was-really-weird-being-there," I say. "Opposite of Woodstock. Or the anti-Monterey Pop. Or something."

Speed rapping. "I'd been to free concerts in the Park. Speedway Meadows. The Polo Field. Those were groovy, man. Not same as the bullshit in the straight mags. *Time* and *Life* and *Look*."

We smoke the finality of that doobie 'til there's no roach. And me, talk, talk, talk. "Everyone trippin' a love high in the park. Sittin' in the grass, chicks dancing and shaking their tits. First I saw tits for real, and not in a magazine was that time up on Mt. Tam in '67. Janis screaming 'Down on Me.'"

Lord Jim raises the lid of his record player. He don't want to hear my reverie, and I get this feeling things been shit for him when the Freak Scene Dream was in full effect, and not the echo of an echo. Altamont. By then the scene was done.

Lord Jim drops the needle onto the groove, and then *he* starts to groove as this Fifties R&B deal starts in. He got the volume cranked so loud it's same as the band is in the room. And that's when Lord Jim begins to imitate Floyd Dixon. One-man band, *Thee* Freakster Bro. A rude sax riff, a minimal beat and Dixon sings, *Went ballin' the other night, started drinking and got real tight.*

The chorus is swinging, I'm snapping my fingers, man, and this walking bass and a piano join in. Dixon got a classic R&B voice—kinda deep and smoky—and me, I got a stonered beatific smile. *We were having so much fun, didn't know it was half past one, sat down to have one more, looked at the clock and it was almost four.*

As the song played on Lord Jim became the barrelhouse piano man, fingers pounding an invisible keyboard, shifted to air-sax for the rip-roaring solo, all the while singing away with that ragged-ass voice. *Draw one, draw two, draw three four glasses of beer.*

Oh fuck.

Ghost of 'lectricity. Early summer of 1971, first time I got drunk. We'd gone to this club in San Anselmo, the Lion's Share. Me and Polanski and Faithfull, well I mean her real name is Ruth, but we call her Faithfull 'cause she's so into that British chick who was Jagger's girlfriend. Oh man, Polanski's chick, what a babe. Mom and Dad gone to Sacramento to spend the night at the Cohens' place. Deborah Cohen been Mom's best friend since high school. Me and Polanski, we're 17, and Faithfull, she's 16. Afterwards we come back to my house. They want booze, and I'm the big man. Break into Dad's liquor cabinet, bottle of Jameson Irish, three of us at the round mahogany dining room table finish the bottle. And I gotta run to Dad's bathroom and puke. Polanski and Faithfull are supposed to sleep on the foldout in the den, but instead they fuck in my folks' room. In the morning my head got a whole team of carpenters working the nail guns. Polanski and Faithfull asleep naked on my folk's bed. So fucked-up, man. I yell and yell, and finally Faithfull said she'd wash the sheets. I tell 'em get dressed, but they lie there, don't get up, and soon enough I can hear Polanski grunting away, hear Faithfull moan a moan that can only mean the Forever Infinite Ecstatic.

Thee Freakster Bro sings, and he's so loose. Hardly knows me, yet there he is. Fearless. Don't give a fuck if he makes a damn fool of himself. Eyes closed, overwhelming oblivious, oh man, freakster bro so happy. And can I risk acting the fool? But how foolish is Lord Jim? He's got me total impressed, him letting it all hang out. He's not trying to control every damn thing about himself.

That day I remember about living in the moment. Not looking back, not looking forward. That's when your authentic self can shine. All your worry, gone baby gone. In the moment there is no worry, there is only the moment.

Un moment decisif.

I step into the moment. The groove's got me, tap my right boot, my head movin' to the rhythm, and I sing the chorus.

Yeah, well, that's when I see my reflection in Lord Jim's mirror, and fall right out of the moment. Suck in my cheeks, shake my hair, and yeah man, tell myself I look the cool scene. Well I'm high flyin' and flyin' high, and what the fuck do I care if I look cool or not? *Like. It. Fucking. Matters.* So cool, and never gonna live the authentic real.

"Hey, Bartender" ends, and Lord Jim's fist jabs up into the air. "Yow!"

Freakster bro grins at me same as an idiot. "Gotta hear that again. Let's rock!"

An audience, me, and it ignites Lord Jim. Freakster bro's fingers fly along the imaginary keyboard. When it comes time for the sax solo he's ready, rockin' back, hands grip the invisible instrument, face puffed as if he took a huge gulp of air in preparation.

Hey, bartender!

Oh man, I can't sit. Can't. Got to live. In the action, not on the sidelines. Jump the fuck up, frantic strumming the air, and I sing along. *Hey man lookie here!*

Bros-in-arms. We sing together off-key, drunken harmony. Keith and Mick sharing a microphone. Sal and Dean. Jules and Jim. *Draw one draw two draw three four glasses of beer.*

Both there for the finale. Lord Jim shouts, *Hey, bartender!*

I catch the next one, my voice tentative, *Hey, bartender!*

Lord Jim raises the volume, *Hey, bartender!*

My voice loud, more confident, *Hey, bartender!*

Lord Jim smiles his beatific Dean Moriarty smile, *Hey, bartender!*

And me, don't give a fuck what I look like, what I sound like, none of it. *Hey, bartender!*

All together now, *Draw one, two, three four glasses of beer!*

Another "yow," fist in the air.

Give each other the dotted-lines eyes. Lord Jim laughs his too-too-loud-smoke-scarred laugh, and I laugh my you're-too-too-fucking-much-man laugh, both bent over, and we can't stop. That's when I fall right out of the moment again, and I do stop. Did I expose too much too soon? I feel the embarrassment deal on my face, and yet it felt good to let loose. God-who-probably-don't-exist only knows how long since I let myself go. I always hold back. Even when I fucked Sweet Sarah it was same as I stood in the doorway of her bedroom watching. I want so bad to let go. Don't wanna watch no more.

Talk talk talk record talk. Make noise, fill the room—anything but dead air. "Never-heard-anything-quite-like-*that*," I say. "I mean I'm into the blues, man, but that's a whole other deal."

Lord Jim, man, he's got the confidence from another freakster bro digging his scene. The room hazy with reefer smoke, and he opens a window, gets himself a Pall Mall.

"A man's cigarette," he says. "Filters are for chicks, and *pussies*."

I never smoked a cigarette, not ever.

Un moment decisif.

Funny how easy it is. I shake one from the pack, get out The Dylan, which is what I call this stainless steel cigarette lighter I got 'cause once it was Bob Dylan's lighter. Well, that's the story, and back then I wanna believe the story.

Ghost of 'lectricity. July of 1969. Me and Big Man Bobby are shaking, man, total nerves. We've made it into Jerry Garcia's Spanish-style stucco house in Larkspur, and while Mountain Girl, that's Garcia's chick, goes to get him, I'm busy with the reel-to-reel. A guy sits in an upholstered chair reading a book about Indians; turns out it's Robert Hunter, you know, who writes the lyrics to Garcia's songs.

I'll tell you about Garcia's living room 'cause everyone asks about it. Everyone asks what he's like and his house and all that. Imagine someone went to the Salvation Army and buys up two upholstered chairs and a couch and a low antique coffee table and ancient brass floor lamps with the big frosted glass around the bulbs and a worn-out rug old enough for Kerouac to have brought it back from Mexico in the Forties. There's a framed collage over the fireplace that's the cover of the first Dead album, and some ancient landscape paintings that might as well been by William Keith or Manuel Valencia, that kinda late-19th/ early 20th century California trip I never figured would be up in Garcia's house—although these days it makes sense. That living room, comfy as a pair of old moccasins.

Garcia comes in, trips when he steps from the hardwood onto the rug, manages to catch himself, yeah he's messed-up. His hair's not long as it was back in '66, '67, a frizzed-out halo circling his head kinda same as Lord Jim, only Garcia's hair is black, and he got the full beard and mustache, but trimmed, not out-of-control. Has on black jeans and a lumberjack plaid shirt, black and red. He reaches out his hand and that's when I see the finger. You know, the finger that got chopped off when he was a kid. Fuck, two-thirds of Garcia's middle finger isn't there.

"Hey Hunter, man," Garcia says. "Got a number to cheer me up?"

"You smoke up your stash already?" Hunter says.

Hunter starts rolling a fat one, I start the recorder and Garcia starts to talk. It's when Hunter passes the joint that Garcia pulls out The Dylan.

"Dylan's lighter, man," he says.

"You mean *Bob Dylan?*" Big Man Bobby says.

"No, I mean Dylan Thomas," Garcia says. "Yeah, Bobby Dylan."

He told us how Dylan and Albert Grossman, you know, Dylan's manager, showed up at a gig the Dead and Big Brother did at the Straight Theater. He said Grossman thought Janis was a star and wanted to manage Big Brother.

"Bobby dug *our* set," Garcia says. "Back in the dressing room him and I jammed. First time I played 'It Takes a Lot to Laugh, It Takes a Train to Cry.'"

Garcia said he produced a joint and that's when Dylan got out his lighter, you know, The Dylan. "He tosses it to me," Garcia says. "I light up and I'm giving it back, he said for me to keep it. 'Jerry, man, it's something to remember me by.' Bobby laughed that high sarcastic laugh. 'If you ever run into hard times you can sell it.'"

"That isn't what you told me, Jerry," Hunter says. "You told me Grossman whispered something to Bobby and Bobby got paranoid and split out of there real fast. You said he forgot the lighter."

"All I know," Garcia says, "is next day I had it."

I figure it's a put-on, but then Garcia's tripping on how it's got the letter "Z" engraved on one side, and he shows me.

Fuck, the letter "Z."

"Sure doesn't stand for Zorro," Garcia says. "Abram Zimmerman, that's Bobby's dad."

He set The Dylan next to my tape recorder, and we talk some more, but all I think about is the shiny lighter with the "Z." *Bob Dylan's lighter.* Probably used it when he recorded *Blonde on Blonde.*

Well, somewhere along the way Hunter splits upstairs, and when the interview's over Garcia splits the house to go jam at the Keystone Berkeley. I pack up the recorder, and there it is on the table.

The Dylan.

Garcia don't need it, and anyway that Hunter guy said Garcia stole it. I got as much right as him. Big Man Bobby's over at the fireplace digging the collage. I pick up The Dylan, and the cold metal feels good. It's as if I know Dylan if I have the lighter. A talisman. Who knows the good luck it'll bring.

There in Lord Jim's dorm room I take a hit of the Pall Mall, and maybe 'cause I'm stoned, right away I dig how the nicotine makes me feel.

"Let's rock!" Lord Jim says, sets the burning end of his cig in the ashtray, and gets another album.

Shouting too too loud. "*THIS* IS THE NEW TESTAMENT!"

Holds up the cover, *Houses of the Holy,* and I fall out of the moment.

"Uh, no man," I say. "Not into Zeppelin, man."

They're crap. Anyone who got taste knows it. Well Lord Jim don't know it. And what if I'm wrong?

Un moment decisif.

Is this the end, or the beginning? But something *is* happening, and it's easy to give it up to the heavy sound, "The Song Remains the Same," let it fill the room, fill my head, and I become one with the rhythm. Page's monster guitar riff, so fucked-up, and Robert Plant, that high, sexed-out scream of a voice, that's real too. Hear that scream, hear my soul, hear the authentic real.

Lord Jim stands front of his desk, a mutant freak acting out Page and Plant, right arm thrashing an invisible guitar, ragged voice singin' along, and I get it.

Right then, best band in the world. Goddamn goddamn yeah.

3. FEEL NOTHING

WELL THAT WAS HOW it started, *Bodhi,* the day I began to
live every day again same as it's a Days of the Crazy-Wild day.
But it was more, 'cause the years when I was in flux also began
that day, and it wasn't only me, 'cause everything was changing.
Day by day the Freak Scene Dream would keep receding as I
fumbled through the darkness in search of me. Not the me I'd
been with Sweet Sarah, not exactly, and not someone brand new
either. It's more subtle, how a human changes, but change was
the only way out.

In my room. In *my* room. The night of the day I meet Lord Jim.
Jukebox in my head, and I hear the voices. "Honky Tonk
Women." Lord Jim's ragged-ass voice, and Mick's voice. So
amped-up. Flyin' high and high flyin'. Flyin' high from the weed,
but high flyin' from the rush of what gone down. Smoked two
joints, me and Lord Jim, talk talk and more talk, and so many
fab records. Maybe three joints, and how many Pall Malls?
Coulda been four joints. Go ask Lord Jim if you gotta know, I
mean it's his weed.
    Well it's time to put my mark on it. My Room. I'd done
nothing other than drag in a second single bed from the lounge
at the end of the hall where there's all this extra furniture, and
pushed the two together for a makeshift double. For when I
bring a chick up here. Hey, man, nothing wrong with high
hopes. Give up your dreams and you'll go crazy, you know, what
Mick sang in "Ruby Tuesday." Then again, hope is the most evil

of evils because it prolongs man's torment, what Nietzsche said. And so on. And so on.

My room's a cell. White walls, beige carpet, and one of those empty freestanding clothes closets. Particleboard or some shit. Empty bookcase. Desk with nothing on it but the white candle I put there. I got the bed running lengthwise under the windows. Got it covered with a paisley madras bedspread— yellow and red and black. Made in India, where The Beatles hung out with the Maharishi. So for sure it's groovy.

Blank canvas room. All my shit in boxes. Suitcase open, and my other worn-in bell-bottoms on top, the pair I wore to Altamont. Wear those jeans, feel death swoop in. I can see my Boy Scout binoculars there in the suitcase. Why the hell did I bring them?

I'm gonna tell you some about where I'm from, and if you or Salinger think that kinda stuff is boring, well no one's forcing you to pay attention. Grew up in Marin County, not the fancy-ass idea some people got of it. I grew up in the closest Marin got to a no-name, one of those places you pass going from here to there. Lowland Drive, that half mile snake in the side of a hill, curves up from Tiburon Blvd. just off Highway 101, takes a right and it rises, up, up, up, and it peaks, rolls down and dips to a valley and up again, before winding down and around to reunite with Tiburon Blvd.

There's more than one way to clue you in to Lowland Drive's place in the social hierarchy relative to the towns and neighborhoods in its vicinity, but finally—whether compared to upper middle-class Strawberry, a shit-white suburb that starts in the flatlands on the other side of Tiburon Blvd. and ends on a hill about a half mile south, or old town Mill Valley to the west, other side of Highway 101, with its majestic redwoods, and those stately houses hidden in the hills behind the town square, or Tiburon to the east where the doctors and lawyers and financiers who don't live in Ross or Sausalito or San Francisco's Pacific Heights built their mansions overlooking the Bay, the view of the San Francisco skyline out in the distance—the bottom line, in comparison to all that, or taken on its own, Lowland Drive is a barren, semi-lifeless stretch of road where white collar workers built the homes that would entomb them for 20, 30, 40 years, living out their middle class lives, and no, that's wrong, 'cause they're not living. No Days of the Crazy-Wild for them. No, man, it's a slow death. And it's midway along Lowland Drive, where the road dips to its lowest point, where in 1953 my dad finished building our house just in time for my unheralded arrival on the planet.

He painted the house gray. Hellfuck gray.

Lowland Drive. Shoulda called it Dry Grass Hill Drive 'cause from our driveway you got a view of a hill covered in dried-out weeds most of the year. Coulda called it Car Sounds Drive too, all the cars whizzing by down below on Tiburon Blvd. Those cars on their way from here to there, here being elsewhere, there being Tiburon. Course don't matter what it's called, 'cause it might as well *be* a no-name. The coup de grace, no one on their way from here to there has to actually drive on Lowland Drive—when they get off 101 they can stay on Tiburon Blvd. all the way out to Tiburon.

Me and my folks might as well live on a dead-end.

All you see from the road is the rectangular garage.

It's hellfuck gray too.

A black asphalt driveway butts up against the slab floor of the garage, and the house is maybe 12 feet behind the garage and lower by the height of a not particularly tall human. My dad designed the house, which is sad, man, 'cause he's no architect.

If you drew a line with a zero at the left end and 100 at the far right, and the closer to 100 you get means you got artistic talent, well my dad is negative 30. Maybe even negative 40. I guess he was trying for low-rent Eichler, that kind of boxy minimal style, only there's a grace to those Eichlers, and it's actually really clever how Joseph Eichler made maximum use of space, with big picture windows looking out on the private back yard, and hardly a window looking out on the street, which created a serene peaceful vibe. I know about Eichlers 'cause my kidhood buddy Rock 'n' Roll Frankie grew up in one. Our house is an ugly box, and no grace, and no clever use of space and every window got a view of the other lame suburban houses in the neighborhood.

The house falls short of 1000 square feet and except for the living room, with a ceiling that starts at 9 feet over by the picture window and slants up to 12, the house has 8 foot ceilings so it feels cramped, as if you got to lean over to not hit your head. The front door opens into the living room, but there's a 4 foot wide entry area created by a wood divider to your right. There's three pots set on that divider, each with some kind of house fern in it. The flooring in the entryway and leading to the kitchen are these crappy vinyl tiles. Brown with phony marble-like streaks—makes me think someone puked when I look down at 'em.

From the front door, past the coat closet, there's a mirror. An oval mirror with an elaborate gold frame, mock Louis the 14th. I call it the Versailles mirror. Coming or going I always look into the Versailles mirror. If I don't look so cool, I fuck with my hair or change my shirt. Gotta look the cool scene. Past the Versailles mirror is the kitchen, but right before it, to the left, a narrow hallway covered with those same puke-ugly tiles that leads past Dad's little shit-hole of a bathroom, and Mom's slightly bigger bathroom, and on to my room and my folk's room and the den where we watch TV.

The kitchen, piece of work. It's the smallest room in the house, other than the bathrooms, and it's where we spend most of our time. I guess it's maybe 6 feet by 10, but I never measured. Along one wall there's an ugly-ass Formica counter with the telephone and the stone-age white stove. Take a right and there's a white sink and the white Kenmore refrigerator with the hum, and a window over the sink looks onto this cement patio where Jamie the dog used to shit, you know, before he died, and the steep hill covered with ice plant, for sure the lamest plant ever. Along the wall opposite the sink and refrigerator is a Formica counter where we eat most of our meals and argue. There's enough room for me and Mom to sit on stools facing a wall covered with that stupid flowered wallpaper. Dad sits at the end, his rear facing the phone and stove. And the floor: tiled with shit-white-with-speckles cheapest on-sale vinyl tiles you can buy. Got the picture? So that's the shit-ass I left when I split for The University, and I couldn't split fast enough.

Blank canvas room. Snakeskin boots on the carpet near the suitcase, and I wanna feel the danger. Keith Richards boots. As if wearing the boots makes me same as Keith. The danger. Well there's no danger. Only a cool pair of boots I think will bring me good luck. Got those boots after I blew it with Sweet Sarah. Got them to replace the suede cowboy boots I wore all the time Sweet Sarah was my old lady.

Change my boots, change my life.

Grandfather owned a shoe store, Mel's Shoes, in San Rafael, which was maybe 15 minutes north of the no-name, you know, Lowland Drive. He had a marketing slogan: "Mel's Shoes. A miracle for your feet on the Miracle Mile." Mel Malamud. That's Grandfather. On my mom's side. The other one, Dad's dad, dead and buried before Mom born me. Grandfather came up with that slogan. Printed it on his bags. Used it in his ads. Had some plastic giveaway shoehorns with the slogan on them. "Mel's Shoes. A miracle for your feet on the Miracle Mile."

It's funny, man, calling that mile or so strip of fast-food joints, discount flooring stores and used furniture deals the Miracle Mile. The miracle though, Mel's Shoes was Grandfather's golden goose. Mel's paid for a fancy-ass ranch house in the nice part of San Rafael out near the country club, and a new Mercedes *and* a trip to Asia or Europe every year.

I'd looked at those suede cowboy boots a lot. At Mel's. Hellfuck expensive. But when I asked, Grandfather gave me a pair.

"My pleasure, Mike," he said.

Took me years to learn. How doing something for someone else, someone you love, or someone who's in a bad way who you don't even know, how it gives you pleasure.

The day Grandfather gave me the boots he was a portly man with a potbelly from all the halvah and cheesecake and apple strudel he ate to soak up his anger, and he got plenty 'cause of what his parents did to him. I get to that soon enough. And 'cause of Nana, and I get to that too. Grandfather had a bald head, big and shiny with gray hair at the back and sides. He wore his usual deal, the gray wool dress slacks over a perfect pair of shiny black dress shoes, a yellow and brown and green plaid short sleeve shirt under a camel hair vest that buttoned up the front. He had a metal shoehorn in the sweater vest pocket, and a pair of bifocals hanging from a string around his neck.

Grandfather was the only one who could call me Mike without pissing me off. Something about the way he said it, and the special bond between me and him. I mean the reason I hate Mike so bad all the years I was growing up is 'cause Mike Stein is Leonard and Esther Stein's son. Mike Stein is the four-eyes who got Bar Mitzvahed, and according to my dad, couldn't do nothing right—a good for nothing. With Grandfather it was different. How he treated me. He was never mean, not when I fucked up sometimes as a kid, not never. He didn't think I was a good for nothing.

I hated it when Nana snapped at Grandfather. Nana's a bitch. I love Nana, but man, if she were my wife I'd divorce her. Nana's got the personality of a Florida alligator been living in the swamp too long. Nana's 5 foot 4 and so thin she gotta weigh around 95 pounds. Has a whole oriental trip going. Chinese-style silk pant suits and blouses. Her bleached blonde hair is always up in an elegant do copped from Coco Chanel, who Nana idolizes; it's fairly short, brushed back off her forehead, and bobbed above her shoulders. Her face reminds me of that comedienne Joan Rivers, only Nana's face is skinnier and her nose longer and on occasion, when she turns her head a certain way, her nose looks pointed. She also copied Chanel's deal with the pearls, you know, conceptually, 'cause instead of pearls, Nana wears a zillion gold strands. And a zillion thin gold bracelets hanging from her wrists. And two rings. An elaborate gold wedding ring Grandfather had custom designed, and the huge 2-carat Tiffany. Grandfather, man, he had the patience of Job to put up with Nana. Don't know how Mom managed either. Nana was always rubbing it in how Mom married the wrong man. How she shoulda married a doctor or lawyer who could provide for her same as Grandfather and Nana did, you know, for starters buy her a decent size engagement ring instead of the sad-ass she got. Whenever we visit my grandfolks, at some point Nana would hold up the hand with the diamond so it caught the light and say to Mom, "Look how beautiful—my 2-carat Tiffany. Too bad Len didn't buy *you* one, Esther."

When I started college, wasn't Dad who paid the bill. Mel's Shoes on the Miracle Mile, man, the fucking golden-ass goose. How Nana looked at it, Grandfather was an easy touch, and Dad might as well been stealing Grandfather blind. Grandfather didn't see it that way. "What's the point of money," he said, "if you don't spend it on family?"

What sealed the deal regards Grandfather happened when I was in grade school. Grandfather was the only one who when I told him I liked to write stories, asked to read a few, and after he read 'em, said he was absolute positive I could be the next Mark Twain or even Michener, his favorite, if I put my mind to it. The difference between Mom and Grandfather is Mom said I could be anything, only if it wasn't on her short list of approved career choices I got an *oh Mike!* Grandfather only wanted for me what would make me happy.

Mom told me how Grandfather came to be a success. When he was 8 his folks, who were Russian and who are dead, put him on a boat to Ellis Island and he never saw them again. His Aunt Sophie and Uncle Charlie in Brooklyn raised him, and when he was 11 he got a job at Klein's Shoes. Uncle Charlie's friend, Mr. Klein, owned the place. Klein's sold shoes but also had a repair shop where they could replace worn out soles and heels, polish and waterproof, and sell you new laces when the old ones broke. I figure all the anger in him regards his folks he put into that job. Mom said Grandfather would get to the store before it opened and get the lights on, the heater going, make the place nice for when customers showed up, and he'd be the last to leave. Grandfather got to be Mr. Klein's right hand man. When Mr. Klein kicked it due to a heart attack, Grandfather inherited the business. He was 22. First thing he did, renamed it Mel's Shoes.

I was 15 the day Grandfather gave me the shit-kickers. Made him feel I was safe if I was walking in his shoes. Yeah well, that was a long time ago. Those boots had had it, and even if they hadn't, they were the boots I wore when I was with Sweet Sarah. I'm not superstitious, but right after I blew it with her I got the Keith Richards snakeskin boots at this boutique in Sausalito and the shit-kickers went into the garbage. The Keith Richards snakeskin boots, man, supposed to be the start of the New Trip.

Blank canvas room. Everywhere, cardboard boxes. My books. Fitzgerald, Salinger, Kerouac. Faulkner, Huxley, Miller. Hemingway, Dostoyevsky, Wolfe. And the rest of what John Fante calls the Big Boys, only they're not boys. I call them the Big Men. Melon crates of my records. Stones and Dylan and that crazy-ass Vanilla Fudge album with the 7 minute 20 second version of "You Keep Me Hanging On." John Mayall and Pink Floyd and The Band. Bessie Smith and Joni Mitchell and Van Morrison. And all the rest. That plastic case over there holds my shit-ass Smith-Corona, and I already told you more than enough about that goddamn thing.

I guess I better tell you how it was with me and Dad. What I'll tell you happened too many times. This time, the time I'm telling about, summer of 1963. I stand in the garage. Ten years old and Dad tells me to help him change the oil. I don't know a car has oil. He's got the garage door open lets light in. He's under the car—the white '59 Rambler with the little stupid fins—has a pan to catch the oil and he's swearing, everything bugs the hell out of him, and every time he yells some obscenity, my whole body does a nervous jerk. I got the Jewish guilt as if I done something wrong, even though all I do is wait for him to tell me what to do. He loses hold of the wrench and it slides under the car, and he's trying to reach it, can't get to it and yells that bark of a yell he uses on me, yells out my name so it's a brick hitting a cement wall, brings me into the mess, and I don't know it then, but now I do. I'm the fall kid.

"*Mike*," he says. "Get me another fucking wrench."

I don't know where another *fucking* wrench is, "Dad, where should I look?" and more swearing, hits his head against the bottom of the car and "goddamn motherfucker. Mike. *Mike!* Wrench or a pliers."

I get myself outta my stupor and over to his workbench, get the overhead light on, and look all over, I mean everywhere. I want the pliers to be there so bad, but they're not. I'm like "Dad, where are they?" That's when I find a wrench, take a breath, a deep deep breath, and bring it over.

His greasy hand sticks out from under the car, fingers moving, and I put the wrench in his hand. He pulls it under, "goddamn know nothing," 'cause it's the wrong size. He crawls out from under that car, stands up, and his khaki pants stained with oil and dirt, same with the white wife-beater, and a bruise where he hit his forehead. Don't even look at me, and the deal that happens when he's furious. He don't know it's happening, the end of his tongue folds back on top of itself and his teeth dig down into the top of that doubled-over tongue, and it makes his face look total horror show.

Goes over to the workbench, opens a drawer and under a bunch of stuff finds a pliers. Crawls back under, gets the damn bolt unscrewed and oil drips into the pan. He finishes the job and walks out of the garage and into the house, takes a shower and he's on that couch, glass of Jameson, yells at Mom what a good for nothing I am.

That was the good ending. Well there was another way it went down. The horror show with his tongue, and he says, "You're good for nothing," and he comes at me, hits me upside the head with the flat of his hand, right above the left ear, as if my head been cracked with a baseball bat, hurts bad as hell, and Mom screaming. "Len, don't hit the boy. You're going to give him a concussion. How's he going to be a doctor if you destroy brain cells." My mind gone baby gone, and after a while I come back and my head hurts. He's in the dining room drinking that Jameson he loves.

Hellfuck motherfucker, my dad.

Blank canvas room. Time to make the room mine. Get the big poster of Lennon with the beard and the wire rims. His working class hero look. Tack it above my desk, along with the Peter Max "LOVE" poster. On the opposite wall I tack my peace symbol poster. It's funny 'cause lookin' back to the late Sixties and early Seventies, for some people all they remember is protesting the War. *Peace my brother.* But the War wasn't the only scene unfolding, and by the time I got to The University I had other shit on my mind.

But I digress. Got this thick cardboard poster that's the cover of *Blonde on Blonde.* Dylan out of focus with his hair frizzed and the brown double-breasted leather jacket and the black and white striped scarf. Tack it next to the peace symbol. There's comfort in that Dylan poster being up in my room. I still got that poster. Now it's tacked above my desk, you know, where I write.

Unroll the Indian rug from Cost Plus and it fits between the bed and the door. Groovy, man.

Sit on the bed, and out the window across the quad, one floor below mine, *Thee* Freakster Bro's room, he got his light on, dark rectangle shape of the Black Sabbath poster taped to his window. I seen that poster in the afternoon. Has a tombstone, and the words "Black Sabbath." Fucked-up tombstone. Fucked-up Sabbath. Fucked-up heavy metal sludge. But I'll give Lord Jim a break on his Sabbath shit. Maybe he's right, same as he is about Zeppelin.

Next to Dylan and the peace symbol I got up this sexed-out psychedelic poster for the Avalon Ballroom, where all the stoned freaks go in '66 and '67 and dance the night away to Big Brother and Captain Beefheart and the other groovy bands.

Silhouette of a naked chick, a spiral of colors—red, green, yellow, orange, purple, blue—spinning out from her pussy.

Forever Infinite Ecstatic, man.

And this is good a time as any to clue you in. Forever Infinite Ecstatic is a moment that stretches to infinity, and it only can happen with my Visions of Johanna chick. She's the flesh and blood human who completes me, and me her, *and* she's the transcendent purity of love. The Forever Infinite Ecstatic is an endless moment of erotic ecstasy, and in that moment, a moment that while it happens is all eternity, you get so down and dirty and raw sex orgasmic, *and* reach a place so high and fine, a place of spiritual transcendence, simultaneous *inside* the fucking, and in that moment, and for that moment, two become one.

Oh yeah, baby. Blow your fucking mind, baby.

Past 11, and I'm crashing into bummered-out bummerosity. I got the heavy curtains closed, yeah they don't let no light in, I mean if there been any light. Lying there and my wrist aches and my palm aches. Remember the scars I told you about? Well that day I met Lord Jim I had two of them. The true love scar on my palm, and the Bell Jar scar on my wrist.

Ghost of 'lectricity. Summer of 1970, and *un moment decisif.* The day me and Sweet Sarah made the cuts that became the true love scars. Cut the smallest X into her palm, X into mine. Palm against palm, my blood and her blood, 'til death do us part. Another lie. Death didn't part us. And the lie of *un moment decisif.* You think you come to this fork in the road, and once you make your choice, well that's the end of it. But it's not the end of it. 'Cause later you come to another fork, gotta make another choice, only you might not know that's what it is 'cause it's not a road we're talking about, and when you come to that fork, or rather, I came to the second fork, another *un moment decisif,* I didn't know what it was. Here's some advice. Direct from Tim Hardin to you, via me. His deal about not making promises if you can't follow through on 'em. If you can't keep 'em.

That's sort of a joke, only I'm dead serious.

Ghost of 'lectricity. Fall of 1971, freshman year when I get the
Bell Jar scar. This was a few months after me and Sweet Sarah
split up. This was in my room, the downstairs bedroom, in this
married students apartment I shared with these two guys, Tom
and Wolf. Tom had a different chick he was screwing in the
room right above mine seemed like every other night. Wolf
looked like Attila the Hun only he was this soft-spoken guy who
wrote poetry, thought he was Walt Whitman reborn.
     But anyway.
     It's near midnight, the witching hour, when a guy's thoughts
can turn darker than dark. Get a small piece of cardboard
around a twin-edge razor. An inch past my wrist up my left arm,
please, someone find me, I run the blade across my skin, *get me outta
here*, and it cut though the skin easy as cutting paper, *please*. Drop
the razor. *No one.* Not much blood. At first. *No one.* More blood,
and more blood. Hellfuck hurts. Kleenex and first aid cream
and Band-Aids. My big fucking suicide move. *Not a one.* Fucked-
up loser. Don't got the nerve to end it. And if you want an
example of what's not *un moment decisif*, that would be it.

Two scars. True Love in the middle of my left palm. If you look
close it's there. Bell Jar on my left arm past the wrist. True Love
is a reminder: don't make promises I can't keep. Only I can see
the Bell Jar, it's so faint. A reminder: never be a fuck-up loser.
Never start shit I can't finish. And if I want life to be the
authentic real I better know what I'm doing before I do it. Got
that third scar. You'll have to wait on that one.

Don't know why, but I put on the Grateful Dead's *Anthem of the
Sun*. Don't make sense to listen when I'm bummered. Weird-ass
musique concrete and cut-up tapes of live performances.
Burroughs cut-up trip, only the Dead did it with music.
Burroughs didn't invent it—the cut-up trip. Burroughs
popularized it, if you can say Burroughs popularized anything.
This Dada guy, Tristan Tzara, used it first back in the Twenties.

You take a page of writing, cut it up, small strips with three or four words on each, rearrange 'em random, and voila, a new piece of writing. There are things that on the surface, taken literal, don't make sense, and still they feel true. Burroughs said, "When you cut into the present the future leaks out."

Past midnight, but I'm not tired. Open the window, let the cool air in. Smell the ocean and the trees. I get out The Dylan, light the candle. The smooth metal against my palm, rub my thumb on the "Z." Dylan held this lighter once. This is gonna be my lucky year. I know it. The breeze causes the flame to flicker, and cast a warped version of my silhouette onto the poster of the naked chick with the rainbow colors spiraling from her pussy, and the peace symbol and the *Blonde on Blonde* poster. And is all I am a collection of pop culture references, refried ideas and secondhand philosophy—all I've heard and read and seen? Like Dylan's fucking lighter means shit. Who the fuck am I, man?

Anthem of the Sun often makes me feel as if I'm with an old friend. Been listening since '69. Some nights it's so groovy. Not tonight. Tonight it's a weird-ass weird old friend, one I lost touch with, haven't seen in 10 or 15 years, and in the interim he got into Persian Brown. It's creeping me out, *Anthem of the Sun*, and I turn it off.

I didn't know the hellfuck of what the next years would bring. You can't know. If you did it would be too much to bear. There's this Chet Baker album called *Let's Get Lost*. Well that year, the year that began that day I met Lord Jim, we were all looking for a way out. Me and Lord Jim, and the others. You'll meet them. None of us ready to feel. The drugs and booze and cigarettes and coffee and music and sex—all the ways we didn't feel. Well there were times when the future leaked out. When we had to feel something. Mostly it was *let's get lost*. We tried so hard. To feel nothing.

TWO

1. GIRL BY THE WHIRLPOOL

NOW WE'RE GONNA TIME trip, gonna go back to 1968. I'm gonna tell you about me and Sweet Sarah, some of what went down, so you understand what I been through, what I did, and the ruin of it. So you understand how lost I felt the day I met Lord Jim.

Yeah, so you understand.

The first time I see Sweet Sarah, oh but before I get to that, I gotta tell you about Lauren. 'Cause Lauren was the first chick I had a serious crush on. It's the day after Christmas, 1968, the day I first see Lauren.

I'm in Mill Valley, at Village Music, you know, John Goddard's record store, and I'm in the Dylan section. Been a year since *John Wesley Harding*, and every time I go in there I look to see if there's something new.

John Wesley Harding, such a mindblower. No one had a clue before it came out that the rock 'n' roll Dylan of '66 was gone baby gone. We should have expected something outta left field. I mean if Dylan could go from folk music to rock in '65, certainly he could flip the switch again.

I knew that day I wasn't gonna find something new. I mean I read *Cream*, read *Rolling Stone*, so if there been a new Dylan in the wind, I'd know about it. Still.

A lot of times I'd hang out in the record store waiting. All the grooviest chicks came into the record store. Waiting. Yeah, I was waiting for one of 'em to notice me.

That day, sure I was looking in the Dylan section, but really

I was there for the chicks. The chicks who wanna be hippies. The groovy chicks all born too young.

To be hippies.

All of 'em wanna be part of the Freak Scene Dream scene.

Born too late, born too young, but still.

I had this fantasy. I'd be standing there with an album in my hand, something obscure and sophisticated, maybe *Trout Mask Replica* or *Freak Out* or even an oldie by Carl Perkins, and a knock-me-dead gorgeous chick would come up to me and wanna know about the "intriguing" album I was holding.

Oh man, and then I'd reel out my deep knowledge, you know, about how Zappa was influenced by Erik Satie or the roots of Beafheart's hoodoo Dada sound, or something about the Memphis rockabilly cats, that kinda hipster inside shit that none of the chicks my age had a clue about, and the chick would be bowled-over impressed and right quick-like she'd be my first old lady.

Yeah. I had it all planned out. Only that scene's never how the scene unfolds in real life. So many times I'm in that record store only chicks don't even give me the once over once, let along the once over twice.

So I'm resigned it's not gonna happen. No chick cares about the musical knowledge I been accumulating. Or if they do, no way to get the conversation started.

Until this day when Lauren shows up, and oh man, that chick is a fireball, and she's walking down the aisle same as she's headed right for me.

Me, man. And I mean I don't know this chick. Still.

Lauren is one of 'em. Born to young. Born too late. To be a hippie.

She's heading right for where I stand and I swear she looks same as Suze Rotolo, the chick holding onto Dylan's arm as they walk down Jones Street in the Village on the *Freewheelin'* cover. Since that day I can't look at that *Freewheelin'* album without thinking of Lauren.

Crazy how that is, you know.

Nah, she don't actually look that much same as Suze Rotolo,

I don't know why I told you that. Lauren had an angular Picasso
nose, and wore basement clothes. Had sad sad eyes same as
smoke, where the moonlight swims, and a mercury mouth. Had
a ghostlike soul and a voice same as chimes. And Spanish
manners, and the sea at her feet. Maybe that was her, or maybe
that was the chick in "Sad-Eyed Lady of the Lowlands."

No, man, Lauren didn't look same as Suze Rotolo.

Overwhelming extravagant heavy traffic Dylan freak
Lauren, but she tries her best to look same as Sara Lownds, who
Dylan married. Not to be confused with my Sweet Sarah, who I
haven't met. Who's not my Sweet Sarah. Yet.

Lauren's Siren brown hair the color of polished mahogany,
and the red and white polka dot scarf, same scarf I'd seen in a
picture of Dylan and Sara Lownds, and the scarf covers
Lauren's head, holds her long hair back, and I knew that Lauren
chick was trying to look same as Sara Lownds.

I didn't know it in a way where I say to myself, this chick is
trying to look same as Dylan's chick. No, it's the deal where I
see the chick, and without even saying anything to myself it
registers. The hair pulled back and the red and white polka dot
scarf covering her head, and the other stuff.

The other stuff.

Lauren wears a cotton dress, mostly off-white but blue
leaves on it. The blue leaves look drawn on the off-white fabric,
beautifully drawn with a black pen, a pen with a super fine tip
that draws a super thin black line, makes me think the dress is
from France and some incredibly slender and beautiful French
artist chick drew the leaves and colored them a faded blue, even
though they weren't for real drawn on Lauren's dress. I don't
know nothing about fabric and dresses, but someone
somewhere did a drawing of a leaf and then however they print
onto fabric, well they printed that leaf all over fabric and made
them all that faded blue color. The dress comes down past
Lauren's knees and it's tied at the waist with a cloth tie of the
same off-white-with-blue-leaves-printed-on-it fabric, tied in a
bow below where Lauren's belly button is, well where I think
her belly button should be, if I could see it, which of course I

can't.

Of course.

More other stuff.

Lauren's shades, same as Sara Lownds wore in the photo of Sara Lownds and Dylan I told you about where she has on the scarf. Round granny glasses with the dark purple lenses. And it was funny 'cause Lauren was this thin, almost skinny, no, that's wrong, actually and definitely skinny, feminine looking chick only she had this tomboy vibe.

I got *Bringing It All Back Home* in my hands when Lauren shows up. I'm standing just to the left of the Dylan section. Lauren stops so close I can feel her warm breath, gets her Sara Lownds shades off, got 'em in one hand, and with the other she's flipping through those Dylan albums desperate.

I do my best to be the cool scene, nonchalant, you know, looking at the back cover as if Lauren don't exist. But I'm excited. I never been so close to a chick, I mean other than that one time when Jenny kissed me. And this chick, I mean for sure she gotta dig Dylan.

Yeah I got my head aimed down at the back of *Bringing It All Back Home*, but my eyes scope out what Lauren's up to, and even as she flips through the albums, she keeps looking over at the album I'm holding.

I didn't know this of course, not that day, but later I find out from Lauren that Christmas day her mom, drunk how she gets, came into Lauren's room, grabbed the album off the record player right during "Maggie's Farm" and broke it over her knee, told Lauren she was sick to death of hearing that godawful accusatory Dylan voice coming out of Lauren's room morning, noon and night same as some plague inflicted on their home.

So Lauren spent over an hour walking and busing from San Anselmo where she lives to Village Music, where she knows they'll have *Bringing It All Back Home*.

Only it turns out there's one copy, and I'm holding it.

Lauren finishes going through the Dylan albums, let's all of 'em fall against the back of the bin. She looks at what I got in my hands, and says to me:

You don't need a weatherman to know which way the wind blows.

She quotes Dylan, and me, I think it's fucking hip, her saying that. To me, man.

This groovy Lauren chick says that to *me*.

"'Subterranean Homesick Blues,'" I say.

And she says:

Girl by the whirlpool, lookin' for a new fool.

And I stand there, slowly turning my head, first to the left, then to the right, 'cause somehow I know already how it's gonna end but I don't let myself believe it.

"You found him, man," I say.

Fuck yeah.

And somehow that Dylan album gets from my hands into Lauren's hands.

"You found him."

So let me tell you about it.

You know, my one and only date with Lauren.

And how uncool. A date. I wanted to hang out with her, listen to some sides in her folks' living room and talk, or sit on a bench in her back yard, if she had a bench, if she had a back yard. And later, up in her room. If her room was up, only turned out it wasn't up, it was on the ground floor. I never saw her room, but something she says. No, that wasn't it at all, it was when her mom went to get her, this is later in the story, but anyway, when her mom goes and gets her, after she tells me, "Let me go get Lauren, she's in her room," her mom went somewhere on the first floor, didn't go up those stairs in the entry.

But anyway.

Would have been cool for me and Lauren to check out a band playing a free concert in the park on a Saturday afternoon.

Some kinda hang loose deal.

But no, I went on a *date* with Lauren. And it *was* a date, and we both knew how straight-ass lame it was, and I never knew why she even agreed to it. Maybe she liked me some after all, still don't know. Maybe Lauren wasn't as certain about everything as she seemed. Maybe Lauren had the mixed-up confusion same as every other chick. None of them know what they want, even when they think they do.

Back then I thought it was just the chicks and pretty much everyone else but me. Now I know different, I mean if anyone was mixed-up confused it was me.

But anyway.

About two weeks after I met her at the record store our date happened.

I'm 15, same as I told you before, which means I can't drive. So on a Saturday I get my mom to drive up to San Anselmo where Lauren lives. Yeah, I know it's fucked, but what can I do?

On the way to Lauren's house, Mom and me in the car, the two of us in the front seat, Mom at the wheel, me on the passenger side, Mom on a fishing expedition.

"Is she a nice girl, Mike?" Mom says.

Mom did the quick look over in my direction, and that was the don't-you-lie-to-me look, her needing to keep her eyes on the road, but she can't help it.

No mom, she's not a nice girl. She's a whore, a nymphomaniac, a rabid cocksucker. She's a total love child sex freak, and she's gonna let me do it to her every possible way a guy can do it to a chick.

I don't say nothing but I turn to look at Mom. She's 38 that day. That year.

That day in early January of 1969.

I don't say nothing.

Is she a nice girl? No, she's a junkie, she's a cokehead, she drops acid morning, noon and night. And that's how I get her to do what I want—with the drugs.

I don't say a word.

My mom's a brunette, her hair piled up in one of those bouffant deals that were popular in the Fifties. She has the tortoise shell librarian glasses, the lenses kinda egg-shaped only if you pulled at both sides of the egg so it was flatter and wider, and then the frames come up in each upper corner.

She had a sweet face, my mom did, a kindly face back then, before all the trouble started. Her face was kinda pudgy. She was at least 25 pounds overweight, and it showed in her face and that rounded look made her seem a gentle soul and she was, so even though she hated being overweight, it helped people see the real Mom. It would have been weird-ass weird if Mom looked same as Rita Hayworth or Bettie Page, you know, having the personality Mom had and all.

"Well," she says.

"Well, what?"

Mom has on this blue and green and yellow Madras dress cinched at the waist with a shiny brown leather belt and big-ass gold buckle. She sewed that dress, bought a pattern and the material and used the sewing machine in my folks' bedroom. Mom made a lot of her own clothes. I thought her sewing her own clothes was lame, something that poor people did and no way did I want to think of myself as poor.

Actually, we were in the middle class, my family. Only I wanted to be a rich fucker same as Bruce Wayne or Gatsby or Lennon so I could do shit I wanted and not worry where the dough gonna come from. I was special, you know, so why should I ever have to worry about money, or a job, or any bullshit whatever. That was how I thought back then, when I was 15. Thought that way later too. That think-you're-special deal, beyond the rules that everyone else has to obey, can get you into all kinds of trouble. I know all about it.

Just trying to clue you in.

"This girl we're gonna pick up," Mom says.

"She's not 'this girl,'" I say. "She's got a name Mom. Her name's Lauren."

"But what's she like?"

Having Mom drive me to pick up Lauren seems an even worse than bad idea, and more so all the time. If I'd been a smoker that day, for sure I'd have lit up. Instead, I did this slow elaborate yawn, which, authentic real of it, almost not worth describing. Figure I open my mouth slow, real slow, slower than that even, bring my left hand up and cover my mouth, head back.

The slow slow elaborate slow yawn deal.

Yeah, that kinda trip.

"She's a chick, man," I say. "Lauren digs Dylan."

My mom gives me the quick look.

"Don't all the girls your age dig Bob Dylan?" Mom says.

"Don't say dig, Mom," I say. "Especially after we pick up Lauren."

"Well don't they?" she says.

"No Mom," I say. "All the girls my age don't dig Bob Dylan. Not like Lauren."

We were in the newer car, the '67 green Rambler, and that car had separate seats in the front, and there was a lever you could move to adjust the back of the seat, so now I got it so it was angled way back, so I was almost lying down, my sand-colored suede cowboy boots up on the dash.

That got Mom all distracted and uptight, I could tell 'cause there was a slight jerkiness to her driving when she was tense and her eyes blinked too much. She told me if we were in an accident my legs would go through the front window, and was that what I want to do to her, leave her behind mourning her dead son. Lays it on heavy, so I got the seat back up and my feet off the dash, but I take a real long time doing all that, and she don't ask any more questions about Lauren.

Thank God-who-almost-for-certain-don't-exist when we finally get to Lauren's place in San Anselmo. I gotta go in and get Lauren and her mom answers the door. It was kinda shocking, seeing Lauren's mom, because she was a sad version of what Lauren might look like in 20 years if a lot of things went wrong. Her mom's face was bloated and had that reddish thing going that comes from drinking too much on a regular basis. She didn't care about her clothes or her hair, that was obvious. She was wearing some kinda wrinkled beige pant suit pants with an elastic waist that was stretched to accommodate what can happen if you eat two or three glazed donuts for breakfast every day, and snack with frequency. Her broken blonde hair was straight same as Lauren's only had that faded, stringy look that happens when hair has been subjected to hair dye for too many years.

She stood there chewing gum, filling the doorframe.

"Whatcha want," she says.

I don't know what to say to Lauren's mom, say some shit about us both being into Dylan and her mom nods, and I can't tell if she approves or tolerates or thinks Lauren's whole trip is lame, and she takes a few steps down the hall, yells in a deep scratchy voice.

"Hey Lauren, some moony-eyed boy's here to see you."

Lauren's dad split when she was 9. Lauren told me that. I guess living with Lauren and no husband was more than her mom could deal with, I mean Lauren was more than anyone could deal with, but anyway, nothing else of interest happened there in Lauren's house right then. I tried to get out of there with Lauren quick-like as I could, and then we're in the back seat of the green Rambler and my mom's driving.

Lauren was all tomboyed up that day: oversize black and blue and white plaid flannel shirt that Neil Young would look right at home wearin' and some kind of Army green parka and the baggy blue jeans chicks trying to downplay their bodies wore back then, and fucked-up worn brown leather hiking boots proof she wasn't some girly-ass girl, no man, those boots proof she was tough. Or thinks she's tough, and I'm impressed, makes me think she's tough.

She's not wearing the Sara Lownds scarf and her hair is free, and she was free, that's the thing about Lauren, she makes me feel us two can hitchhike to Oaxaca, Mexico, or steal a car and drive to Santa Barbara and camp on the beach or dream up a couple stallions and ride off into the ocean.

That kinda chick.

My mom gonna drive us all the way up to this cool place I know on Mt. Tamalpais, you know, that mountain whose name is the Miwok Indian word for "sleeping maiden" 'cause if you really look at it, you can see the Tamalpais mountain range is the outline of a sleeping woman, a woman sleeping on her back, face to the heavens, or whatever's up there 'cause I mean if there's no God, there's no heavens. We drive through San Anselmo and turn onto Sir Francis Drake, drive along Sir Francis Drake, past Ross, past the JC in Kentfield, fuck, just the start of it.

To get to that place on Mt. Tam where me and Lauren are gonna take a walk and eat the lunch I brought along, we stay on Sir Francis Drake, drive past the shopping center, and onto 101, all the way past Corte Madera and further still, take the Mill Valley exit, drive along East Blithedale and Camino Alto and up Miller and take a left at the 2 A.M. Club and up the damn winding road twist and turn, another 20 minutes 'til we get near the top of Mt. Tam.

Normal deal, this drive takes forever, but my mom driving it takes fucking forever forever and longer still. And all the way, me and Lauren don't say a word to each other 'cause what you gonna say to a chick you dig but don't hardly know when your mom's right there and this silence is the goddamn elephant-in-the-Rambler. Yeah it's awkward. The elephant. The silence. The awkward.

Biggest idiot in the world, man, that was me, needing my mom to get me and Lauren somewhere, sucked so bad, and why didn't I suggest we get milk shakes in San Anselmo, or take a walk around her neighborhood or something, anything. There had to be something we could have done near where she lives, but too late for that, and since me and Lauren say nothing my mom starts in conducting the grand inquisition. Mom's got a serious voice, a voice where she's the college professor and you're the freshman, or maybe even the high school senior, and that's the voice she uses.

"So Lauren, are you planning to go to college?" Mom says.

Last thing I want is my mom grilling Lauren.

"Come on, Mom," I say.

"I'm talking to your friend, Mike," Mom says.

And oh fuck. *Mike.* She called me Mike in front of Lauren. How lame is that, and what's Lauren gonna think. Fucking *Mike!*

So Mom's question hangs there and we all know. If big red plastic letters hung in the air spelling out that question, it wouldn't be any more obvious.

So Lauren gets this mischievous smile going and she turns my way, and she says to my mom, *losers, cheaters, six-time users* and my mom don't know what Lauren's talking about, and it's the awkward silence in the car, and Lauren settles back in the seat, and I swear I wouldn't have been surprised if she'd gotten out a smoke and lit up, she was so cool.

Up in the front seat my mom's total mixed-up confusion. She don't know Lauren's quoting Dylan, can't make any sense of it. I know it freaks Mom 'cause of that jerky way she drives when her nerves go haywire, plus from where I sit, in the rear view I can see her right eye twitching.

I figure that's gonna be it for the questions, but I'm wrong, Mom storms ahead with another doozy.

"So Lauren, what does your father do?"

Lauren don't look at me this time, and her face dead serious, no smile, and she's the coolest of the cool, and to my mom she says, *Shakespeare, he's in the alley, with his pointed shoes and his bells,* and my mom just keeps driving, but Lauren's trip totally throws Mom off this time, she got that queasy face going, and she slips back to her normal sing-song cheerful voice same as the Fifties are alive and well in a '67 ugly-ass green Rambler.

"Well that's very nice, Lauren," Mom says. "I've always been fond of 'Romeo and Juliet' and 'King Lear.'"

For the rest of the drive Mom keeps quiet, humming some Frank Sinatra song, 'cause Sinatra been her favorite since she was my age.

Lauren gives me her mischievous grin and I give her a me-too smile back, and for right then we were in the pocket, that conspiracy of two deal—united in opposition to the lame-ass adults of the world. Kids man, they think they know it all. Only it wasn't so simple 'cause in the back of my mind I didn't feel so good about what gone down.

I mean on the one hand, it was cool 'cause my mom was lame, but she was *my* mom. Made me feel kinda weird, Lauren making fun of Mom 'cause in a way she was making fun of me too. It was my mom, you know what I mean. Still, it made me admire Lauren, her having the guts. I've always dug chicks who got the guts. Those are the chicks that can really get a guy in trouble.

Finally we pull into the parking lot which is maybe a mile, maybe more from the top of Tam, right near this cool-ass hiking trail I been on many times, and after the car comes to a stop, motor still going, my mom says she'll be back to pick us up in two hours *and don't get into any trouble you two.*

And we're out of that ugly-ass car and Mom drives off, and this is the first time I'm on a date with a chick. And actually, it's the first time I've ever been alone with one.

A chick.

2. MY DATE WITH LAUREN

ALONE WITH A CHICK.

Oh my God. Only there isn't any God. I'm so sure.

I'm freaked and jazzed and buzzed to the nth squared.

But to clarify, 'cause I wanna get this right, it's not totally true what I said about being alone with a chick. I was alone for about two minutes with Jenny that time, you know, the freshman chick who gave me my first joint.

And my first kiss.

This is different, and I know it and my body knows it. I'm more than buzzing, my whole body lit up. Fuck, man, a groovy chick I dig, out on a date with me, us two there by ourselves on Mt. Tam for two hours!

Right quick-like Lauren's laughing and dancing this freaky rock 'n' roll dance there in the dirt parking area, spinning around, I mean those hiking boots might as well been ballet slippers, and her arms up in the air same as a ballerina I guess only the way she did it, it's some crazy-wild Desolation Row carnival ballerina Dylan would sing about, and I try to laugh too, hope hope hope Lauren laughs about my mom, not at me.

Please don't be laughing at me, Lauren.

Please.

We get on the trail, the meadow a wave of wild grasses to our left, the ground angling up to our right to a row of huge Douglas firs parallel to the path. We walk along and I ask Lauren how she got to be such a heavy traffic Dylan fan and she's like *come on, man, how can anyone not dig Dylan, you know, other than your mom,* and we laugh, and I'm like yeah, sure, of course

but actually until I met Lauren I figured I was absolutely
positively for sure the world's biggest Dylan fan. Other than
Rock 'n' Roll Frankie, I didn't know any other hardcore
Dylanophiles.

Right then, us walking along that trail, the air having an ice
cube chill to it 'cause it's still winter so even with the sun out we
need our coats, Lauren in that Army green parka and me I have
on my Navy pea coat with the two rows of large black buttons
with an anchor shape somehow indented into each one, I need
her to understand about me and Dylan.

Me and Dylan, man, yeah. *Yeah.*

And so I tell her about the first time.

The first time I heard him.

Him. Dylan. Yeah.

Him.

The first time I heard Dylan was "Like a Rolling Stone," and
that song changed my life and everything.

And *fucking* everything.

"This was back in 1965," I say.

"Of course it was," she says.

We're still walking along the upper border of the meadow
which is huge and which is where I used to play capture the flag
when I was in Cub Scouts, and the scoutmaster was a man
named Dr. Clark and there was another doctor, Dr. Snark I
called him, who was good friends with Dr. Clark, yeah those
two were bosom buddies they were such chummy chum chums
and on one of the camping trips my dad came along and I
watched how condescending they were toward him.

Those two had expensive camping gear and camping clothes
—special waterproof jackets and polished brown leather boots
and these pants that looked perfect for a safari where you could
unzip the lower half of the legs and turn the pants into shorts
—and my dad coulda just got himself out from under the
Rambler, he had on his grease stained chinos and a moth-eaten
wool shirt he'd had since the earth cooled and ocean creatures
crawled onto land, and beat-to-hell hiking boots. Well those two,
Clark and Snark, I see them judging Dad and Dad not fitting in,

not part of their groovy doctor scene.

Man I had to shake all that shit off me and try not to think anymore about it. Here I got my chance to hang with Lauren and I'm letting the bad vibes of the past do a number on me.

Fuck it, man.

The path is damp, not muddy 'cause it's been a few weeks since the last rain, but it's damp, and the meadow is lush overgrown, you know, the way meadows are, or anyway, the way I think of a meadow.

"July 20, 1965," Lauren says.

"What?" I say.

"That's when it was released," Lauren says. "The single."

"I remember, I heard it in July," I say. "My mom driving me into Mill Valley, and right after we got over the 101 overpass, that song came on and it was like I'd been struck by lightning. Twice."

Lauren talks real fast, walking ahead of me, she's got a stick —a piece of broken branch—she's picked up that's maybe twice the length of her arms she uses as a staff, talk talk talk, and the path narrow for one person, and anyway, she was that kind of chick, take the lead no matter what, no way to keep up with her, no way.

Talk talk talk, and she's excited. She remembers the first time she heard that song too. She'd had a fight with her mother. She was at the end of the line, sulking in her bedroom, listening to her transistor radio hoping something good would come on but there was nothing, one sad sappy song after another and she was ready to explode when "Like a Rolling Stone" started and she wasn't in the bedroom anymore, she was in the Dylan Zone for the first time.

It got me all jacked up, Lauren's excitement, and I forgot about it being awkward, me and her. Us two jumping out of our skins to talk about what happened, and I mean right to this day it's still a mystery.

"Like a Rolling Stone," fucking mystical mindblower, man.

"A lot of radio stations back then just played the first half," Lauren says.

"Yeah, I know," I say.

I want so bad for her to know the serious of my Dylan trip.

"The record company didn't think anyone," I say, "was gonna play a song that was 6 minutes and 8 seconds long on the radio."

Lauren stops walking and she turns fast, so fast, throws the stick into the weeds, closes her eyes behind the shades, and, right there on the path, imitates Dylan's nasal whine. Should have been funny, this 15-year-old chick with a thin high voice imitating Dylan, but there was nothing funny about it.

I felt something in my heart, a joy, yeah, overwhelming extravagant heavy traffic joy so strong it was all over me same as being soaked from the rain. I thought I was gonna fall over, and I don't know when I ever felt a feeling same as that. I mean this chick there with me and she's singing that song, a song I'd listened to alone in my room all those times, all those years.

Lauren stood there in front of me on that path, her face screwed up in pain, you know, how a singer really feeling it screws up their face, Janis singing "Ball and Chain" or Billie Holiday singing "Strange Fruit," and she sings.

Her naked voice.

No surging organ. No pounding drums. No high-voltage guitar. But still, the way she sings, landing hard on the rhymes of "time" and "fine" and "dime" and "prime," making it as much an indictment as Dylan.

Once upon a time you dressed so fine, you threw the bums a dime, in your prime, didn't you?

She's dancing again, and she dance-skips right around me going off the path and into the weeds, yeah, she feels it too. The two of us sharing that moment, and the power of two people feeling so strong about something that means so much.

And she sings.

People'd call, say, "Beware, doll, you're bound to fall" You thought they were all kiddin' you.

And I'm talking. Talk, talk, talk. Talk too fast, the excitement overwhelming us both.

"They put half the song on one side of the single and the

rest on the other side," I say. "But KEWB, it was so cool, that station played the whole thing—totally blew my mind."

She stops dancing, and from behind her shades she's looking at me funny. She don't know what to think. She reaches up, grabs at her Sara Lownds dark purple shades, got 'em clenched in her hand, her jade green eyes x-raying my eyes, and there's a defiance, I mean she got the look of Victorine Meurent in that "Olympia" painting Manet made.

"You better not be fucking with me, Michael," she says. "'Cause it would hurt me bad if you were."

We stand there and I'm desperate, throat choking up, and I croak out some words, I'm gonna say how into Dylan I am but I don't get the chance.

"It's OK," she says.

She reaches out, her hand on my arm, she's touching me and my body levitates and everything goes blurry.

"I, I mean it means so much," she says. "I wouldn't want, it would kill me to have someone joking me about Bobby."

"When I heard 'Like a Rolling Stone,'" I say.

Her voice gets that wide-eyed sound, you know, same as when a kid sees something they dig so much for the first time, that look, only it's her voice.

"It was the *best*," she says.

"It was the *best*," I say.

Me and her stand there on the path, talk about Dylan, talk about the best song ever, and thinking about that now, I can't help but smile. I mean that chick Lauren so into it she couldn't contain herself how excited she was, and me, oh man, to be so close to a girl who felt same as I did about something, and I mean not just any old something, this was the overwhelming extravagant heavy traffic something.

This was *Dylan*, man.

To agree on Dylan the way me and Lauren agreed on Dylan right then and there on that path, well fuck, I thought that was love.

For sure that was love.

Had to be love, man.

For sure us agreeing on that Dylan song the way we did meant we were soul mates. Of course. Yeah, you know. You get it. Yeah, well, I didn't know any better back then.

"He wrote that song for me," she says.

"You know him?" I say.

First time I heard that Dylan song it saved my life.

A song can do that.

Reach out of the car radio, save my life.

Reach out of the car radio that other day, day I first hear it, late July 1965, that voice singing to me and only me, and you know, that other day, day I was with Lauren, early January 1969, I couldn't even really say all that song meant to me. In my heart I knew, but I didn't have all the words. I mean the music the best music I ever heard, like if that Dali painting, "Dream Caused by the Flight of a Bee Around a Pomegranate, a Second Before Awakening," with the naked chick lying above the ocean and these tigers leaping at her and all the weird-ass weird Dali shit going on, was music, well that's what that was the sound of, that Dylan song.

Somehow that song summed up exactly and for certain how I felt that day, summer of '65, every loner feeling, every put down I ever suffered, every bit of existential angst, I hear it all in that song and then, top of all that, that Dylan voice which broke every rule which I didn't actually know back then, but still I knew, in my body I knew, and what I knew was that every damn thing I'd been told was wrong 'cause if a voice like that, all sneer and sarcasm and ragged and strange, could be on Top 40 radio, anything was possible. And all the rules they taught me didn't mean shit.

I knew.

Anything, man, anything possible.

"After I heard that song on the radio," I say. "That was all I thought about all the rest of the day."

And me and Lauren, we still stand there on the path, not going anywhere, shiver in our coats but we don't care, no we don't care at all.

She had her hand still on my arm, and I don't know how it happened, but we were holding hands and I worried my hand was sweaty. Oh man, to hold a chick's hand! Bottle rockets exploding under my skin, and if that been the last thing happened to me and I was dead and gone, it would have been enough, that's how I felt right then. Her little chick's hand, warm and smooth in mine, and her hand was kinda damp, which shoulda told me something, but I was too busy worrying 'bout what it meant, a chick letting me hold her hand out in the middle of wild nature, no one around but me and her same as we were the only humans on the planet.

"I kept singing it to myself," Lauren says.

She sings the chorus, sings it the way she sings, all high and girl and the echo of Dylan's overwhelming extravagant whine.

How does it feel, to be without a home...

"I had to own that record," I say. "It was like I was an addict and needed a fix—a desperation."

...like a complete unknown.

"I walked the mile from our house to the record store," I say. "When I got there, I went looking in the Rock section and there were no Dylan records."

"'Cause they were all in Folk," Lauren says.

She knew. Of course Lauren knew.

At the record store I looked under "D" and then I looked under "B" and there was no Bob Dylan in Rock and I had to ask the guy behind the counter and he was like, *Dylan's a folk singer, he's in the Folk music section,* and right then I thought this is weird-ass weird 'cause the song I heard, that was rock, that wasn't folk music, but he showed me where the Folk section was and damn there's all these Dylan records, like this guy been around.

Can you comprehend the magnitude of the whole deal? Never heard of Bob Dylan, know nothing about him. Not one single thing. And I hear the song on the radio, the greatest most overwhelming extravagant heavy traffic song, a song he might as well wrote for me, a song that was everything I felt, and I go to the record store and discover he has five albums! Five goddamn goddamn overwhelming extravagant heavy traffic albums. I mean something same as that give you a heart attack, man, only I'm 12 when I first hear that song, so I don't gotta worry about heart attacks.

But anyway.

"I didn't know which of his albums 'Like a Rolling Stone' was on," I say.

On the path, somehow we're side-by-side, managing to walk together, holding hands, my insides doing somersaults, me talking to Lauren, and we're walking, walk and talk, talk and walk.

"I checked out each one," I say. "And looking at those albums, on every one, Dylan looked different."

Lauren lets go of my hand, turns to face me, and she's walking backwards, and even with her shades on I knew her eyes were wide, and there were fireworks in those eyes, sparklers going off and Roman Candles and Crackling Comets.

"I love that about him," she says. "He's never the same. Just like how the world changes, everything changes, and Dylan, he never stands still."

She turns again, and I'm looking at the back of her head, brown hair falling past the collar of that Neil Young flannel shirt and maybe this could turn into something, me and Lauren.

I mean why not? It wasn't every day a chick would find a guy into Dylan same as me. She gotta dig the scene of that scene.

Only we're not holding hands no more.

At the upper edge of the meadow the trail comes to a fire road, and there's rustic worn wood signs on the other side of the road from where we are.

"I mean he's this scruffy folk guy on the first album," I say.

We look at the signs, one has an arrow points up the road, says "water tower, 1.5 miles," and another arrow below all that, points down the road, says "parking lot, .8 miles," and another sign has an arrow points to the trail that continues in the direction we've been walking, says "Mt. Theater, 1.1 miles" and an arrow points the opposite direction, says "parking lot 1 mile."

"Then he's got the cool leather jacket," Lauren says. "And this hair that's starting to look rock 'n' roll and Suze on his arm. That's *Freewheelin'*."

Talking fast fast fast, me, then Lauren, Lauren, then me, yeah, that hyped-up talk talk talk talk fast talk deal.

"Yeah and then he's this total serious dude," I say. "Close up portrait in black and white on the third one."

We start walking up the road to the water tower, 'cause I been up there before and I know two things, first being that the view from up where the water tower stands is a groovy trip, San Francisco in the distance and the Bay and the Farallones, and it's gonna blow Lauren's mind for sure, and I'm hoping she'll think I'm cool knowing about that view and all, and the other thing is that there's a trail from the water tower back down to the Mountain Theater that's groovy too, so that's the way to go, for sure it is. I mean there are some things I know I know, and that's one of them.

"My friend Danny," Lauren says. "He looks how Dylan looked on *The Times They Are A-Changin'*."

That should have stopped me, her talking about some other guy, some guy friend when she's on a date with me, and if I had paid more attention, I might have heard something there in her voice, a thin tremble beneath her words, but I was too caught up in talking to a girl I dug about Dylan. I mean I'd never talked about anything with a girl the way me and Lauren were talking.

"And with *Bringing It All Back Home* in March of '65, now he's this rock guy, his hair and his face is another person," I say. "This weird-ass weird baroque deal, he's in some old Victorian room and the ornate fireplace and that gorgeous chick in a dark red blouse and red pants smoking in the background."

"That's Sally Grossman," Lauren says. "The wife of Dylan's manager. You know Albert Grossman, right? You seen him in 'Don't Look Back.' That's the Grossmans' living room."

"How do you know?" I say.

"I *know*," she says.

Her voice was rock solid, and there's no doubt of her certainty and I looked at her, man, she's young and beautiful and such a tomboy with that flannel shirt, shirt tails out, brushing her hair out of her face, and she had a birthmark at the edge of her jaw right under her right earlobe, a small brown splotch.

I don't know why but that splotch of a birthmark killed me.

"He got the idea from Fitzgerald," Lauren says.

I didn't know what she was talking about, and I guess she could see that all over my face.

"Gloria and Daisy and Rosemary and the girl in 'Winter Dreams.'"

Still I didn't get it, I was so dense, and by that point in the day, I was in love. Mistaking a crush for love. I was so starry-eyes back then.

"It's where he got the idea for 'Like a Rolling Stone,' silly."

And I got it. The debutantes and stuck-up rich girls, so fickle and selfish and egocentric.

And she started to sing, and her voice was her chick voice, her high chick voice, but it was Dylan too, it was Dylan's whine, it was the cynical. So starry-eyes.

You've been through all of F. Scott Fitzgerald's books, You're very well read, It's well known.

So obvious. I mean I'd read "Gatsby" and "Winter Dreams" and maybe half of "The Beautiful and the Damned." Never for a minute did I put it together.

"Love is just a four-letter word," she says.

And she smiled this mischievous smile, you know, the kind of smile a chick can have when they know something they're not gonna tell you. Lauren, man, she was proud of all she knew about Dylan, and no way was she giving her sources away.

Well what the record store clerk told me that day, July of 1965, was that "Like a Rolling Stone" song wasn't on any album yet; turned out the album it would be on, *Highway 61 Revisited,* wasn't coming out 'til the end of August.

"So I bought that 'Like a Rolling Stone' single that day," I say. "But about a month later, day it came out, I bought *Highway 61 Revisited.*"

"Damn right you did," Lauren says.

And she's standing there got her shades off again, twirling them by one of the metal temples, and with her other hand, snapping her fingers and her face all smirked up.

"Why'd he call it that?" she says. "Come on, Mr. Jones. Let's see how much knowledge you got."

And I don't know about the crossroads or Clarksdale, Mississippi, none of it back then. I mean I'm 15.

"Highway 61," she says. "Where the blues got its start."

"Yeah?"

"So Dylan's goin' back there to revisit the old haunts," she says. "Only he got new stories to tell."

"Groovy," I say. "I dig."

Only I didn't dig, didn't understand, not at all.

"That's not the end of it," she says. "You know Hawthorne, 'The Scarlet Letter'?"

"Got no time for that musty shit," I say.

"You really are a new fool," she says.

And before I figure a comeback she tells me about Hawthorne's "Twice Told Tales," how he wrote another history of America in those tales, revealing a secret history of classism and religious discrimination and fucking over the Indians and drowning women they decided were witches, and there's more and he gets into how all the surface piety and good manners and Puritan righteous deal conceals a darkness of adultery and boozing and lust and devil worship and Dylan wrote his own twice told tales, called it *Highway 61 Revisited*. He got so much to tell about this America he discovers on *Bringing It All Back Home* at the start of the song he called "Bob Dylan's 115th Dream."

And I thought about it often what Lauren said that day, and started to understand about the surface of the surface and how almost nothing is what it appears to be and I think that's when I got it in my head I got to figure out the authentic real, see the world for what it is and not the façade of delusion humans erect in front of the truth.

"There isn't just one good song on *Highway 61 Revisited*," I say. "Every song is groovy."

That day, August 30, 1965, in my room listening to that album, every song was the best song I ever heard. Dylan's stream of words going on and on and on, and the music, rock 'n' roll never been played same as that before, and while all that was going on I stared at that photo of Dylan on the cover wearing the motorcycle t-shirt and the shirt over it with the weird-ass modern art designs printed on it like Dylan himself was a work of art, and there was someone standing behind him, this camera dangling from a strap that person was holding, that cover so laden with symbolism and I didn't know the code, like what did all of it mean?

I needed to know so bad.

"That's how I felt when I listened to it the first time," Lauren says. "Like I wanted to know what every single thing meant, every line in every song, who the musicians were playing on those songs, who that producer Tom Wilson was who produced 'Like a Rolling Stone' and how come there was a different producer who produced everything else."

"And what kind of guitar he was playing," I say.

"The thing I wanted to know the most," Lauren says. "Was about that look."

"What do you mean?" I say.

"The way he's looking out from that cover," she says. "Lookin' at the cover for hours while I played it over and over, that's when I knew he wrote them for me."

She said it like how could I not know what she was talking about.

"He's looking right at the camera," she says. "But he's looking right at me when I look at that cover. What's he saying with that look? What's he saying?"

I sure didn't know what to say.

Lauren was a trip. She was what Winston Churchill said about Russia: a riddle wrapped in a mystery inside an enigma. I mean she would just go off and say some shit like Dylan's the Picasso of rock and compare him to Picasso, and she'd talk about Picasso's women and Dylan's women and Picasso's paintings and Dylan's lyrics and how the images in Dylan's lyrics were same as the fractured Cubist shit in Picasso's paintings and she knew about the time Dylan and Ginsberg and McClure hung out at City Lights, Ferlinghetti's book store, in '65, this summit of the hipster poets, the old guard, The Beats, passing the torch to the young word-slinger.

Sometimes Lauren would be doing this monologue same as I wasn't even there. We'd walk along and she'd start dancing to some song in her head, the sunlight glinting bright off the dark dark purple oval lenses of those granny glasses and then, all of a sudden, she'd shout out the lyrics to "Stuck Inside of Mobile With the Memphis Blues Again" or "Leopard-Skin Pill-Box Hat." She was like that—total unpredictable chick.

I couldn't really talk to her. I said something like *look at the light coming through the leaves of that oak*, me trying to be poetic and sensitive and impress her, and she goes off about light, starts talking about all the Dylan songs with light in them, you know, "Chimes of Freedom," Dylan singing *electric light still struck like arrows*, and "Don't Think Twice" with the *light I never knowed*, and "Highway 61 Revisited" with *come here and step into the light*, and "Visions of Johanna" where *lights flicker from the opposite loft*, I mean that Lauren chick could have taught a fucking college course just on Dylan and light.

That kinda deal, yeah, for sure.

3. TO TOUCH HER

WE'D BEEN WALKING MAYBE an hour up to the water
tower and down that trail I told you about already, and we
ended up at the Mountain Theater, this stone outdoor
amphitheater where they had plays and folk music shows and
for a while in 1967 cool-ass rock festivals. I saw Big Brother and
the Holding Company and The Doors and The Byrds at this
one festival, and even Captain Beefheart and His Magic Band
was there. Last show Ry Cooder played before quitting
Beefheart, and they played "Electricity." I was 13 and that was
the freakiest music I'd ever heard.

And on this day, though the amphitheater was empty except
for me and Lauren, I could see it full of crazy Freak Scene
Dream freaks and Janis up there on the stage they set up with
big psychedelic flags and she's screaming "Down on Me," and I
knew that somewhere in the universe, light years away, some
creature watching earth was seeing Janis on that stage singing
that song.

Once something happens, it happens forever.

Forever, man.

You think about it you can total lose your mind trip, the
images and the sounds heading out into space, and they keep
going and if you had a fast enough space ship, you could get
ahead of them and see the shit play out again and again and
again.

Crazy, man, crazy.

Me and Lauren find a spot about halfway back from where
the stage would be, if there was a stage, which of course on this

day there isn't, sit on a couple of flat stones, she gets off the parka and I take off my pea coat, let the bright bright midday sun warm our bones, and we make sandwiches from the food I brought along. Out of my back pack I get a loaf of French bread, hunk of Swiss and some of that dry Italian salami with the paper around it where you cut off some, peel off the paper, that kinda salami. I had two Cokes, a bag of potato chips and a couple Red Delicious apples. Lauren dug me bringing the lunch and me using my Swiss Army knife to cut us hunks of bread and slices of that cheese and salami.

Don't know why I brought the lunch along, I mean it wasn't anything I spoke to her about when I called and asked if she wanted to go hike with me. It was one of those deals where I did it, not even thinking if it was the right thing to do or not. I guess I thought, well, I'm the one asked Lauren to go with me, so I got the responsibility and all, you know, that deal, or maybe it's that Eagle Scout syndrome, always bring everything along, just in case. Swiss Army knife, canteen of water, gloves, hat, jacket—all the shit.

Yeah, me, always bring all the shit, and it's such a burden, all the shit I don't need draggin' me down.

Lauren sat next to me, maybe a little more than a hand's length of pretty flat rock between me and her, and we have our feet on the dirt path right below us. Lauren lifts her left foot, has it on the rock and unlaces that boot, gets it and her dark blue sock off and the other boot and the other sock, sticks her legs straight out, flexing her little toes quietly humming "It Ain't Me, Babe." It was cool her singing Dylan, but I wanted it to be another song, "Baby, Let Me Follow You Down," the one he learned from Rick von Schmidt, or "I'll Be Your Baby Tonight."

Her humming "It Ain't Me, Babe" was a bummer.

Lauren being so close she smelled of Ivory soap, not some perfumed fancy chick smell, but just-the-facts-ma'am Ivory.

And lime, she smelled of lime.

I never figured out the lime deal. Maybe she was into using lime juice for something, I don't know, but I dug it. Lime. Now whenever I smell lime I think of Lauren sitting there in the

Mountain Theater singing "It Ain't Me, Babe."

And I get sad. I can't help it.

I still don't know if she was trying to send me a message, you know, after us holding hands and getting so close, or if her singing that particular song was coming from the unconscious. One can't ever know why a person does something. Even if they tell you why, hell knows if it's the truth. Even if they think it is, might not be.

Lauren didn't wear one of those Sara Lownds kinda scarves that day and now she pulls her hair back in a ponytail. She gets this blue kerchief out of her parka, wipes sweat off her forehead and her nose. It was hot, that cool wind had stopped and the bright bright midday sun overhead, man, me and Lauren sit there on the rocks, and I remember my surprise that chicks sweat too, same as guys. Sure my mom sweats, at least when she played tennis she did, but that was my mom. Never thought of my mom being a chick. You know, my mom was my mom.

Lauren wiping away the sweat from her face made me think for the first time that maybe chicks weren't that different, but I was wrong.

Yeah, of course, of course.

Felt the sweat under my nose, above my upper lip, all along it and my stomach sweating too, my t-shirt damp.

"We oughta build a teepee up here," Lauren says. "And live in it, like the Miwok Indians."

Fuck did that get me all mixed-up confusion.

Such an odd thing for Lauren to say, and I didn't understand. I mean did that mean she *really* dug me?

She picks up one of those apples, you know, the apples I bring for our lunch, polishes it against her flannel shirt.

"That'd be cool, you think?" she says.

She got the shades on, turns her head to look over at me, check my react I guess and my react is this adrenalin rush, like wow, I'm sitting close to this groovy chick and she says *that* to me, that's the coolest ever.

She bites into that apple like the way I imagine Dylan or

even Woody Guthrie biting into an apple or chewing some chewing tobacco or tamping down tobacco in the bowl of a corncob pipe, that kinda hillbilly hobo action.

"Me and you up here in a teepee?" I say.

"For real?" I say.

She finished chewing that bite of apple, but took her time, and when she finished, said the next thing she was gonna say.

To me.

"You could be the hunter out slaying buffalos and rabbits and deer," she says. "I'd be back at the tent, squaw girl, taking care of all the little papooses."

I look at Lauren right then, and her face gives nothing away and my mind tripping, this chick must really *really* dig me, and you know I was 15 and everything so super overwhelming heavy serious, and such a big trip. I mean a chick saying some shit about us living in a teepee, in my mind, we're gonna fuck, the whole deal.

First date and this chick wants me, that's what's running through my brain right then.

Lauren has the apple in her hand, and I see where she took the bite and I see something black same as maybe it's rotten or even a worm.

"That apple looks weird," I say.

And then before I could even say shit about that whole teepee deal, before I really made a total ass of myself, she threw that fucked-up apple as far as she could throw it and she was cracking up, just the idea of that nonsense, me and her playing Mr. and Mrs. Indian in a teepee and her putting one over on me and I fell for it. It was a version of "Don't Look Back," Dylan putting everyone on and I knew I better be careful around Lauren 'cause a lot of times I didn't get the joke and 90% of what she said *was* the joke.

It made me feel sad, that lonesome deal, 'cause for a moment that teepee, I could see it, and it was real for me. Sure it was a crazy never-could-happen day dream, but it was beautiful, what she said, but then it was a goddamn fucking joke.

What chicks do to guys by saying a few words, and a lot of times they don't have a clue how much it hurts. A lot of times chicks don't think guys feel anything.

Lauren knew she fucked-up my feelings, so she tries to be nice, and she has some peanut butter cookies in a small plastic bag she gets out of a pocket of her parka, quick-like, asks if I want one, and I really don't want to be mad at her.

Her offering me that cookie, in my mind I totally forgive her and the two of us sit on those rocks, eat those heavy traffic delicious cookies. Don't know if her mom made 'em but the one I eat, I guess mostly because Lauren gave it to me, is the best cookie I ever tasted. I mean right then it was.

"You know if you grew your hair out a little longer, you could kinda look like him," Lauren says. "Like on *Blonde on Blonde.*"

I look at her, but those round granny glasses with the dark dark purple lenses, I can't see her eyes and her face is deadpan, total serious, not the hint of a smile.

"Wow," I say. "You're kidding, right?"

I wanted my hair to be cool so bad. I'd finally got my dad off my back, had to almost blackmail him. This happened in early August of '67, end of the summer. Back then I had one more merit badge to earn to get my Eagle Scout award. And you know, man, now I have some appreciation for what it took to get it, but at the time it was all about my dad pushin' and pushin' and pushin' for me to get those damn merit badges 'cause he so much wanted to say his son was an Eagle Scout.

All I had left was this Community Service badge and all I had to do to get it was spend an afternoon up at this Scout camp west of Fairfax doing some conservation work. So I'm all set to go up there, it's all arranged, my dad gonna drive me Saturday morning only instead of being ready to go, I stay in my room listening to *Highway 61 Revisited.*

Pretty soon the knock on the door.

"Get out here," he says. "Let's go."

I yell out, don't even open the door.

"I'm not going."

He opens the door, stands himself in the door frame. His hair was short same as it always was, almost a crew-cut but actually he needed a haircut and despite the grease-ball shit he put on it it's all askew, some of it sticking this way, some the other. He got his jaw jutting forward at me and he's pissed.

"What are you talking about?" he says. "This is the last one. You'll pretty much be an Eagle Scout by this afternoon."

His arms are hanging at his sides but I see him clenching, unclenching, clenching his left hand.

"I don't care about it," I say.

He wants to step into the room, but he don't.

"You don't care?!" he says. "I've been working with you, helping you get all these merit badges."

"Yeah," I say. "You should go do the conservation. They'll give you the award."

His face, man, the bones are gonna bust right through the skin, him straining not to just go crazy-fuck wild on me.

"I'd go up there," I say. "But there's something I need you to do."

"Oh I get it," he says. "You want money. A bribe."

"No I don't want money, Dad," I say.

I been lying there on the bed, now I sit up.

"I don't want you to cut my hair anymore."

"You want to look like a girl?" he says. "Like those Beatles."

"No Dad," I say. "Albert Einstein wasn't a girl. John Lennon isn't a girl. Bob Dylan isn't a girl."

I stood up so I could look right straight across from where I stood at him and I wasn't smiling, I was dead serious, holding my lips together real straight until I spoke.

"Come on, Dad," I say. "It's my head, it's my hair. I'm almost 14, in four years I could get drafted and sent off to Vietnam."

I don't know if he bought into my argument, but maybe it helped, and anyway, he wants that Eagle Scout award so bad. He stands there a while, doesn't say anything, just stands, gets his temper under control.

Finally. Finally.

"I don't like it," he says. "But as long as you get the Eagle Scout award, when you start high school I'll stop cutting your hair."

It's not the best, 'cause high school is nearly a month away, but still.

"Deal?" I say.

And then he did something he'd never done before. He walked over and reached his hand out and we shook on it.

"Deal," he says.

So I been growing my hair for over a year now, and I don't know why but my hair grows hellfuck slow, so when Lauren said that about my hair, and Dylan on the cover of *Blonde on Blonde*, it was curling off my head OK, but I needed another three inches at least to get in the ballpark of that John Lennon "White Album" look. Never found out if Lauren was blowing smoke up my ass, or she meant it.

She got the shades up on her head, the temples disappearing in her hair, and my eyes and her eyes, her Victorine Meurent eyes of defiance and I didn't understand, had I done something wrong, or was this one of her moods. That's another thing about chicks. They all got their moods. I guess guys got moods too. Picasso got moods. Hemingway had moods. Fitzgerald had 'em. But chicks, man, oh Jesus, I mean if there ever was a Jesus. I look into her eyes but I don't know how to see into her, I'm dazzled by those eyes, the beauty of them, and I don't care if she's looking at me same as Olympia looks at her john, those deep green eyes, man. There's a way a chick can look at a guy, look right into him, fuckin' kills me.

She starts talking about her favorite Dylan song.

"To Ramona," that's the one.

But why? Why that one, of all the groovy songs Dylan wrote, why would that be the one?

"It just is," she says.

And she sang some of it, and it was sad and beautiful, more sad and beautiful than when Dylan sings it.

Ramona, come closer, shut softly your watery eyes, the pangs of your sadness will pass as your senses will rise.

"There's got to be a reason," I say.

"I guess because of the hope," Lauren says. "He's saying the sadness will pass. He's saying that even the worst, it won't stay the same."

She sighed, and it was the only time I saw who she really was, a 15-year-old chick who didn't know everything, and who didn't have a dad around and had a mom who drank too much and who didn't know what was gonna happen next.

"You know at the end," she says, "Him saying he might be back, that's a symbol for something good that's going to happen."

Maybe, I thought, or maybe not.

That song was a favorite of mine too, but I didn't want to say that because I didn't want her to think I was a copycat.

"It's the changing of the guard, that song," I say. "The end of something and the beginning of something."

"Yeah," she says.

Her voice got that wide-eyed sound again, and it was same as she hadn't quite thought of it same as that until I said it.

"It really is," she says. "The end of something, the beginning of something."

Lauren got her boots back on, and I packed the lunch stuff 'cause it was almost time for my mom to be at the parking area, but still we take our time, walk on the rocks. Lauren skipping from one rock seat to another across the amphitheater, me walking behind until we're out of there and as we walk along the path under the trees I start thinking about my mom in that fucking Rambler and it bums me. I wanna stay here with Lauren, wanna get that teepee and live up here with her like we're a mountain man and a mountain chick, only we're at the fire road and I think Lauren was going through something too, the both of us in withdrawal as we leave the Dylan Zone, materializing back in the fucked-up reality of school and parents and how humiliating to need my mom for a ride back to

Lauren's house. Back in the Dylan Zone I'd have a Harley and she'd climb on behind me, wrap her arms around me, and I'd drive us two into some crazy-wild future.

Only the Dylan Zone was fading, and the world was spinning away from me.

I wanted a tree to fall on me or a mountain lion to rip me to pieces.

Or the Devil to drag me off to Hades.

There'd been moments so beautiful on that mountain with Lauren, moments when we weren't teenagers, when we were a guy and a chick, passionate about the truth, 'cause that's why Dylan meant so much to the both of us. He was truth in the guise of a man. His songs were a blueprint for how the world really was, and not the Hollywood façade the straights used to hide everything that meant *anything*. Moments so beautiful, and it would never happen again. I knew it, even if I didn't realize I knew it.

There are things you know, even if you shouldn't know 'em.
When you cut into the present the future leaks out.

By the time we got back to the parking lot we were two teenagers again who needed my mom to drive us, and sure enough she was parked there waiting, her window rolled down. The Rambler is the only car there, but soon as she sees us she calls my name too loud, a hoarse yell that I been hearing since I was too young to remember, all the times I was down at the neighbors' playing with 'em in the sandbox and she wanted me home, or dinner was ready and I was back in my room listening to the records too loud that took me on a trip far from that suburban gulag, and her hand out the window waving as if we need help locating her and that sad-ass car.

I thought sure she'd be reading a book. That was one thing about me and Mom and even my dad, we almost always had a book or a magazine with us so if we had to wait for anything, we could whip out the book.

You never waste your time if you got a book, my dad said.
Time is short, my dad said.

Before you know it, you'll be old and gray, my dad said.

My dad was full of the homilies and clichés.

When you're a kid you accept what your dad says as how life is, no different than the sun rising and setting each day. Later, if you got a brain, you stop accepting and you start asking questions.

That thing about the book, oh man, so not in the moment.

Later, I tried not to carry a book around.

You want to change shit in yourself, you got to take drastic measures.

And it's hard. To live in the moment when your impulse is to escape into a book or a song or a daydream. To live in the moment. I couldn't do it, and I was never gonna reach perfection. I mean if there's ever perfection, that would be God, but there isn't no God. Well, I mean probably there isn't. Right up to now, this very moment, I mean later, when everything I'm telling you about is over and done, and I'm at the typewriter getting it down, still don't know for sure. About God.

My mom sits there in the front seat of the green Rambler, and she's not reading a book, she's knitting. Knitting is what the truly lame-ass moms do. I know it, and Lauren knows it.

Just trying to clue you in.

Right quick-like me and Lauren in the back seat of the green Rambler and all my mom's knitting junk on the passenger seat, and she's at it again with the third degree.

"Mike, did you two have a nice time on your date?"

There's plenty of wiseass I could give my mom. Why she gotta rub it in regards this being a lame-ass *date?* And why she gotta call me Mike in front of Lauren?

I say nothing, and Lauren says nothing. My mom turns in her seat, looking through those librarian glasses from me to Lauren and back to me, got the quizzical going strong. Lauren's face is a blankness, yeah she knows how to maintain the cool scene.

Mom's working at sounding all chipper, one of those happy tweeting birds don't got a worry in the world.

"Did you have a picnic?" Mom says.

I know this isn't gonna end, and we're not gonna get goin' until one of us says something, and I'm the Man, so it gotta be me.

"Yeah Mom, we had a *lovely* picnic," I say. "Lovely as Manet's 'Luncheon on the Grass.'"

Mom don't like the sarcastic, and I guess she thinks me bringing up that Manet painting, you know, with the naked chick, now Mom thinks me and Lauren did some sex deal 'cause she looks at me with the hard look she gives Dad or me when one of us fucks up, and she looks at Lauren, trying to break through the blankness.

The cool smooth surface of the surface.

Lauren's fooling with her shades again, twirling them by the temple, and they're a hypnotist's spinning wheel and she's lost in the twirl.

"Well I hope you didn't get *fresh* with Lauren, Mike," Mom says. "He didn't did he, Lauren?"

I know Lauren wants to laugh 'cause she gives me a wink, a quick exaggerated wink of her left eye, one of those conspiracy of two winks, and it cools me out 'cause we're on the same page regards Mom.

Mom starts the car, pulls out, and she's driving that winding twisting turning road down the mountain, and I wish she'd zip that mouth of hers.

She's given up on the sex angle, got her voice all happy tweeting again.

"I'd *love* to meet your mother some time, Lauren."

Lost in the twirl.

"Lauren, did you hear me?" Mom says. "Maybe you and your parents could come for dinner."

Lauren puts her shades back on and she's like, *Here comes the blind commissioner,* I tell you someone might as well dosed me with a tab of uptight. I'm all mixed-up confusion 'cause on the one hand I dig it how Lauren's dealing with Mom, and Mom's like, "Mike, did you hear that?"

"Lauren lives with her mother, Mom," I say. "Her parents been split up since she was little."

Well for once the mouth stops flapping, but not for long 'cause Mom got a way of rationalizing everything, fitting it into the world as she knows it, so don't matter how bad a scene is, Mom turns it into business as usual.

"Oh I'm so sorry, Lauren," Mom says. "It must be so difficult, just you and your mother."

I can tell this has all of a sudden gotten way too intimate for Lauren, but still she keeps her cool, and she's like, *They've got him in a trance,* and I got this world-gone-wrong shiver on my insides and I'm really not so sure about Lauren's trip, 'cause this is my mom, the woman who born me and raised me and cares about me, and if Lauren don't respect my mom, how's she gonna respect me, and even if she does respect me, *it's my mom.* I can put my mom down, but what gives Lauren the right?

"Mike, your friend alright?" Mom says. "She wasn't out in the sun too long was she?"

And Lauren's like, *One hand is tied to the tight-rope walker,* and my mom says "was there a circus at the Mountain Theater today?" and Lauren keeps going, and with a this-is-the-end-my-friend finality, says too hellfuck loud, *THE OTHER IS IN HIS PANTS,* and that shut my mom up for the rest of the drive. Oh yeah, for sure it did.

Oh I was so sure I loved her in that moment, so sure, and no hesitation, I mean I was looking at Lauren, I was in awe and I didn't give a fuck about my mom no more, Lauren was my whole scene.

Lauren had her left hand on the beige Naugahyde seat between us and so did I and I still don't know where I got the nerve but I put my hand right on top of hers, didn't say anything, I just did it and her hand tensed up but she don't take it away. My palm right against the back of her hand, her skin smooth and cold, and I have my fingers so the tips are down between her fingers, and I'm shaking, so excited to touch her again.

I don't know why Lauren left her hand there, but she did, maybe 'cause for right then we were partners in crime, you know, conspiracy of two deal. That was the first time I ever done anything like that. Touching a chick's hand as if she's my chick. Sure we were holding hands before during that part of the walk I told you about, but this was different.

Touch a chick.

My hand on her hand.

So we get to Lauren's place and I tell my mom to wait in the car, I'm going to walk Lauren in and after her keeping her hand under mine for most of that drive back, I'm trying to get it together to ask if she wants to do something with me another time. I mean even though a lot of shit was awkward and her making fun of me, and how she acted around my mom, that hand thing made me think I had a chance. I was gonna wait 'til the last minute, and we go into her place and her mom's right there and before I got a chance to ask Lauren, her mom says "Lauren, your friend Danny's here," and oh fuck!

Big fucking grin on Lauren's face, first time all day where her face is a total natural relaxed joyful kinda deal and she runs down the hall, and I'm behind her, her running and me walking as fast as I can, and we get into the kitchen and there's this college guy, looks that way to me, at least 18, tall 6-foot something skinny with short hair same as Dylan on the cover of *The Times They Are A-Changin'*. I swear he looks same as that scene in "Don't Look Back" when Dylan sings "Only a Pawn in Their Game," a song that's partially about the black civil rights activist Medgar Evers who got shot and killed by a KKK member.

Yeah this Danny guy in Lauren's kitchen looks exactly same as Dylan that day he sang that song at the Voters' Registration Rally in Greenwood, Mississippi, 1963. He stands there, puts his arms out and she's right up against him, glued to Danny boy and they're hugging and he lifts her up off the ground and there is no way in the world that me, 15-year-old high school lame-ass me, can compete, and I know it.

When they finish their lovers' hug and their lovers' kiss, Danny looks at me standing there awkward and embarrassed, and the guys with the nail guns have at it inside my skull, and he says to Lauren, "Who's this, one of your little high school friends?"

It was cold how Lauren was right then, she'd turned into a stranger.

"Yeah, this is Mike, he's sorta a friend of mine."

Sorta a friend! *Mike!!* Oh fuck.

"Well I gotta go," I say. "Maybe we could do something some time Lauren."

She don't wanna get into that, not with her for real college-type boyfriend Danny there.

And I'm hearing Dylan.

I used to be among the crowd you're in with.

And feel like shit.

Me seeing the two of them all lovey-dovey right after she let me keep my hand on her hand, all the good way I was feeling, gone baby gone.

First time my heart got broke.

4. MY VISIONS OF JOHANNA CHICK

THE FIRST TIME I saw Sweet Sarah, really *saw her*, you know, that Buddhist deal where your senses absorb what's around you, no preconceptions getting in the way, where you take in the authentic real of what's there, well that was a hell of a Days of the Crazy-Wild day.

It was at this Freak Scene Dream meditation center, out past Woodacre, which is way past Fairfax on Sir Francis Drake when you're heading for Point Reyes.

Sweet Sarah was the innocence. I mean the innocence of the Garden, before the snake and the apple, if there ever was a Garden and a snake and an apple.

And even if there never was—that kinda innocence.

Somewhere around late January of 1969. This was maybe a week, coulda been two, after my date with Lauren, and me and Sweet Sarah are both 15. What happens happens at this freaky place Rock 'n' Roll Frankie drags me to where they do a version of vipassana meditation, and if you need the details, you can find an encyclopedia easy as me. I mean what the fuck? Meditation? But what got me to listen up was when Frankie told me about the groovy chicks who come to this meditation place.

I needed a chick bad.

We're in this big Buckminster Fuller dome. We sit on the beige rug, and through the windows, even it being evening and dark out, the movement of branches in the wind, the sound of the leaves, always the mystery of the wind and the branches and the leaves, and there's a bunch of us, freakster bros and chicks in a circle.

Finally I've found my tribe, man. I ended up going out to that meditation place a lot that year.

I thought I knew something about meditation, but I didn't know nothing. Real meditation, you have a mantra and keep repeating the mantra to clear your mind. Or watch your breath, and keep the thoughts away. I don't know what everyone else does when we're supposed to be meditating. Me, I look at everyone in the circle, check out if they got their eyes closed or if they sneak a look. But that first time out there, mostly I look at the chicks and wonder which one I like the best.

We hold hands, Rock 'n' Roll Frankie on my right, and this chick Trendy Wendy with the black hair twisted into a pony tail on my left. That's what I call her, Trendy Wendy, when I'm thinking about her, which is not often. Later I tell Sweet Sarah that's my name for Wendy and we laugh about it. There in the circle her hand is cold, same as her personality. I mean she's OK, just not a chick I want for an old lady.

When we meditate we're supposed to focus on a big problem, usually the War. We really believed meditation would end the War. Seems crazy, but that's how we thought. We let go of the hands we're holding, place our palms on our thighs, and close our eyes. Right quick I open mine 'cause even though I'm against the War, on that particular day I don't think about peace on account of this chick.

Sweet Sarah is a lily floating on the pond in those dreamy late period Monet paintings. Her auburn hair luminous even in semi-darkness falls wild around her face, she hasn't brushed it, falls just past her shoulders, and that hair is a melody sweet and true, and her face, when I first look I know she been hurt in some deep way. Right as I'm looking she opens hers, and in those tired blue eyes I see her pure heart, and it's as if the look I give her is a special kind of light. My Visions of Johanna chick. That look I give her, it's a look that contains love and hope, a look that says I see the compassion in your eyes, I see the heartache, I see *the sad*.

I see you for who you really are Sweet Sarah.

And in seeing that look she came alive right before me, and her eyes brightened and the glow of her face, it was sequins and glitter falling from the sky and she lowered her eyes, I guess because of my look making her feel all that and me seeing into her the way I had, she didn't want me to know that she knew that I knew.

Something else, Sweet Sarah bathed in the look I gave her, me seeing her come alive, well it changes me, I come alive too, and feel the self-confidence and the strength and the power. So so strong. I'm the Man, and I know it, for the first time I know it, and don't matter Dad's a goddamn loser, don't matter Mom's a sad case, 'cause fuck yeah, I'M THE MAN, and I *know*. Last freakster bro standing, guns a-blaze.

After the meditation session is over we all stood around casual talk, and this part I remember real good. Everyone's getting ready to split, and I go to Sweet Sarah, and she's putting her Great Depression coat on, the gray wool overcoat that goes down to her ankles. I always thought of it as the Great Depression coat 'cause it made her look same as those chicks standing on the street in photos from the Great Depression. Only none of those Great Depression chicks could ever look beautiful as Sweet Sarah looked to me that day.

I tell her my name, no chit-chat, man, and I get right to the heart of it.

"I gotta talk to you," I say.

Sweet Sarah, oh man, a teenage Ali MacGraw, you know, when she was in that film "Love Story," if Ali been even more crazy-beautiful, if Ali been pure and bright and smart enough to beat her dad at chess. Frankly, I don't know that much about Ali. Sweet Sarah, that's who I know about. Her straight auburn hair parted in the middle, and a smile that takes over her face, and when that smile is for me, feels same as I snort a line of coke, although back then I hadn't done coke yet. So even though it feels same as that, I don't know that's what it feels same as. Not yet. Now I do, and that's what that smile did to me. Only better. Forever Infinite Ecstatic better.

Oh man, Sweet Sarah's body. That day of course I hadn't seen it, but later I see it plenty and it's perfect, man, perfect how only a 15 or 16 or even 17-year-old chick's body is. She wasn't one of those waif chicks. She had some meat on her bones, as Nana would say.

There's this special deal about Sweet Sarah's mouth I saw right then. I guess it's her mouth and jaw. When she closed her mouth, lips together, she had this serious, upright, do-the-right-thing vibe, and something about it, this beautiful fragile lily of a girl with such a serious expression, seeing her that way I wanted to hold her and tell her everything gonna be alright, I'll take care of you 'til the end of time, that kinda romantic sap talk that if someone else tells me about it happening to them I laugh my ass off, except it happens to me right then, and I don't laugh, nothing funny or sapped-out about it.

Sweet Sarah gives me that serious lips together look, and the deal with the jaw, and her voice, well if shy has a sound, that's the faint sound of it.

"What about, Michael?"

Oh man, to hear her say my name for the first time. *Michael.* It was soft and fragile how she says it, and this is kinda weird and maybe I imagined it, but even though she moved out West from Tennessee when she was five, I could hear this subtle southern accent, hidden in her voice. My name. From her lips. My name.

Michael.

I'm so intense, man, and she feels my vibe, and no way she ever had a freakster bro come at her with the high wire intensity of me. That was the first time I ever talked the authentic real to a chick I dug, and I was 15 and I didn't know no other way. I didn't know how to flirt or talk bullshit, none of that. Had to speak my heart.

"About what *happened*, man," I say. "Between *us.* You and me, Sarah. In the circle."

I flash on Gatsby that first time he's alone with Daisy, and the guy in "The Laughing Man" when he falls for Mary

Hudson, and Dylan singing *she aches just like a woman, but she breaks just like a little girl*. And that's the first time I felt *the wanting*.

When you feel it, *the wanting*, I mean I don't know if chicks feel it the same, but for a freakster bro, I was possessed, had to fight to keep it from bringing me to my knees, and it isn't only the sex deal, no man, all-consuming desperation to be with the chick. Stand there right close to Sweet Sarah, and she's the fresh cold forest after the rains and the frost on the outside of the tent, and icy water rushing by in the creek on its journey to join the Forever Infinite Pacific.

Yeah, man, Sweet Sarah, wild-nature to the max.

"What *did* happen?" she says.

Never gone up to some chick I haven't talked to before and said what I need to say. But I gotta talk to her. I should be embarrassed, scared to death and the shakes, and in a way I'm all that, but I'm not gonna show it.

"This is so weird-ass weird," I say.

How sad she was in the circle, before she saw me looking, well I see that again. And something else. It freaks her, me talking authentic real about it—none of the usual chitchat. It's heavy what I lay on her.

"There's connection," I say.

"I don't understand."

"Yeah you do," I say. "Between me and you. It's deep, and I *saw*."

Sweet Sarah's serious, I get the vibe this is as life and death for her as for me, and she pushes through her fear and there's an eagerness in her next words, she rushes them.

"You saw *what*?"

I move in closer, my hand on her arm, her arm in the sleeve of that Great Depression overcoat.

"You came alive," I say. "You *felt* it," and I got my other hand on her other arm, and through the wool coat I feel her tremble.

"I know you did, Sarah."

I expect her to pull away, or look away or both, but she don't, she keeps looking right back at me and now her blue eyes aren't tired, they got that spark—they're alive.

"I don't think a girl is supposed to say something like this," she says. "To a boy she's never talked to before."

"Say it anyway."

Her voice is that faint shy voice. "I felt," she says, and her words are the breath you see on a freezing cold-ass cold day. "I do, I mean I did feel something."

I step forward, my arms around her, my hands on her back, my fingers against the rough wool of her coat and her arms around me, I feel her small fingers press against my back and we hug, this awkward attempt to hold each other and we don't know how close and where our hands should go, if we should barely touch or more than that, and what if she feels my hard-on? I never hugged a chick before, but then we go for it, and she presses her body tight against mine and even with that coat on I feel her, and her head against my shoulder, her soft auburn hair and the side of her face warm against my face, and I feel her tremble and I'm so hard, but authentic real, bottom line deal, it's not about getting laid or sex, even though it's that too. It's so much more 'cause for the first time in my life, after all those years of the lonesome, a chick feels what I feel, and we're destined, I know it, and it's one of those times, those rare times in my life when I come close to believing there's a God. I think that's the moment I came the closest. No, that's not right. There was one moment still waiting for me.

5. THE PHONE CALL

I GOT SWEET SARAH'S phone number that night after the meditation, the night I saw her for the first time, really saw her, and I told her for sure I was gonna call.

She gave it to me, her number, printed her name and the number, but I could tell she didn't believe me. It was in her eyes, the sad, and I knew it would break her to pieces if I didn't call. Just the idea of her waiting for the phone to ring, well it fucking killed me dead.

For sure I'm gonna call Sweet Sarah, man.

Wild horses couldn't stop me calling Sweet Sarah.

Want to call so bad, only the freak of calling her, the freak-out of it going terrible bummered-out *wrong*.

The freak of it 'cause of Julie, you know, that chick Julie, only you don't know, only now you do. Julie the one chick I called in the past. I first dug on her in eighth grade. She was this 13-year-old with freckles and red hair, and she reminded me of those British Go-Go chicks on "Hullabaloo" who dance in the raised light boxes that if you think dirty look kinda like cages, and looking at that Julie chick in her mini-skirt across the room in Mr. Harris' English class gave me a hard-on for sure.

Thanks to God-who-almost-for-sure-don't-exist for those one-piece desks with the seat attached to the desk part, and no way anyone could see my boner 'cause the desk hid it.

But anyway.

Never went to a party or anything where that Julie chick was at, but in high school she's in my math class, and I see her sit with her girlfriends on the front lawn at lunch on sunny days, and in my mind I know me and her would be perfect together if only she knew what I was about, which of course she don't 'cause I never talk to her other than maybe a couple of times when I said hi.

Somehow I get up the nerve and I call that Julie chick on the phone one time, this is freshman year high school, probably late September of '67.

It's Julie who answers the phone, not her mom, and I say, this is Michael Stein, remember, Mr. Harris' fourth period English class, and I'm in your math class, and she's like, oh yeah, you're the boy with the thick black frame glasses, and I'm like yeah, that's me, and she says, well OK, hi, what do you want, not friendly at all. I think her saying hi was only 'cause I surprised her, she don't know what to say, maybe she expects a call from someone she wants to talk to, but anyway, I'm like, well I just thought I'd call you, hey what's goin' on, and she says, I have to study now, real cool chick irritated kinda voice, and I know this is going down so wrong, I mean my fantasy of us getting into it about The Beatles who have "Hey, Jude" on the radio, or the Stones' new single "Street Fighting Man," this total cool ambivalent revolution trip or Dylan just because I assume back then every chick wants to talk about Dylan, but anyway none of that's happening. She makes that total clear, she gotta go, so I say, I was wondering if maybe you'd go with me to the Harvest dance next month, which was pretty funny, 'cause there was nothing anyone was harvesting in Mill Valley and I guess they had some reason to call it that, but I mean it was such a lame thing to call a dance, especially in 1967, but anyway, that was what it was called.

So I ask her, you know, if she'll be my date for the Harvest dance, and there's a silence, probably lasts a flash of a moment, a beat of dead air, but for me that moment of silence, oh man, I was in that moment and it stretched and stretched, seemed like the forever infinite bummered-out moment.

You know that in-the-moment deal, well this was one of those times when I don't want to be in-the-moment, one of those times I want the moment to be so long gone, man, want the moment to never have happened, and I wish I could forget about it only it's gonna stay with me the whole rest of my life.

Beat of silence, dead air, and then she's like, no, I'm going with someone else, and I don't believe that for a minute which makes no sense, I mean she's this total groovy chick so of course other guys want her, but whatever, don't matter 'cause she don't want nothing to do with me, only I don't think about that right then, instead, me being me, I push it, 'cause I always push it, and I say to her, well maybe we can go to a movie sometime, you know, only she don't know about that, she's awful busy, and she's certain that won't be able to work out, and she says she gotta go and next day her and her girlfriends out on the lawn with their sandwiches and their Cokes look over at me and giggling like it was the most fucking hysterical thing, me with my short hair—'cause it only been a couple weeks since my dad took that electric razor to my head for the last time—and those black rectangular-frame plastic glasses, I might as well had a sign on my back that said "square" or "dork" or "four-eyes," actually asking that chick Julie for a date.

Man, chicks don't get it, don't understand what they do to guys. They think a guy has no feelings. Some guy could have a chick pull that number on him, never call another chick again, you know, that kind of freak out neurosis.

Ruin a freakster bro for life.

Well I'm not that freakster bro, maybe that's the Jew in me, or one good thing I learn from my dad, or some genetic deal that started back in the caveman days of the Stein family, don't matter where it came from, it just is. I'm the guy who keeps knocking at the doors. One door shut on me, I knock on the next, and the next, nothing easy in this life, and anyone who thinks shit is easy don't understand.

Don't understand nothing about nothing.

Just trying to clue you in.

I'm scared to call Sweet Sarah 'cause what if it's the Julie deal all over again only I keep thinking about Sweet Sarah sitting across from me at the meditation circle and then I remember the time I called Lauren and that worked out, well I mean it sorta worked out, but anyway I got myself pumped up and I'm gonna do it, 'cause like my mom told me, there are some things you do even though you're scared, even though it hasn't always worked out before. You gotta take a risk for anything real important. Sweet Sarah was the most important person in the whole damn screwed up world and I was gonna take the risk, Wednesday night, 8 p.m., no matter what, I was gonna call her.

No matter what, man.

All day Wednesday at school I think about that call, what I'm gonna say to Sweet Sarah, what we're gonna talk about, what if I can't think of something, what if she can't think of something, what if there's silence and there can't be silence 'cause if there's silence she's gonna hang up 'cause what's the point of being on the phone if no one has anything to say.

No point. And there has to be a point. There has to be something me and her need to say to each other. And if there isn't, but I can't think that way, that's a one-way trip to downer city and no way I'll go there. No fucking way.

Ride my bike from school, get home around 3:30 and get some cookies and a Coke, well it wasn't really a Coke, it was this shit-ass off-brand cola that my mom bought 'cause it was cheaper, and there was a reason that shit was cheaper, and I go right to my room and get to work on my geometry homework 'cause I gotta get the homework outta the way so I can call Sweet Sarah at 8 p.m. 'cause of that promise I made to myself. I mean you tell yourself you're gonna do something at a certain time and then let it slide, your whole life is gonna slide.

Way of the world, so get a fucking clue.

Anyway, my mom comes and knocks on my door and she's like, hi Mike, how are you, how was school, how come you're not in the kitchen talkin' to me, million fucking questions, same as she's always asking, and I'm like, I just want to get my homework done so I can—and I stop for a moment, a beat of a moment—listen to music.

Beat of a moment.

So short my hesitation only she caught it, she knows something's up but she don't push it. When I get done with the math, I have this idea, and I know this sounds lame, but I get a piece of binder paper and make a list of shit I can bring up in case my mind goes blank when I'm on the phone with Sweet Sarah. I rack my brain, write down favorite poets and whether she's into Joan Baez and what's she think of that movie "The Swimmer" that's been in the theaters, that kinda stuff.

My dad gets home right at 6:15. I hear the door slam, he always slams it even though my mom ask him like 10,000 times not to and I'm lying on my bed reading "A Separate Peace" for English, but I know he's standing in the kitchen doorway while she gets some broccoli steaming or the lamb chops in the broiler or cuts up vegetables for a salad, and he asks her if she took care of some stupid thing like did she go to the four supermarkets, one in Mill Valley, one in Strawberry Town & Country Village, one at the Bel Air shopping center and one up in San Rafael, to save a nickel on potatoes or those lamb chops she was broiling or some shit and he yells 'cause she went to the one nearby in Bel Air and paid the extra nickel and then I can hear him in their bedroom, other side of the wall from mine, and he's taking off his charcoal gray suit coat and undoing the tie, takes off the white short-sleeve polyester dress shirt and his charcoal gray suit slacks, puts on those gross motherfucker stained brown and white checked pants and one of his polyester short-sleeve shirts that are so hellfuck ugly, like some garish yellow and red and bright orange Hawaiian print thing that total clash deal with the pants and even on their own those shirts are way more ugly than any sin I can think of, and he's heading for the dining room, pours himself a big glass of Jameson, and into the living room and sits on that threadbare couch and he's into his brood routine about some shit.

It's 6:50 now and my mom calls out, Mike, dinner, and I got my homework done like 15 minutes earlier, and right when she calls my name I'm reading this weird-ass weird sci-fi story, "All You Zombies," by Robert Heinlein, same guy who wrote "Stranger in a Strange Land," trying to distract myself from the phone call I'm gonna make in about an hour.

Authentic real of it, that "All You Zombies" story is kinda sick. It's about going backward and forward in time. This guy goes back in time and fucks this chick but it turns out she's his younger female self, only she has a pussy and a cock and after they fuck, she gets pregnant, and when she has the kid she also has this sex change operation to become a guy and it turns out that the guy who goes back in time and her and the kid are all the same person, and this old fart who is narrating the story when the story starts, well he's the same person too, like everyone in the story turns out to be the same person.

Yeah, kinda sick.

I come into the kitchen, take my seat at the Formica counter and my mom is like, get your homework done?, and before I say nothing she calls, "Len, dinner," and I hear the ice in the glass as my dad drains his drink and he comes in, sits on his stool, and that big dark cloud is floating above him.

He picks up a spoon and dips into this bowl of minestrone soup and that spoon into his mouth, not even waiting for Mom to sit, and she looks at him, Len, that's really bad manners, what kind of example are you setting for Mike?

My dad don't say nothing to what Mom says, instead he starts in about college, what college will I be able to get into and how if I'm not careful I'll end up a good-for-nothing. He always threatens me with that good-for-nothing deal. Says it so many times I start to think I oughta take on good-for-nothing as a career goal, I mean if he don't like it, got to be some merit there.

"You don't get yourself into a good college," he says.

Takes another spoon of that soup, and he keeps on.

"Get a college degree and a law degree or get yourself through medical school," he says. "Otherwise, end up a good-for-nothing."

He's said this shit so many times, same as it's engraved in my brain, not worth the grief to argue with him about it. One time when I told him I'm gonna be a writer, and not just any old writer, but a rock critic writer, 'cause that's what I thought back then, well my fate as a once and future good-for-nothing was sealed for all eternity.

"How does anyone make a living writing about that crap," my dad said.

And said. And said. And said some more.

Yeah that was a sentence he loved the sound of almost as much as telling me I'd wind up a good-for-nothing.

How does anyone make a living writing about that crap.

If somehow everyone ignores my wishes and instead of the cremation deal and tossing my ashes off the Big Sur coast out into the deep blue of the Forever Infinite Pacific I end up buried somewhere with a headstone, that's what I want chiseled right into the stone:

How does anyone make a living writing about that crap.— Leonard Stein

And later, years later, even after I tell him I'm over the rock critic deal, that I finally figure out I'm gonna to be a novelist, tell the story of the world heavy with symbolism and arcane allusions and the total self-referential deal, my own version of "The Odyssey" or "Moby Dick" or "The Adventures of Augie March," and all the others, my own revelatory novel of self-discovery and lessons learned and debts paid, he sneers.

"Gonna end up pumping gas," my dad said. "If you're lucky. Could be worse. Much worse."

He had a list.

List of shit-ass jobs and he's sure I'll end up doing at least one of 'em.

He's been working on the list since I was a kid, and he keeps updating it, refining it, adding new shit jobs to it.

Goddamn fucking list.

Pumping gas or repairing cars or washing dishes in a greasy spoon or mopping floors or driving a garbage truck or driving a school bus or driving a delivery truck or the guy stacking boxes in the warehouse or delivering mail or selling used cars or painting houses or putting unwanted dogs and cats to their death at the S.P.C.A. or pumping out septic tanks or exterminating termites.

He always comes up with super boring jobs he knows would suck the life out of me if I don't become a doctor like my mom's cousin Larry or a lawyer like her cousin Albert or a dentist like her brother Pete. Yeah, I'll be doomed to a purgatory worse than death.

"Your choice Mike," he says between spoonfuls of soup. "You get the law degree and you're on Easy Street, or you can pretend you're a writer and end up in the little booth collecting a dollar bridge toll from each car crossing the Golden Gate. How'd you like to sit in one of those little toll booths eight hours a day, five days a week. That how you want spend the daylight hours, Mike?"

Course Larry the doctor is a plastic surgeon, spends his days cranking out nose jobs and boob jobs, some shit like that, and Albert the lawyer is one of those ambulance chasers who advertise on late night TV and Pete the dentist is a pediatric ivory snatcher, which made him the Mr. Rogers of the dentistry biz, which made him even lamer than Larry the plastic surgeon pseudo doctor.

Yeah when my dad starts in on the college deal, I start into my bowl of minestrone soup, hope my mom can run interference. I mean it's five minutes past 7; I gotta call Sweet Sarah in less than an hour.

My mom sits down, still wearing her apron, my dad going at that soup, making slurping sounds, and me and my mom start eating, and now he's done with the college deal, with the good-for-nothing deal, yeah he's got a new topic.

"You water the plants?" he says.

And fuck, total forgot I'm supposed to water the goddamn plants 'cause it's Wednesday and every Wednesday I'm supposed to do that as part of my chores to get my allowance and I need that money 'cause I hope Sweet Sarah is gonna let me see her on Saturday, and if that happens I need money to buy us real Cokes or ice cream cones or milk shakes.

"So you water those plants, Mike?" he says again, and I'm

like no, forgot, I look down at my plate, don't look at him, I'll do it tomorrow, don't worry about it, and he's like, you'll do it right now if you expect to get your allowance, and my mom is like, Len, let the boy eat his dinner, he's been working on homework for the past three hours, he needs to eat and I get up, don't say nothing, don't look at either of 'em, don't get a coat, get my ass out of the kitchen, into the dining room, and out the sliding glass door and slam that fucker closed and it's getting dark fast and fuck that asshole, and where's the goddamn hose.

I'm freaking because Sweet Sarah told me her mom didn't want her getting calls after 8:30 on a weekday, and watering the plants takes an hour, and I haven't started yet and it's nearly 7:15, so I won't be able to call her until maybe 8:20, and how fucked is that.

I walk around the side of the house where I always start watering but the hose isn't there and I got to find it. Out to the front walkway and take a right and now I walk on the cement walkway past the living room window, between the house and the brick patio in front of the house and past the front door on my right and the hose is screwed to the faucet at the far left of the front of the house and I unscrew the damn thing but the sprayer nozzle is missing so I get the hose and drag it around the side of the house and screw it to the faucet there. Then it's around the corner, up the three cement stars and into the garage and pull the string to get that bare bulb on and I'm looking on his built-in work bench and the nozzle isn't there and it's not on the counter to the side that my photo enlarger is on and I'm outta that garage slam the fucking door and walk down the three cement stairs onto the back patio, past the sliding door on my left, past the outdoor table on my right where we have dinner sometimes on summer evenings, and that hill covered with the shit-ass ice plant and there on the left, on the patio by the faucet coming out of the wall below my bedroom windows, is the fucking nozzle.

And the time is going by, and no fucking way I can get this all done by 8, or even 8:20.

I'm so screwed.

It's 7:30 and not only do I gotta spend an hour on the watering, but I haven't eaten dinner, and I'm hungry and it's getting dark, getting cold. Back to between the house and the garage, get the nozzle screwed on that fucking hose and turn the water on and start in with the plants on the garage side of the path. Normally it's boring as hell watering the plants, time slow as molasses, but tonight it's slower than slow, every minute I'm out there is forever and then some.

Supposed to take an hour but fuck that, and I rush it. It's excruciating, never has time passed so slow, and this is another in-the-moment where I hate the moment, don't wanna live in that moment, only it just stretches and stretches and stretches, and after 45 minutes I'm done, and if anything worth your time had happened during that 45 minutes I'd tell you all about it, but nothing, not a fucking thing, most boring dead slow slow slow excruciating in-the-moment 45 minutes of my life.

I run back into the house, into the kitchen, and it's nearly 8:20, take a seat. My dad is back in the den, I can hear the TV, the "Dick Van Dyke Show" and another Jameson, my mom finishing up the dishes, stands there washing them, and my salad sits there and the plate with the hot food all cold, broccoli and rice and a lamb chop and a roll and the bowl of minestrone soup, that's cold too.

My mom is like, I could heat it all up for you, Mike, and I'm like no mom, it's alright, I don't wanna wait and I'm chowing down that salad fast as I can get it in my mouth, and she's like, chew your food, you're gonna choke yourself to death if you don't watch out, and I skip the soup and the rice, go for the broccoli and the lamb chop, finish eating that shit and it's nearly 8:25 and my mom says, I've got some chocolate ice cream, and I'm like, no, I'll maybe have it for a snack, and I'm outta there, down the hall, into my room, door closed, and I feel my heart, man, there's a construction worker in there taking a sledgehammer to it.

It's 8:25 when I sit down in the wood captain's chair at the shitty built in desk and I get my list of conversation topics, and get Sweet Sarah's number out, and fuck up dialing it the first time. I hang up, pick the phone up again, dial real careful and the phone starts to ring.

Oh man, one ring, no one picks it up, and what if they gone out for dinner, or who knows what, just not home. I mean I been waiting for this since Friday night after the meditation circle when me and Sweet Sarah had the heavy traffic intense conversation I told you about, and if I have to wait another 24 hours to call, oh please God-who-almost-for-certain-don't-exist, please don't make we wait.

One ring, nothing, two rings, still nothing, another ring, oh thank-you, who ever I should be thanking, 'cause her mom answers, and I say I'm a friend of Sarah's, Michael from meditation, you know, and her mom's like, yes, Michael, I know what that is, and I'm like, well Mrs. Winton, is Sarah around and her mom says, well she's upstairs in her room, maybe I could get your phone number and if she's done with her homework she can call you back, and what can I say so I give her the number and that's that, and now I sit here, I know there's no way she'll call back, I mean girls aren't supposed to call boys and it's after 8:30 so that's two legit reasons she won't call.

Hellfuck of a bummered-out bummerosity, and it's my fault. All on account of me forgetting I had to water the goddamn goddamn plants. I could've done all the watering but instead I was reading "All You Zombies," could've called Sweet Sarah at 8 and plenty of time for her to call me.

And now I have to wait 'til Thursday night to try again, and how fucked is that, fuck my dad, fuck that goddamn stupid watering and I feel I'm gonna die if I don't talk to Sweet Sarah tonight, and how could I blow it so bad, and she's gonna think I'm a loser calling so late, she's probably even glad I called so late, she probably has second thoughts about me, and that stuff I said probably scared her, me coming onto her so intense. I should have played it real cool. Yeah this is gonna be same as that Julie chick, same as the deal with Lauren. I'm never gonna have an old lady.

I try to get back into "All You Zombies," and even with that story being so weird, I mean that chick with the pussy and the cock and everyone being the same person, the freakiness of all that, but it's no use, can't read a single sentence without looking at the phone, without thinking of Sweet Sarah up in her room though I don't know what her room looks like, so I just imagine her in some cool, really groovy chick's room, and so I do what I always do when everything is crashing down. I put *Blonde on Blonde* on, and Dylan singing "Visions of Johanna," and these visions of Johanna that conquer my mind, and I think of Sweet Sarah, see her stand there in that Great Depression wool coat, her hair so crazy-wild, her saying she felt something too, oh yeah she's one of those Visions of Johanna chicks that conquer your mind, I mean for sure she listens to Baez, that kind of sad, arty chick.

Holy Grail of chicks, that was Sweet Sarah.

I guess that's when I knew she was my Visions of Johanna chick for sure.

And the phone rings.

I turn the stereo down to zero, pick the phone up quick-like, got that list at the ready, and I'm like, hello, and I hear the extension phone in the kitchen picked up and it's my mom and she's like, hello, and I'm like, Mom, it's for me, and my mom hangs up. For once my mom don't start with the questions, and then I'm like, hello, and I hear Sweet Sarah's voice, and oh sweet Jesus, oh man oh man oh man, if shy has a sound.

"Hey," she says. "It's me, Sarah."

I know that.

Before she says word one I know that, only when I hear her voice, her tremble of a voice, there's conspiracy of two deal, the casual confidante intimacy, nothing formal, no man, and it's as if we been doin' this—talkin' on the phone—for years.

"Thanks for callin' back," I say. "I thought maybe it was too late."

"It is," she says.

She giggles, this shy girl laugh. Hearin' that, her on the phone with me, and she's sharing the joke, we're both pulling this fast one on her mom. Oh man, Sweet Sarah sharing a joke with me, that was so groovy.

"My mom's a little mad," she says. "She didn't want me calling back tonight."

"It's too late," Sweet Sarah says. "But I told her there was some important meditation technique we had to discuss."

"Groovy," I say.

And then the silence, and we haven't done this for years, this is the first time, and I better say something quick-like. Look down at my list.

"You been doing homework?" I say.

"Yeah," she says. "I have to write a paper on 'Pride and Prejudice.' You read it?"

"No way," I say. "Sounds like one of those old timey books."

"It's kinda hard to get through," Sweet Sarah says. "It's by Jane Austin, she wrote it in 1813."

And then.

"What are *you* reading?" Sweet Sarah says.

"For school?"

"No, anything you're really into?"

I can't lie to Sweet Sarah. If this is gonna work I have to tell the truth, always the truth. I mean how could I ever become one with a chick, merge souls, the Forever Infinite Ecstatic, all of it, if I lied. Has to always be the authentic real, has to be.

I just know lies are bricks, and if I tell one lie, pretty soon there'll be another, and one day there'll be a brick wall, taller than the sky, and I'll be on one side and she'll be on the other, and there'll be nothing left of whatever there once was.

"It's called 'All You Zombies,'" I say. "It's a short story."

And is it a lie to withhold info?

"You ever heard of this writer, Robert Heinlein?" I say. "You know 'Stranger in a Strange Land'? He wrote it. It's this really important book. Had this overwhelming heavy traffic influence on the hippie trip."

"Really?" she says. "But what's the one you're reading about?"

And how I gonna tell her? She'll think I'm a pervo, and why the fuck did I have to be reading "All You Zombies" the night I call Sweet Sarah?

"It's pretty strange," I say. "It's about time travel."

"Like 'The Time Machine'?" she says.

"Kinda," I say.

"What happens?" she says.

"I don't think you'd like it, actually," I say.

"Why won't you tell me what it's about?" she says.

For a second I don't say nothing, and then I realize the silence I dread, it's happening and if it goes on any longer, well there won't be any more reason for her to stay on the phone.

Deep breath, man.

"OK," I say. "It's about this guy who goes back in time and has sex with this young chick he meets there, in the past, and they have a son and later you find out the son is actually the guy who went back in time and had sex with the chick, so the father is also the son."

And the dread silence, oh fuck, and then she speaks.

"That's icky," she says.

"I'm sorry I told you about it," I say.

"Well I asked you to," Sweet Sarah says. "It's OK."

Man was I glad I left out the part about the chick being the same person as both the guy who fucks her, and her son, and her having a pussy and a cock.

"That does sound like a strange story," Sweet Sarah says. "Maybe we can talk about it another time, maybe if you came over."

"I was going to ask you, Sarah," I say. "If you want to do something, maybe go for a walk or listen to some records, I have this Dylan record I think you'd really dig. Maybe Saturday?"

"You want to come to my house?" she says.

Oh God-who-almost-for-certain-don't exist, maybe you do exist, and if you do, well thank-you, thank-you, thank-you.

6. CRAZY LIKE ZELDA

SWEET SARAH. HER NAME was Sarah, still is, far as I know, I mean she's not the kind of chick to change it. But I always thought of her as Sweet Sarah, still do, you know, when I think about her. I mean the innocence of course, but more than that, how she was in the world back then, well, how she was in the world when it was us two. Soon as I talk to her that day she's Sweet Sarah. Just the way it is, and nothing more to say about it.

Writerman and Sweet Sarah.

All my friends called me Writerman, except for Sweet Sarah, 'cause she called me Michael. She said my name made her think of the Judy Collins song, "Michael From Mountains," which she loves even before she knew me. Even before she loved me. I could tell you about how we fell in love, how our trip got so deep, and the hikes we went on out to Arch Rock and Sky Camp in Point Reyes, and up on Mt. Tam, all that happened between us after the meditation circles, and in my room, and hers. Two things, though, right off I better fill you in on.

Mid-February of 1969. It's over a month since me and Sweet Sarah talk for the first time. She lives 30 miles northwest of my house, but sometimes distance can be more than a literal measure, more than miles traveled. Where Sweet Sarah lives might as well been some other side of the world—might as well been Park Avenue or one of those entire floor kinda apartments overlooking Central Park or that villa in the South of France where Dick Diver and his wife Nicole live, you know, before everything goes to ruin in their world—in terms of the unfathomable chasm separating the austere million-dollar serenity of the four-story Victorian Sweet Sarah calls home and that cramped dump on Lowland Drive where I grew up.

Somehow I get to Sweet Sarah's house—I guess my mom must have dropped me off but really I don't remember—and her mom answers the door and she's overweight, not fat but on the heavy side and she got the beginnings of a double chin. She got auburn hair too, wears it cut so it just touches her shoulders. She's dressed OK, khaki pants and a blouse, that kinda mom deal. She invites me in and closes the door and we're in the entryway and I figure her mom gonna ask me to wait while she gets Sweet Sarah, but that isn't what she does.

It's hard to hear Sweet Sarah's mom, what she's saying, 'cause she whispers. She says since me and Sarah became friends, Sarah has changed 180 degrees. Her mom says that before I started spending time with her, Sarah was down in the dumps, and how her mom explains it, man, it was the total heavy traffic bummered-out bummerosity. I didn't want to hear it, and it was creepy, her telling me that bummered-out shit, same as the world had come to an end.

She says she wants me to know how important my friendship with Sarah is, tells me how her and Mr. Winton both approve of me dating Sarah and hope I'll visit often. Her voice gets quiet and real serious, tells me she'd really appreciate it if I wouldn't tell any of this to Sarah. I try to get an expression on my face that's got a real understanding vibe, *of course, don't worry about it, mum's the word*, that kinda thing without actually agreeing to anything with words 'cause that would be a betrayal. Even if what her mom said is true, I'm not gonna promise to keep a secret from Sweet Sarah.

No way, man.

Not in a million fucking years.

Early March of 1969. The other thing that happened, well it's part two of what I already told you. We're still 15, this is when holding her hand is almost enough. Still can't believe I got a chick who loves me. Once again I'm visiting Sweet Sarah at her folks' house, and it's a Saturday, one of those Marin County days, the bright bright sun so bright and the blue blue sky so blue and it's warm but not too warm, and there's a breeze, that kinda groovy day and I got a present for her, a necklace. I guess it's a go-steady necklace, but in those days it wasn't cool to ask a chick to go steady. Yeah well that's what the necklace meant. Gotta wait for the right moment.

Sweet Sarah asks me if I wanna go for a walk and of course I do, I wanna do anything she wants to do, you kidding? You know the first time, when everything about being with a chick is new, I mean *everything*. I burst with excitement, don't know what's gonna happen next, every minute with her is an adventure, anything possible. Every word she says I want to hear and every book she reads, I wanna read it. What she wears, every blouse and pair of shoes and pair of socks, I notice. A different hair clip, or if she got that Great Depression coat buttoned or unbuttoned.

Absolutely everything about her I'm seeing.

Her house was built in the late 1800s, set up on this hill, way back from the road, and the road is narrow, two cars barely get by, and it's a dirt road, and there are hedges and trees all around the property, I'd say a half acre of driveway and front yard. Huge-ass oak with the swing hanging from it out front of the house and an old garage where her dad parks his black Jaguar XKE, and right front of the house is the circular driveway. A six-foot stone wall surrounds the property. No gate, but on either side of the entrance these stone lions, ready to rip a trespasser to pieces.

We walk past the swing and along the driveway, me holding her hand, and we start swinging our arms in sync, forward and back, and she's laughing, tells me about some silly thing her younger sister Esmé did and I talk about "Strawberry Fields Forever." Sweet Sarah's into folk music, so she's never heard "Strawberry Fields Forever," which is so crazy I can hardly believe it.

"Sarah, it's the most groovy psychedelic song," I say. "It sounds like what an acid trip must be like. Strange watery guitar,

I mean you see God when you hear it. I mean if there is a God. It's the world through a kaleidoscope."

What happened next, we walk for 10 maybe 15 minutes, down the road, past this groovy pond and into town, this one block business district, get ice cream cones. Sweet Sarah gets cherry vanilla, and I get butterscotch. As we walk back to the pond she says, You want to try mine? and she reaches out so her cone is in front of my mouth and I take a small bite, and it's the sexiest thing ever, tasting some of the ice cream her mouth touched. I let her eat some of my butterscotch and we keep walking, eat our ice creams, let the other one have a taste, and so on and so on. I don't think either of us taste the cherry vanilla or the butterscotch, we so trip on tasting each other, and on sharing them, you know, everything of mine is yours and yours is mine, that vibe.

I am he as you are he as you are me and we are all together.

At the pond we sit on this stone bench, her body close against me, hold hands, look at the calm water, and we can hear kids playing somewhere nearby. There's ducks in the pond, and once in a while they quack at each other.

"Sarah," I say. "There's something I've been wanting to ask you about. But, you know, if you don't want to talk about it I'll understand."

She gets quiet, the shy quiet deal. "When I looked at you across the circle," I say. "That first time, I saw this hurt in your face, a sadness."

What I don't bring up is what Sweet Sarah's mom told me. Sweet Sarah looks out at the pond, tightens her forehead.

"Sarah, whatever it was, it doesn't matter," I say. "It won't change anything about me and you."

She turns her head, her blue eyes into my brown eyes— hellfuck serious, man.

"How do you know?" she says. "You don't know."

"I *know.*"

"What if I'm crazy," Sweet Sarah says. "Crazy like Zelda."

"I'll take care of you," I say. "No matter what."

"I don't know," she says. "If you were me and I were you,

and you were crazy like Zelda, I don't think I'd stick around."

"Well I'm not crazy same as Zelda or nobody," I say, and that's when I give her the present. She takes the folded lavender tissue out of the box and unfolds it and there's this thin silver chain and a small silver heart, and on the back of the heart, etched into the silver, M + S.

"A heart close to your heart," I say. "To always remind you."

There's a look on her face, she's so touched, I mean it coulda been one of those sentimental sapped-out scenes, only it wasn't, it was *so real,* man, and she gets the necklace over her head and she gets it under that white blouse in the back and in the front it's hanging so the heart is a few inches above right between her tits. I lean in and my lips against her lips and we kiss, this gentle romantic first time in love kinda kiss. Afterwards we sit quiet side-by-side looking out at that pond, the ducks floating the way ducks float, and that's when she tells me.

"A lot of the time, from when I was little, there are days when my mom doesn't feel so good," she says.

Her dad had to hire a nanny to take care of Sweet Sarah and Seymour and then later, her sister Esmé. It wasn't like her mom was always sick. There were whole years when her mom seemed pretty much OK.

"I really don't remember when *I* got *the sad,"* she says. "That's how I think about it. I got *the sad."*

"But why?" I say.

"I don't know," she says. "Be careful what you ask for. You thought I was kidding."

"What do you mean?" I say.

"Crazy like Zelda."

7. TRUE LOVE SCARS

SO MUCH HAPPENED BETWEEN me and Sweet Sarah during our first year and a half together, and it seemed as if our love got stronger and stronger, so strong, man. I mean how could it ever go wrong?

Well the first of the troubles came the day I drove her to the doctor's office in my folks' '59 white Rambler, the car with the stupid tiny white fins and one seat in the front same as in a booth at a Fifties-style diner. That was the car I got to drive. The other car, the green '67 Rambler, was off limits.

Sweet Sarah was worried she was pregnant, but that wasn't possible.

We hadn't fucked.

She wasn't ready, that's what she told me, and I sure wasn't gonna push it, and I didn't push it. If and when, well she'd tell me.

Her period being three weeks late had to be something else. I figured chicks' periods were just late sometimes. I mean what did I know?

It was a Wednesday, summer of 1970, must have been mid-June 'cause school was already out, but not July 'cause I was still 16. She was 16 too.

Sweet Sarah was back in the examining room with him, the doctor.

I was sitting in the waiting room.

Yeah, you been there.

It was same as every doctor's office waiting room I ever been in, you ever been in, bunch of chairs, each with the patterned light brown and beige, or olive green and beige cloth-covered seat cushion, and some end tables with out-of-date magazines and the beige wall-to-wall carpet and a counter with a chick receptionist behind it, bored, wishing she was on a date or somewhere she could meet some guys, anywhere but there.

I'm alone in the waiting room trying not to think about what that doctor is telling her. Ellingsworth. That's his name. Dr. Ellingsworth. He's a good friend of Sweet Sarah's dad. I'm reading "Tender Is the Night" for the second time, which is about that doctor, Dick Diver, well he's a psychiatrist, which is a kind of doctor, I guess, head doctor. He starts out so handsome and charming living in the South of France with his wife Nicole, but by the end of the book he's this pathetic alcoholic middle-age loser living alone in one of those no-names somewhere in the U. S. of A., I forget the town, but you know, one of the ones you drive through to get from here to there, or worse, one you never even drive through.

I try to focus on the book, ignore the "art" on the wall. There's three ugly-ass framed 16" by 20" color photos of sailboats on the Bay. The one I really hate is a closeup of an immense fancy-ass boat that's got "Mr. Lucky" on the bow. The doctor, Ellingsworth, stands on the deck, holds onto the mast with one hand, champagne glass in the other, and his mouth got an idiot grin.

I start the page over, but all I think about is Sweet Sarah in with the doctor, and those ugly-ass photos mocking me, their goddamn existence a big fuck-you to art and photography and all that's beautiful groovy in the world. Whoever took them never heard of Henri Cartier-Bresson or Man Ray or Robert Frank. Even now I bet he never heard of William Christenberry or William Eggleston.

He don't deserve to own a camera.

The door the nurse opened when she came for Sweet Sarah opens. There's Ellingsworth in his doctor's coat, old fucker with white hair and those glasses where the frame is around the top half of each lens, kind of glasses people who are 100 years old wear.

Sweet Sarah comes into the waiting room, and she might as well been dizzy.

"I really am sorry, Sarah," Ellingsworth says. "But you'll get through this, you're a strong girl. You've got character."

He looks over, scopes me out, and he don't like what he sees, me in my paisley cowboy shirt with the string tie, my Lennon part-in-the-middle hair frizzing out and curling down past my shoulders, the brown corduroy sport coat with the peace symbol button pinned on the lapel, the fucked-up blue jeans with the names of rock stars—Dylan, Lennon, Richards, Zappa, Beefheart, Buckley—hand-written indelible ink all over 'em, me stretched out same as this is my room, leaning back in the chair, feet on the coffee table, heels of my suede shit-kicker boots dig into Nixon's ugly-ass face on the cover of *Time*.

No, man, old fucker Ellingsworth don't like one damn thing about me, and he shoots me dead, those hard eyes, raises a nostril, sour mouth, and he don't think I got even an inch of character. Well he's gone, back through the doorway into his doctor's lair.

Sweet Sarah don't cry, not yet. As she stands there she touches the silver necklace I gave her, you remember, the silver heart got M+S etched into it.

She's wearing the usual: blue jeans and a white blouse, and the Great Depression coat I told you about. She walks to where I sit but she don't sit. Normally, when she's serious about something, there's that special deal with her mouth and jaw, but on this day that's not her scene.

Something is terribly wrong. This bummered-out bummerosity, well she's Degas' "Absinthe Drinkers." You seen it, right, sad, broken chick sitting in a café. I feel Sweet Sarah's sadness, but I can't deny the poetry. There's beauty in that heartbreak.

I get my feet off the table, stand up tall, try to act same as an adult or at least a responsible kinda freakster bro, you know, who got character.

"Sarah, you look like a wounded dove," I say. "What'd he say?"

"Can you take me home?" she says.

We split out of that office, get in the car and I turn to her, my elbow against the wheel, try to get comfortable, take her hand, and it's cold. I hold her hand between both of mine and try to warm it up. The hand with the scar.

The true love scars. The scars that mean eternal love, which was our love. The scars that symbolized our promise, me to her, her to me. Promise of forever infinite ecstatic true love more sacred than any wedding vows.

We were up in her room, sitting on the edge of her bed, side-by-side, feet on the wood planks floor. I'd just turned 16, and she was still 15; it was the six-month anniversary of me and her. I took a brand new razor blade, dipped it in rubbing alcohol. Got her hand face up on my thigh, and the razor blade in mine.

"You sure?" I say.

She said nothing, but she wants it. I hold the blade so maybe an eighth of inch, just enough, sticks out from between my thumb and index. I don't want it to go in too deep. I don't want to hurt her. I never wanted to hurt her. Oh man oh man oh man.

"When I say 'now,'" I say. "That's when I do it. OK?"

I look over and her blue eyes are closed, and she's so crazy-wild beautiful, and I can't do it. Can't cut into her perfect body.

"Do it, Michael," she says. "Come *on*."

I tell myself it's OK, tell myself she wants it, tell myself I gotta do it.

"Now," I say.

She goes all tense, and I make two quick cuts, X marks the spot. It cuts into her so easy. Her hand so small and pale white, only it's not only white no more 'cause the dark red wells up, runs along the lines of her palm, the lines a palm reader would read, and overflows out of those lines. Oh fuck, and what the fuck have I done?

I know it hurts, but she don't make a sound. Down the line, after that day at the doctor's office, when I look up what that word character means, yeah that's Sweet Sarah, of course it is.

"OK," I say. "You cut *me.*"

I get the blade flat on my palm for her to take. With her free hand she starts to go for it only she stops. She still got her other hand on my thigh, and where I cut into her, blood still leaking onto her palm.

"I can't cut you, Michael."

All the blood on her palm, and I take her hand and press it into my thigh, blood on my jeans. She's shaky looking at the blade.

"Come on, Sarah," I say. "It's no big deal."

The blade lies there on my palm, and there's dark red on the tiny part that cut her. Something about it freaks her, she won't touch it. And how she was all tensed up when I cut her, well it's worse. And her face sickly pale.

Yeah, well, and I pick up the blade.

"There's nothing to it," I say.

I see real fear on her face, her mouth open and her eyes scared, and she's not gonna do it, *no way no how.*

"Oh, damn," I say. "Well *I'll* do it."

She gets the hand that don't got blood under my t-shirt, the flat of it against my back, and I feel love how she touches me, and her voice shy like the first time we talked, which seems such a long time ago.

"It's OK, Michael," she says. "You don't have to."

Oh I have to, I mean no way gonna pussy out of it. I hold my left hand palm up in front of me. *Don't think about it, do it,* and cut into myself. Once, twice. It hurts same as shit, and the blood, there's blood on Sweet Sarah's palm but I went too deep into mine, so much blood. But I don't care.

"Your hand," I say.

I press my cut hand down on hers, press our palms together, the cuts right top of each other, blood dripping onto my jeans. Palm against palm. My hand aches, and if this is the price of true love, let it ache forever.

Sweet Sarah twists to face me there in the car, and her truth-seeking eyes are tired as the first day I saw her, before the brightness showed up. She pulls her hand away, and it scares me, the cold front coming in, only it's not a cold front, it's a hopelessness cutting into me.

"So are you?" I say.

She moves her head up down once. The white Rambler falls away, and the medical building and the parking lot too, and the world could be burning up but I wouldn't know. All I see is Sweet Sarah, and a newborn wrapped in a white blanket, pressed to her chest.

"How the fuck?"

She looks at her knees, I mean she got on those jeans, so she looks at her denim-covered knees.

Well I gotta say it, I gotta. "Sarah, we didn't have sex. We didn't fuck."

For a flash of a moment I don't get it, but then I do. Knocked Sweet Sarah up without fucking her. Some guys, if that happened, they know their chick two-timed 'em, but I know Sweet Sarah and that isn't what happened.

My cock, my sperm, my fault, but her fucking nightmare.

I get my arm around her, take a clean white handkerchief from my back pocket, and she dries her face.

"Michael, Dr. Ellingsworth wanted to know how it happened. He said to me—."

She's total freakin', only she isn't gonna let it stop her; she gotta tell it.

"He said, 'Sarah, you're still a virgin and you're—.'"

She got her palms against her cheeks, fingers against her forehead, and in a rush, "He said, 'Sarah, you're still a virgin and you're pregnant, have you gotten religion all of a sudden?' And he actually laughed. Said that to *me*, and laughed."

She looks out the windshield, her face kinda pink, and I guess she feels all over again how it felt with the doctor when he said it.

"You know how embarrassing that is, having to tell him we

didn't do it, you lying on me, your sperm all over me down there. Oh God!"

"But I *wasn't* in you."

Spring, 1970. We're upstairs in her room, naked on her bed, crazy-wild nature outside the window, a harsh wind shakes the leaves of the old oak, and the crack of a branch. Together near to a year and a half, she still isn't ready, but it don't mean we don't make out, and every time we go further. Kissing, touching, and today I'm on top of her, and the cold harsh wind rattling the windows. I'm not in her 'cause of my promise, but still I come. Afterwards I look out the window, and that cracked branch hangs there, a tree creature's broken arm, and from high in the tree I was sure I heard the strange cry of a bird.

Caw caw caw.

"Dr. Ellingsworth said the sperm must have just got into me," she says. "Like it dripped into my vagina, and it isn't that uncommon actually."

"There was a lot," I say.

It's funny 'cause talking about my sperm and her pussy and all that, I should feel the embarrassment deal, only I don't, and it seems the total normal scene.

"It was a mess," I say.

Sweet Sarah's back in that moment, and her smile, it's for me.

"It was beautiful," she says. "You were so —."

Oh man, the hellfuck of it, and how unfair, me getting off, and Sweet Sarah pregnant.

"Horny for you," I say.

"Yeah, you were that," she says.

Still got my arm around her. "I felt like a beauty queen," she says, and her chick hands feeling my face as if she's blind trying to "see" my features.

"No, that's not right," and her fingers move on, push into my hair. "I felt like I was really your old lady, that I could make you do that."

She pulls my head toward her, and she kisses me, and something was different, a desperation in her kiss. When it's over she's all blissful.

"You wanted me so much," she says. "You were on top of me, your hands on the bed, your arms holding your chest and shoulders up, and your head above me."

"You trusted me," I say.

Her head on my shoulder, her cheek so warm. "I was looking into your eyes," I say, and her silky auburn hair falling across my arm. "They were so alive," and she smells of the forest, pine and redwood and oak. "That birthmark below your nipple," and yeah, she's the wild nature. "First time I saw it, Sarah. So groovy."

She's holding onto my arm and her jaw relaxes, the weight of her against me, her blue eyes so bright in this moment.

"You looked down on me and your face," she says. "I thought you were in pain, your forehead clenched and every muscle tight." Yeah, she's on her bed, looking up at me. "You told me you were gonna come."

"And you said it was OK," I say.

"Your eyes got wide when you came," she says. "And across your face this wave of relief and joy. So pure your face."

"But you're pregnant," I say. "I *never* imagined," and it brings her back from the beauty of that afternoon to the fuckedness of us in the shit-ass Rambler.

"Dr. Ellingsworth tried to make a joke. How I didn't even get to experience the fun part of sex, but it wasn't funny."

There were dark brown water stains on the stucco wall in front of us.

"Nothing's funny, Michael," she says. "I think he was trying to make me not feel so bad. I don't think I've *ever* felt this bad."

She was bawling then, and I'd never seen her such a ruin. And I hear it again. *Caw caw caw*, and these big black birds on the roof of the medical building.

"Look at the crows, Sarah."

"Oh *no*," she says. "Those aren't crows."

"Quoth the raven, nevermore," I say, but I know I shouldn't be joking.

"Isn't funny, Michael," she says. "Those are the black-billed magpies that bring trouble. I've seen them for years. I call them Doom and Gloom."

That's when she tells me about the magpies. Doom's the one got a bigger beak, she says. That bird knows all the troubles that can befall a human. Gloom's usually got some detail to add to what Doom says that makes the whole deal even more blue-turns-to-gray than how Doom sees it. Seen all the horror of the world gone down, those two.

"Damn," she says. "Why? Why me?"

"What do you wanna do?" I say.

And how the fuck we gonna get out of this alive?

That day we find out she's pregnant, as we sit there in the Rambler I wonder how it would be if Sweet Sarah has the kid and we get married. We'll have to drop out of school, and I'll have to take some shit-ass job to support us. Gonna be damn hard to maintain as Writerman if I'm wearing one of those baby blue McDonald's hats all day, or stuffing ground beef and refrieds into tortilla shells at Taco Bell.

She's hellfuck sure not thinking about us up in her room no more either.

"I can't keep it," she says.

She's so sure, and it don't really matter what I want. I can see by her grim determination, you know, the deal with her mouth and jaw, and hear it in the unemotional of her voice. She's thought about this long and hard for the three weeks her period been late. Authentic real, the kid's in *her* body, and how can she count on me being there. Even if I wanted her to have the kid, what if my parents split back to Brooklyn, or sent me off to boarding school. Yeah, she's got to make the right choice. Don't matter what I want.

"I'm 16, Michael. I'm going to college in two years. I gotta get an abortion."

I don't know where you get an abortion. Well Sweet Sarah

knows. She knows 'cause of her dad, the $300-an-hour activist lawyer who pledges allegiance to the Sierra Club and drives to work in that black Jaguar.

"They do them at this hospital in Berkeley," she says.

It's scary how she can turn her emotions off, and I got good reason to be scared. Right then she didn't really understand that the beginning of a human was in her. Of course Sweet Sarah's right, and I'm glad she says it. If I say it, would make me sound like I'm not a stand-up guy at all, some fucker who don't got even an inch of character.

"When are you gonna tell your folks, Sarah?"

And when am I gonna tell my folks? I know what my dad gonna do. He'll have a major conniption, tell me I'm a good for nothing, tell me I gotta keep my dick in my jeans. And then he'll be all yelling and screaming about who's gonna pay, and after some time passes he'll get all crafty, figure out how he's gonna weasel out of it.

"When I get home," she says. "I'll tell my mom."

She's so detached, in a way she's in shock, as if she's removed herself from the situation, and talks about someone else.

"Dr. Ellingsworth said he'd wait until tomorrow before calling my dad. To give me time to tell them."

"That's *real* nice of him."

"Don't be like that, Michael."

"He hates me."

"He doesn't know you."

I reach for her, but she pulls away and faces the front of the car again.

"Look at me, Sarah," I say, but she shakes her head as if she's shaking something creepy off her.

"Sarah," I say. "*Look at me.*"

Her head turns, and there's more gray in her blue eyes, I guess it was just how the light was making them look, but whatever it was, the brightness from before is done.

"It's gonna be *all right*," I say.

Me telling her that, well I don't know shit about how it's

gonna be, but still I say it and she stops crying, and she trusts me, she believes what I say and I know it's all on me. I gotta be strong no matter how I feel, no matter the doubt I got. It fucking well got to be all right, and I gotta believe it and if I believe it and I keep saying it to Sweet Sarah with a firm and confident and self-assured kinda voice, she'll keep believing it too.

She kisses my cheek, falls back against me, and she wants to keep believing, and so do I. And maybe I do—for a moment.

She takes my hand, holds it palm up, and kisses the true love scar.

"Fuck yeah," I say. "Fucking die for you!"

I turn off the road, drive past the stone lions, and down the long driveway. I park in front of the house. I tell her I love her; I tell her I'll call in a few hours; I tell her I'll come see her tomorrow. She nods sorta absent-minded. I don't feel like Writerman no more, it's Mike there behind the wheel. She gets out, and stands staring at me through the side window with her truth-seeking blue eyes. She looks abandoned. Her auburn hair messed up and wild, and she's trying real hard to keep it together. Her Great Depression coat looks way too big, and she looks so young, and slight, and lost. No 16-year-old girl should have to be pregnant. I drive slow toward the road. From somewhere behind me I hear a cry, *caw caw caw*, and I'm certain Sweet Sarah hears it too.

8. HER PARENTS

THE DAY AFTER WE found out she was pregnant, I drove the '59 Rambler with the stupid fins, such a lame ass car, from our middle-class shit-loser-side-of-the-tracks new-kid-in-town-section of Marin the 30 or so minutes to the Wintons' upper crust deal.

You know that East Egg place in "The Great Gatsby" where Daisy and her husband Tom Buchanan live, that's kinda how I think of where Sweet Sarah lived, I mean Sweet Sarah's family didn't have a mansion or grounds as expansive as those East Egg estates, but still it was a grand old place, and their neighbors were doctors and lawyers and bankers.

Mr. Winton, Sweet Sarah's dad, he opens the door, and he's impressive looking, 6 foot something, muscular 'cause he skis in the winter and swims in the summer, and those brown eyes and the black hair, he reminds me of Gary Cooper, you know, who's so serious, man, in the movies. He got his law degree from some fancy-ass school. Usually Sweet Sarah's dad acted formal and when he spoke the words were stiff like he was reading out of some Miss Manners proper English book, you could hardly tell he was from the South, and the thing was, I think he kinda liked me, but not that day.

No man, not that day, hellfuck no.

Grim overwhelming serious face and he needs to talk to me, leads me right into his too overwhelming extravagant groovy study, all Danish Modern shit, those light teak bookcases floor to ceiling jammed with all his important law books and philosophy books and art history books and books about the environment, the guy was some kinda brain for sure, and the walnut desk with the brushed aluminum drawer pulls and the drop down leaf, man he was so fuckin' proud of that desk, and right then, way I felt, wanted to take my pocket knife and carve Kilroy Was Fuckin' Here! into the top, and his big important Eames black leather chair with the matching ottoman and this orange and black Calder mobile hanging from the 12 foot ceiling and he had me sit down in there and closes the door and then in a hard voice I haven't heard from him before he starts to talk.

"Mike, I could have you arrested for *statutory* rape."

And fuck-to-hell I'm not thinking about the furniture no more.

"You understand what you've done to my daughter?" he says. "She's 16. That's statutory rape. That's juvenile hall. You understand?"

And thing was, right then I hated Sweet Sarah's dad.

And the other thing, he was wrong, I hadn't fucked Sweet Sarah so it wasn't statutory rape. What it was was her pregnant from my sperm, only I didn't know what statutory rape was that day, I was 16, who'd ever the fuck heard of statutory rape?

Not me. And another thing.

Authentic real of it, I didn't hate Sweet Sarah's dad at all, it was me I hated. I wanted all of Sweet Sarah's family to like me, wanted them to think I was the right freakster bro for her, that I'd be able to take care of her, that I was someone special.

You know, I'M THE MAN, last freakster bro standing, guns a-blaze.

Only now I'd fucked it up so hellfuck bad.

I never told anyone this, not even Sweet Sarah, but her dad, he was the kinda guy that I wish my dad was, kinda guy who would sit at the dinner table with his family and introduce some serious intellectual deal into the conversation, ask Seymour what he thought about some foreign policy decision of Nixon's that had been in the papers that morning, ask Sweet Sarah about "Pride and Prejudice," the novel she was reading for English, and what she thought were the major themes, that kind of smart conversation where everyone has something to say. Even Sweet Sarah's younger sister, her dad would ask her just the right questions so she could talk about something she'd learned.

Man, I would have died to have grown up with that going on.

So yeah, I wanted Sweet Sarah's dad to think I was cool only I'd knocked up his daughter and you know, even a liberal in Marin County, member of the Sierra Club and everything, still, punk like me gets his daughter pregnant and he can't help himself, he wants to lash out, tell me to go fuck myself, never come around again no more only he can't 'cause he's not that kinda man.

So instead he said what he said, that statutory rape deal.

"Yeah," I say.

Said it right quick-like so he knew I did understand just what he was saying about juvey. And for maybe a minute I was scared, but then I knew. He wasn't gonna do that shit, couldn't do it, summer of 1970 no liberal dad was gonna press charges against a kid been the boyfriend of his daughter for a year and a half, no fuckin' way. And yeah, he was a liberal, don't know how that happened but he was. I guess that's why he moved out West. He was trying to scare me, but I wasn't scared no more.

I don't want to look him in the eyes, and I start spacing-out on this rug I'm looking down at, this red and yellow and black and green striped hand woven wool rug he has on top of the hardwood floor. Sweet Sarah's whole family kinda collect all this stuff from countries they been to, they got all this native shit, rugs and shirts and blouses and scarves and blankets and little coin purses—you almost thought you were at Cost Plus, only the shit they had was the real deal.

"Press charges," he says. "If it were up to me I would do that."

I don't believe him for even a minute. Not Mr. So Understanding Liberal Jaguar-driving lawyer, fuck no.

He stops talking, looks at me, makes his face as stiff and stern as he can, tries to look the angry deal but he's one of those unemotional men—he's so detached from the world.

"I can't do it," he says. "That would just break Sarah's heart."

He said that and I gotta tell you, all my angry sarcasm deal, gone baby gone and I almost start to cry, only I never cry, but I mean if I did ever cry, that would have almost been the time, when I heard those words. Made me so goddamn sad, to think about something breaking Sweet Sarah's heart, I mean no way I could explain how sad.

"She says she loves you," he says.

Weird-ass weird hearing that kinda talk from Sweet Sarah's dad. I didn't think parents thought about love, couldn't imagine an old guy same as him could know shit about the way me and Sweet Sarah feel for each other.

"I believe her," he says. "I couldn't do that to her."

"Mr. Winton, you probably won't believe me, but I really didn't want to hurt Sarah," I say. "Or you or Mrs. Winton. I mean, we didn't even actually, you know, do it. I mean I was just lying on her."

Oh man did I feel like shit, what the fuck was I thinking, saying that to Sweet Sarah's dad and I thought maybe that old fucker Dr. Ellingsworth hadn't told him Sweet Sarah is still a virgin, and maybe Sweet Sarah hadn't told her mom any details same as that, so he didn't know. He thought we'd done it. He looks at me and for a moment his face got like I thought he was gonna be sick, but he got it under control. And I never knew if he heard me, because most people, they get an idea about something in their brain, might as well be epoxy glued in there, you can never change them.

"I mean I was really respecting Sarah and what she wanted," I say. "I hope you can understand."

I was looking right at him, my eyes raygunning into his brown eyes and he was softening and he managed to ignore what I said about lying on his daughter, which probably wasn't the image he wanted in his brain. So he acts like I haven't said anything of what I said other than maybe the respect deal.

"I know it's strange for me to say this at this time," he says.

"But you've done a lot for Sarah."

Kept my face total heavy traffic serious, but inside I relaxed 'cause it was over, he wasn't going to do shit, and far as me and Sweet Sarah, all would be groovy.

And I was right, and I was wrong.

Where I was right, he never got in the way of nothing.

Where I was wrong, well with Sweet Sarah and me, there would come a time when it wouldn't be groovy. But we get to that when we get to that.

"You two are much too young to be intimate," he says. "But you've brought her out of herself and Louise and I do appreciate that. We just wish things hadn't gotten to this."

And you know how a teenage guy can get all overly respectful and forthright upstanding, well that was me right that moment.

"I appreciate what you're saying, Mr. Winton," I say. "I really and truly do. Thanks."

That shit was hard to say, and I don't even know how I managed to say it.

That was all Sweet Sarah's dad wanted to say so I got outta there quick-like and Sweet Sarah was nearby, sitting in the living room pretending to read my copy of "Tender Is the Night," which I'd finished the night before. I'd told her it was the best novel I'd ever read, which is how I felt about a lot of novels right soon as I finished them. Still, if I had to pick one novel, that would actually probably be the one, or maybe "The Great Gatsby," but right then it was "Tender Is the Night."

"So what did he say?"

We were up in her room, the door locked, lying on her bed, her hand woven wool blanket on us, a candle and incense burning. Sweet Sarah had a single bed lengthwise under the rear windows that looked out on the back yard and that tall oak that towered over the house. There was a small Danish Modern desk in there, and a big closet for her clothes even though she didn't have that many clothes. She had a bunch of cool stuffed animals and an arty photograph of an old barn I'd given her in a frame standing on her desk and a weaving of birds in flight that she'd hung like a painting on the wall across from her bed, and we could look at it as we lay together right then, her body warm against me through her jeans and the white blouse.

"He said he could have me locked up for raping you," I say. "But he's not gonna do that 'cause he knows you love me and he doesn't want to break your heart."

"You didn't rape me," Sweet Sarah says.

"He said statutory rape," I say. "I don't know, but it doesn't matter 'cause he's not gonna do anything. You know maybe you could break the news to him about it."

Sweet Sarah pregnant. What a drag, man.

Goddamn goddamn.

And I knew there couldn't be a God 'cause if there were he would never do something same as that. Not to Sweet Sarah, not to me. This wasn't my fault. Sweet Sarah didn't want to fuck and we hadn't fucked. I could have pushed her into it but I didn't. And this shit happening. Fuck Sweet Sarah's dad and his goddamn Danish modern.

Only I knew it didn't matter what I tried to do, what I hadn't done, none of that was worth a shit 'cause I was the one responsible. My sperm. My fault. And I could hate every old fucker on the planet, every one of them to blame for everything that was wrong about the world. And Sweet Sarah's dad, he should be apologizing to me for all the shit his generation had let go down on their watch. Yeah I could rationalize being mad at all of them fuckers. But the only one who could have stopped Sweet Sarah from getting pregnant was me. I was the one to blame.

Oh yeah, man, that's what I thought there in Sweet Sarah's room. But I didn't say any of that. We lay on her bed quiet for a long time, Sweet Sarah in my arms, I didn't try any sex stuff, listening to the wind and the leaves and the branches against the window. I wanted it to be like that forever, it felt so safe in her room, nothing could harm us there, nothing could separate us.

9. I'M THE MAN!

SIXTEEN YEARS I LIVED in that same god-who-almost-for-certain-don't-exist forsaken house before I got Sweet Sarah pregnant, and that house is where I had it out with my goddamn father.

Sweet Sarah's abortion. Crazy beautiful Sweet Sarah's abortion.

We found out from the doctor on a Wednesday, I had that scene with her dad on Thursday, and by Friday her dad had the arrangements worked out. Whole shitty deal about who would pay, man was that awkward. Her dad calls my dad on Saturday and tells my dad that he, Mr. Winton, got a brother who's a doctor, and her dad and the doctor brother calling in favors right and left, and even with the fee for the operating room and the nurse and everything it's gonna cost $400, and since I got Sweet Sarah fucked-up there's this expectation that my family will pay.

Good luck with that one.

My dad, cheap-ass bastard, tries to get Sweet Sarah's dad to split it.

"Well if your daughter wasn't so loose," my dad says. "This would never have happened."

Hearing him there in the kitchen phone glued to his ear say that, I feel like the lowest fucking heel. Sweet Sarah's dad says something same as this:

"Maybe you should give it some thought Mr. Stein," and he hangs up.

Hangs up on my dad, and my dad's swearing and yelling.

"What the fuck did you have to go start messin' around with that girl like that for, Mike," he says. "I told you to stay out of her pants."

The both of us sitting at the Formica counter, him in his spot at the end, me in mine. Fuck-ass bastard my dad says stuff makes everything seem dirty and cheap when everything with me and Sweet Sarah is so fine and beautiful and soulful. I'm scared 'cause these are the times he hits me. His face red and his greasy black crew cut, five o'clock shadow even though it's 3 in the afternoon, sweating in his short-sleeve plaid button-down, black frame glasses slip down his sweaty angular nose, and I'm detaching, only hear some of it, "pregnant at 16... jailbait little whore."

Un moment decisif.

Am I the scared-shitless twerp my dad bullied since before I can remember, or a stand-up freakster bro, guns a-blaze. Am I in, or out?

"Shut up Dad."

I'M THE MAN, and if I go down, so be it.

"You didn't say what I thought you said, did you Mike?"

His wiry body all tense, blood vessels on his face about to burst. You know when they say some fucker is tightly wound, well my dad was tightly tightly wound.

I'm off the stool standing there in the kitchen hellfuck defiant.

"Shut the *fuck* up Dad," and there's earthquake tremors inside me.

"You're not talkin' same as that about Sarah no more."

He gets off his stool. "Oh, the big shot," he says. "Got the balls to screw your slut girlfriend's life up, and you're ready to take on Dad, huh."

I see it, his tongue folding over, his face a fright mask.

I step back, more space between me and him, us two under harsh fluorescent light on that shit-white-with-speckles vinyl floor. He steps toward me, and always before when he was this mad he hit the side of my head. Always before I took it. His right arm comes up. Veins bulge in his wrist, hand moves fast, on the cliff's edge, the ground so far below. Only this time I grab his motherfucking wrist, get a steel-ass steel grip on him, and I'm 16 and 6 feet, an inch over him, and I been on the swim team and my arms strong from the butterfly and the breast stroke and the crawl, and he's old, nearly 40, works a desk job, and I hold his arm in the air, away from my head, and he yells all kinds of shit at me but I don't care no more 'cause I *know*.

When I was a kid I always looked up at my dad, always thought of him as this strong-ass dad who controlled my life. One time when it was rainin', I was maybe 6, I asked my dad to stop the rain. Well this day I don't look up. I look straight across at him, his face a few feet away, his eyes wide and his mouth open, a shocked kinda deal, and he *knows*. Even in his anger I'm pretty sure I see admiration, same as that time at the Boy Scout ceremony when they gave me the Eagle Scout medal. Only this is different—for the first time he sees me as a man.

Oh yeah, baby, I'M THE MAN, authentic real I am I am.

Any time I hear someone talk about a mooch, first thing I think of is my dad. Even in defeat, he's a goddamn goddamn mooch. There's more than contempt and derision and perhaps even execration in the snide-ass tone of his words that day in the kitchen when he tells me to go get *the damn blood money* from my grandfather.

"He's an *easy touch*," my dad says.

My dad don't got a clue. Grandfather is the best, got so much love for me and my mom and even some for my dad, and my dad saying mean-ass shit about him. *Easy touch* don't got nothing to do with my grandfather. 'Course my dad would call Jesus an *easy touch*.

So I have to drive to the store, you know, Mel's Shoes on the Miracle Mile, and get him private deal in the back where he got the inventory, and tell him my sad-ass. He knows Sweet Sarah, even gave her a groovy pair of hiking boots she wanted. I mean 'cause I asked him. He told me one time she's a fine young lady. I don't need Grandfather to sing praises regards Sweet Sarah, but that's what he said.

He comes through with the abortion dough, I mean he don't dig any of it. But what's cool as cool can be about my grandfather is how he don't say his opinion unless he got something nice to say. Otherwise he does everything he can to keep it to himself unless you *ask* his advice. Most people, they heap the advice on you and first, they don't know shit about what they act the expert on, and second, who asked 'em, not me.

Yeah he comes through, 'cause that's the kind of standup human my grandfather is, no way same as my dad.

My dad the asshole mooch.

And this is the day.

Sweet Sarah's abortion takes place on a Friday.

Black Friday.

Not just any Friday.

Friday, July 3, 1970.

My birthday. Oh yeah, authentic real, my 17th birthday.

That was rich.

Happy birthday, motherfucker.

It's summer, natch, so no problem regards school. Take the old fuck-to-hell white Rambler and drive to pick Sweet Sarah up to take her to the hospital.

Berkeley deal, you know, where the hospital's located.

And this is the day.

Sweet Sarah has to be there at 9 a.m. so I get up super early for me, 5 a.m., and my dad in the shower and my mom still asleep and I get out of the house by 5:10, and I mean who knew it was that dark at 5:10, I never in my life got up at 5:10, but it's so damn dark. Weird the way you learn new shit. So much you stumble into, random trip, and one thing and then another, pretty soon you know a few things, more than a few, a whole lot. About the way of the world.

Anyway.

I have the radio on. Man, there's only AM in the Rambler so I tune in KYA. Yeah, lame Top 40 but KYA sponsored The Beatles' Candlestick Park appearance in '66, have to give them points for pulling that one off. An oldie but goodie, James Brown, Mr. Please Please Please himself. He's singing "It's a Man's Man's Man's World," and no one knows that more than me.

My old lady gotta get an abortion.

Happy birthday, Motherfucker.

No one on the freeway heading north at that hour, up 101 and turn onto Sir Francis Drake, and head west, sun begins to rise, rays hit the top of Mt. Tamalpais, and I don't want music right then, don't need James Brown reminding me of my bummered-out bummerosity, turn the radio off and it's quiet and the world begins to wake up and it's beautiful.

Can't help but see all the beauty.

Total Zen deal.

Drive towards that sleeping maiden mountain, you know, Mt. Tamalpais, the outline of her face set against the lightening sky, the gray streaked with magenta, and I drive past the middle class suburban homes all along Sir Francis Drake, and past College of Marin, and Ross Hospital and all the high priced psychiatrists' offices, and more homes, and all the way through San Anselmo and onward, onward, into Fairfax and up, up into the hills, and the homes get nicer, and the landscaping lush and well-tended, the homes set far back, hidden by fences and tall shrubs and huge trees, many of those big fancy houses on one or two acre lots, each with its own circular driveway, some with elaborate black iron gates and the manicured green lawns, the automated sprinkler systems running, and I can hear the sounds of the sprinkler heads spray water in huge arcs, hear that, and it must be different water than the rest of us get, some kind of special water that makes the grass such a deep rich green. Special water for people who got a lot of dough.

Those are the people I want to be, the people with the dough.

They got it made, man.

But anyway.

Park the car kinda near the pond, you know, where we went the day we got the ice cream cones and I gave her the necklace.

Five-thirty-five, and I'm not supposed to pick her up 'til 7. She could go in with her dad but I want to take her and she wants that too. I can't go into the hospital Sweet Sarah said when we spoke on the phone about it, and her dad would be driving her home afterwards, and I argued about that but Sweet Sarah said that was just the way it would be and I better accept.

The people with a lot of dough, do they have to accept?

I have an hour and a half to kill. Park the car, turn the radio back on, "Bridge Over Troubled Water," and I listen to the rest of it, those voices soothing and the words just right and I'm glad no one is with me 'cause Simon and Garfunkel are lame-ass lame. I mean I dug the *Sounds of Silence,* and the *Parsley, Sage, Rosemary and Thyme* albums but their sound is the wimpy deal for sure. Still, can't help it, they're just what I need.

Some sappy song by The Carpenters comes on next, switch to KEWB, the other Top 40 station, and oh yeah, John Lennon, my *man,* only he sings "Instant Karma," sings how instant karma gonna get me, and I don't need that, turn the radio off.

And fuck-to-hell this is the day.

Happy birthday, motherfucker.

Get out, walk along the dirt path that leads around the pond to the stone bench. Me and Sweet Sarah, we sat on that bench a lot of times, and this morning I look out on the pond, and the ducks and the lilies and some frogs croaking and for a moment I'm overtaken by a nostalgic kinda feeling, this good feeling, but as I sit on that bench by myself in the shade 'cause the sun hasn't risen past the trees, mostly Douglas firs but some pines and sycamores, I'm cold and alone, my Visions of Johanna chick soon to have an abortion and I'm scared and this death shadow on me, this dread, things gonna fall apart, that kinda bummered-out feeling. Somehow my body knows this is the beginning of something.

Sweet Sarah is real quiet as I drive her to the hospital. Turn on the radio, KEWB, James Brown again, screaming about *papa's got a brand new bag,* and Sweet Sarah turns it right off.

"I'm scared," she says.

I look at her quick-like, and my eyes back on the road. She's shivering, a little girl, eyes red half closed 'cause she slept fucked and she hadn't brushed her hair, she looks a mess, crazy-beautiful mess, just makes me crazy how crazy-beautiful Sweet Sarah looks, even fucked up same as she is, so crazy-beautiful in the morning light same as a graveyard looks beautiful at twilight.

For once I don't know what to say.

So we drive in silence out to 101, and then we drive under the freeway and the road winds up and around past San Quentin and then we're on 580, slow among all the 9-to-5 drones, one to a car, heading to their 9-to-5 hellfuck of a day, across the Richmond bridge, the Bay a fury, the water dark and turbulent, past the goddamn oil refinery and eventually I turn onto 80 West.

And all the while I need to come up with something smart and caring and loving to say to Sweet Sarah that's not lame-ass-lame. Everything I think of is a cliché. *It'll be alright* but that's bullshit, I don't know it'll be alright. *Isn't gonna hurt*, don't know that either. *You'll feel better once this is behind you*, yeah sure. *Such a bummer but we'll get though it*, like I know shit about what it is for a teenage chick to deal with the heavy traffic bummered-out bummerosity Sweet Sarah's going through.

Finally, fuck it, man, talk.

"I'm sorry," I say.

"Sarah, I mean I would do anything to undo this," I say. "If I'd known, I'd never—."

Another quick look at her, she nods and a smile, her smile, and I know that smile means it'll be alright, we'll get through all this, our pure good-as-gold love is stronger than any of this, stronger than her well-meaning dad and my goddamn fucking dad, her clueless mom and my career-planning mom, and this abortion and being in high school and all the other shit. But what I know is wrong 'cause what I didn't know was I was gonna keep fucking up, that I was gonna make another wrong turn and then another until it was over and nothing of what was pure and good and beautiful was left.

I get off the freeway at Ashby and another 10 minutes of

driving and I stop in front of the hospital and Sweet Sarah's dad is there in the doorway.

And Sweet Sarah turns to me, pulls her hand out of her pocket and she gives me this small package, from her cold hand to my warm hand.

"Happy birthday, Michael," she says.

I didn't open it right then, but later I did, and it was a ceramic heart, a bright shiny red ceramic heart that Sweet Sarah made and glazed and fired, the whole deal. And I mean later, after she's gone, and I open the package and see that heart, I feel her love. If it hadn't been her and me, if it was a movie or a book or something, I would have thought it was the most corny melodramatic deal I ever seen, but you know, when something happens to you, it's a total different deal. For sure.

Right there in the car she smiles that smile that means everything's gonna be alright.

She turns away and her dad comes to get her and she's out of the car and she has on her blue jeans and her long gray Great Depression coat and her auburn hair, still unbrushed, but just crazy-wild magnificent, man. Sweet Sarah, this 16-year-old hippie ragamuffin princess, and her dad hugs her and they walk to the door and into the hospital and they're gone.

I sit there looking at that stupid hospital door as if, if I look long and hard enough, Sweet Sarah will come back out, get in the car and we'll drive away, get out of fucking Dodge forever, hit the road, start a grand new life elsewhere.

And behind me there's a car honking.

Happy birthday, motherfucker.

Later Sweet Sarah tells me that someone, either the doctor or the nurse, told her she couldn't have sex for a month, which she thinks is funny since in all of her 16 years on the planet she's *never* had sex.

10. THE FIRST TIME

AUGUST 10, 1970. TODAY we're gonna fuck for the first time. She wants to take a shower before we do it, so we strip in my room, and Sweet Sarah is so serious, that thing with her mouth, lips pressed together, and her jaw, unbuttons her white blouse and lets it fall on the floor, and her jeans and the white panties and oh man.

Oh man oh man oh man.

Barely room for two people in there. But that don't matter. I mean come on, me and Sweet Sarah together in the shower! Total fucking turn-on. I soap her back, massage it and work my way down to her ass, soaping each cheek and washing her neck and breasts and stomach, down to her pussy, washing her light brown snatch. I'm gentle, really getting the soap to foam up and the hot water coming down on our heads, streaming down our bodies and her mouth on mine, her lips and everything wet, and it's too much. Man, anywhere on my body she touches got a direct line to my dick. I keep washing her snatch and my index and middle fingers in her, at first tentative and then firm and soon I'm rubbing fast same as she shows me, and touching her that way helps get my attention off my dick. Her left breast against my chest, she licks my face, biting at it gentle, sucking my lips, my tongue, my hand up down up down up down, her breath speeding and I never seen her this way, oh man, it's an ecstasy to see her so into what she's feeling. She makes this moaning sound, pushing into my hand, her eyes closed, she kinda falls back against the white plastic wall and I keep working my fingers and she stops pushing but she wants me to do it more, and I do, and I do, and I do, and she cries out again, and her body relaxes and her hand on my hand, she wants me to stop, and I stop.

She opens her eyes and I'm proud I could give her such pleasure.

"Do it," she says.

I want to fuck her there in the shower, but I can't.

"Gotta get a condom," I say, and she smiles a dreamy smile. "Yeah, you do."

So it turns out that when I fuck Sweet Sarah she can't come. Not the first time, and not any time. If we'd been older and knew something about sex, and chicks' bodies, we'd know that some chicks can't come when a guy is in her, and it don't mean there's anything wrong with the chick or the guy. There's other ways. Cunnilingus or getting her off in the shower same as that other time, or maybe if she got on top of me instead of us always doing the missionary position.

But we don't know. We're 16. How the hell we supposed to know?

We try things. Slow it down, kiss for a long time and me touching her and me trying not to rush it. She reads these how-to sex books. One's about tantric sex. In the book it says the "male" is supposed to put his cock in the "female" and they lie there for hours and hours, this whole mystical enlightenment deal, and when they come the guy has the most intense Forever Infinite Ecstatic orgasm ever, and the chick comes and comes even more than forever.

Well it's one thing for some Buddhist to write in his book about having your cock in your chick for hours, and it's another to do it, and after maybe four minutes at the most I can't help it, no matter what I'm gonna come so I start going at it and when I come I feel so goddamn guilty 'cause I'm getting off and she isn't and that's fucked-up. It's as if she's giving herself to me, but I want her to be doing it for her *and* for us, not only for me. I don't want her to feel it's her duty as my chick, you know, some stone-age wife scene.

Who knew fucking could be such a bummer.

We decided the problem was the condom. It felt like shit, that thing tight around my dick, and it didn't feel any better when I was in Sweet Sarah and even when I came it sucked. It had to be the condom that was keeping her from coming.

Sweet Sarah got an IUD put in, so we wouldn't have to deal with the condom, wouldn't have to worry about her getting pregnant. Getting the IUD was terrible, she said, old fart Dr. Ellingsworth and his fingers in her attaching this little thing that was gonna stop the sperm. I didn't get that, how the fuck is this thing, looked like a tiny tiny little fish hook, gonna stop all those zillions of amped-up search-and-destroy sperm whose only mission in life is to gang-bang the egg.

Fucking without the condom was great for me, the most intense pleasure trip ever, I mean it felt awesome and Sweet Sarah really tried, probably tried way too much and that was the problem, every time we fucked and she didn't come it was another pound added to the weight on her shoulders, and finally she didn't want me to ask anymore, said that if she started coming, then after a while she'd tell me but she just couldn't deal with the pressure.

So after she told me not to ask there was this thin wall between us that I could feel that hadn't been there before the sex. Before, whether she told me everything or I told her everything, it felt like we did and we were totally there with each other but now I didn't know for sure.

Although I knew. I mean no matter how into it she seemed to be, still, I knew.

The IUD didn't work, and this time when her period was a couple of days late we knew. And I was to blame of course, again. Sweet Sarah never said anything same as that and we didn't talk about blame but I was guilty as fucking hell 'cause this was all my fault. I was why we were fucking, I was the one who got off, I was the selfish asshole who couldn't stand the fucking rubber and now Sweet Sarah had to pay.

Only I had to pay too. I just didn't know it but I was gonna pay in heartache and pain and forgetting who I was. I wasn't just going to lose Sweet Sarah, I was going to lose myself. When it was all over I wouldn't be standing on solid ground, and my confidence would be gone and all the cool shit I'd done before — feeling I was a big deal, someone special, the freakster bro who made shit happen, the guy with the coolest music first and hip to Godard and Truffaut and knowing obscure shit like it was Bob Seidemann who took that naked photo of Janis and that Keith played a Dan Armstrong guitar at Altamont, me with the best chick in the world for a girlfriend and not only that, fucking her all the time, that kind of I'M THE MAN kinda shit —that was gonna be just gone, dead in the water, whole fucking life gone to shit. Yeah I didn't know that was coming when she said her period was late. Again.

For a couple weeks after we find out Sweet Sarah's dad is so pissed he bans me from their house. I gotta pick Sweet Sarah up out on the street, and we go to my house to fuck, or go for a hike and fuck on a tarp, some flat spot you can't see from the trail and the ground's hard and she's scared someone will see us, or we make out in the Rambler at the end of some dead-end and she gives me a hand job, the sperm all over her hand, us trying not to get it on the seat.

One day I realize all I think about is sex. All I think about is when's the next time me and Sweet Sarah gonna fuck. Don't matter if we go to a movie or I buy us burgers at the drive-in or we go to the Freak Scene Dream place in Fairfax for veggie soup and spring rolls, I'm always waiting for when I can fuck her. Soon we won't be able to fuck for a month, you know, 'cause she'll be healing. So all I think about is how many times can I fuck Sweet Sarah before abortion number two. I feel same as shit for thinking that way, but I can't help it.

January of 1971. This time there's no talk about who's paying. Everyone wants to get the damn thing over, no one wants to talk about it and that includes Sweet Sarah. Total mixed-up confusion, Sweet Sarah is, sometimes she's pissed at me, sometimes she's pissed at herself, sometimes at shit-ass Dr. Ellingsworth. Sweet Sarah's a chick cares about trees and animals, and the planet. She reads Gary Snyder and "Walden" and calls herself a pacifist. She believes life is precious, so killing this thing inside her that could grow to be our son or daughter, some wonderful human who'd make the world a better place, oh, man. Still, her life ahead of her, and everything gone to hell if she keeps it. This time Sweet Sarah drives to the hospital with her dad and that's how it is and I have to accept.

Things changed after that, and the thin wall I told you about got thicker. Right after her second abortion Sweet Sarah went on the pill, only way to know for certain there wouldn't be a third one. Right about when she started on the pill I started smoking weed. At first it's occasional but soon enough I'm high all the time. So much easier to let the troubles float away. I'm still not sure why I got so into it. Was it 'cause I couldn't cope with Sweet Sarah slipping away, or was it just me digging the high? The authentic real of it, I think the weed took me too far out, where my normal proclivity to push shit right to the edge, well the weed let me push right past it into places I shouldn't have gone. It's what I think, but maybe it's not true. Maybe it's a story. Maybe it takes the responsibility off me, you know, *It was the weed, man.* Same as those lame-ass propaganda films, "Reefer Madness" and "Devil's Harvest." 'Cause everyone I knew who smoked the weed, Polanski and Faithfull and the others, they didn't get freaked-out crazy weird.

When exactly what happened after that, regards dates and times, happened, I couldn't tell you. Sometime after her abortion the heavy scene between me and Sweet Sarah goes down. First she tells me her and Trendy Wendy, you know, the black haired chick with the cold hands and the colder personality who is Sweet Sarah's best friend, when summer comes they're gonna run a kids' art program at Sweet Sarah's house. That's cool, and I said I'd total be there to help. Oh man, she got weird, gave me the hard look, you know, where I gotta accept, and told me she don't want me coming over when the kids are there. She said sometimes I'm so intense it could scare the kids, and on top of that, she don't want the kids around a pothead. Couldn't believe it. Her calling *me* a pothead. Course I was. A pothead.

That's when I got the idea in my head if I gotta accept Sweet Sarah saying I can or can't come around, well she gonna have to accept me doing my own thing. Yeah, there's stuff I could do without her, for sure, only the things I was gonna do, they were gonna cause me nothing but trouble.

If I'd been listening, I'd have heard it louder than loud, *caw caw caw*, Doom and Gloom, the sound of crushed souls, heard their warnings.

11. POLANSKI

AND THEN IT HAPPENED, for the first time I looked at another chick.

It was after Sweet Sarah's second abortion, we were both 17, and I was a serious pothead.

The first time, but it was more than that, more than me looking at another chick, all the craziness, the craziness, man.

Yeah, and I mean later everyone wanted to say weed was the problem. The psychiatrist at the loony bin, and my dad, and my mom, and I mean even Frankie and Bobby bought into it, you know, that it was weed made me crazy. It wasn't the weed, I mean the weed probably helped promote it, push it right out past the edge, but it wasn't the weed. It was my nature, it was me, it was my crazy-wildest freakster bro you ever seen ego blown high as the bright bright sun. I was blinded by my own eye-blinding, self-generated light, man.

I aimed it right in my own eyes.

Sweet Sarah wasn't into the weed, and long as I knew her, never into the weed. Sweet Sarah was into the pure natural innocent trip, I mean she tried to hang on to it despite all we'd been through. But even when we were 17 already she was losing it. The innocence. Only we didn't know it back then.

For all I know, maybe Sweet Sarah never smoked weed. Maybe she always held onto that do-the-right-thing pure heart trip same as a life preserver—to save her life, save her soul —'cause when the darkness came back, that was the one pure thing she held onto. Maybe, but I sure don't know, and I sure don't even want to know what goes on with her now, how she's changed, who she is out there wherever she is, whoever she's with, if there even is a whoever she's with, don't matter.

Don't matter.

And I sure don't want to think about this part of what happened, when the beginning of the end began, first time I looked at another chick, and another chick, and another, so it became just what I did, nothing special about it.

Yeah, what I want to think about is Sweet Sarah before the troubles, when we were 15 and 16 and it was all crazy-beautiful and brand new and we were certain our love was pure and true and forever, only what happened later keeps getting in the way.

Before the troubles, man.

Anyway, I was into the weed. I smoked it. Usually with Polanski, you know, the guy whose dad was a hot shot in the movie biz, top of his driveway in Tiburon where I saw Jerry Garcia and asked him for an interview.

Yeah, that Polanski, Polanski whose old lady is Ruth, you remember, the chick we all call Faithfull 'cause she got that Marianne Faithfull fixation, and he fucks her that time in my mom and dad's bedroom, in my mom and dad's bed.

And Faithfull never changed the sheets like she said she would.

Of course you remember.

Anyway.

Sticky Fingers wouldn't be released for another two months or so, didn't matter though, the seedy nod-out vibe of junk and morphine, of dead sex and dead flowers, of heartache and desire was already seeping into everything.

Into everything, man.

One afternoon, early months of 1971, and I'm on my way to meet Polanski, on the street in Mill Valley, I walk toward the bus depot when I see this dealer. Dealer Cat I call him.

Dealer Cat fucked-up chants quick-like.

"Weed, coke, reds, hash, 'shrooms,

"Weed, coke, reds, hash, 'shrooms."

And I seen a million of this dude on Haight Street, and at

those free concerts in the Park, Speedway Meadows and the Polo Field, and up on Mt. Tam too. Me and Big Man Bobby hitched to those concerts in '68 and '69 and '70.

Always there's Dealer Cat.

The unwashed matted hair, never fucking shaves, thin as a malnourished string bean. Some kinda mud-brown poncho, strands of discolored beads around his neck, the bell-bottom jeans too long drag on the sidewalk torn and frayed and dirt-stained. And if I had a look into Dealer Cat's soul, for sure as torn and frayed and dirt-stained as those bell-bottoms.

And I don't got time for this dude, got to hang with Polanski.

"Peace, brother," Dealer Cat says.

And something about him makes me stop.

"Hey, man," I say.

And he looks at me.

"The end is near," Dealer Cat says.

Oh man, and I brush those words away, 'cause I don't get it. Not that day. Later I get it. Later it's way too late.

Me and Polanski have coffee and a soft drink, me with a big-ass ceramic cup of strong black muck, Polanski with a bottle of Coke. Polanski is what we all call Rodney, you remember. Of course you do, I mean everyone who knows Polanski calls him Polanski, other than his chick Ruth, who calls him Rod, and who, same as I already told you a couple times, we call Faithfull.

Downtown Mill Valley at the former train depot, now a bus depot that's also a café, where the tune-in-turn-on-drop-outs sit around all day, contemplate the universe, talk about their big plans, the play they're gonna get going just soon as they get a sign from the earth mother or the stars or the I Ching, just as soon as the moon and Jupiter and Pluto are in alignment, or the voices tell them *it's time*.

Only it's never time, but maybe tomorrow.

Maybe, but don't hold your breath.

Me and Polanski sit outside out back where there's tables, and past the tables the small cement plaza with benches where the burn-outs who don't have the dough for a cup of coffee and a donut hang out. We sit at a small round metal table, a round metal table with an umbrella coming up through a hole in the middle of it. And I want it to be the kind of round metal table you sit at near the pool of a high-price hotel on the French Riviera, or maybe on a patio overlook the beach, that trip, yeah, you know the deal.

That's what I want that table to be, French Riviera umbrella, the umbrella open to keep the bright bright Mediterranean sun off us. Only it's the bright bright California sun, and there's no pool, no French Riviera, just a view of the plaza, and the burn-outs, and the cars driving up Miller Avenue.

We're stonered for sure, yeah we are.

Smoke the weed out in Polanski's black Mercedes convertible with the black leather seats that already got cigarette burns. Polanski's dad bought it for him 16th birthday, year or so before the day we sit at that French Riviera table, and already Polanski got into some accidents. Big dent in the passenger-side door, and some other shit. Only Polanski isn't the only one.

I drive the white Rambler into a tree not so long before that day we sit there. Well not as bad as that sounds, not as if I go 60 miles an hour when I do it. And anyway, it wasn't really my fault. I was in a rush and high on some weed and gonna park the car off the road in front of this tree, right next to where another car was parked and I misjudged the distance, don't brake soon enough, fucked up the front fender deal.

Yeah I have plenty of excuses back then in early '71 or whenever the fuck it was, plenty of 'em, and nothing's ever a big deal, not when the weed kicks in, hit the front fender into a tree but no big deal, man, you know, don't sweat it, and don't bummer me out. I got enough on my mind.

Too much on my mind. I got my own big plans, and I'll get to them, you'll see. Not same as the tune-in-turn-on-drop-outs, not same as the burn-outs. I got it wired down so tight, man.

But anyway.

Polanski thinks he looks cool as Jim Morrison after Jim

Morrison grew his beard, you know, Jim Morrison on the way down down down, and so fucked up, getting ready to be gone, baby, gone. Getting ready to be dead. Jim Morrison getting ready to get found in the bathtub of a Paris apartment O.D.'d on junk, but that hasn't happened yet, not that day me and Polanski sit at the French Riviera table.

Polanski stonered and me stonered too.

Flying high and high flying, man, and we think we're the crown princes of rock 'n' roll, only it's clown princes of rock 'n' roll and we don't know about the clown part.

Me, I look as crazy-wild freakster bro out-of-control crazy as I ever look, my hair way long, and super curly, and I mean it comes out from my head same as the freakiest freaked-out hippie hair you ever seen. Garcia in '67 when the Dead play Haight Street, that kinda freaky freaked-out hippie hair trip. Got on my cool-as-Dylan Wayfarer-style shades, and I haven't shaved in three, four days, so I got the wasted black-sand-stuck-to-my-face look. And I been wearing the same clothes for maybe a week, all wrinkled and slept in vibe, my old denim bellbottoms and the brown suede cowboy boots, and that golden yellow cowboy shirt with the orange paisleys all over it, wear that shirt over my favorite purple Lennon t-shirt, none of that cowboy shirt tucked in, yeah that whole trip. In my stonered delusions of grandeur I think I look same as a rock star, man, only if I could see myself that day, what I see is a burned-out basement.

Such a hassle to change my clothes.

Such a hassle and the more I'm hanging with Polanski, the more hassle it is, and I don't have the time, I got big important shit to do.

Yeah, burned-out basement, how I look. That day.

That day I sit there and drink black coffee with Polanski.

And I hear it.

Caw caw caw.

I twist around, look up, and there's two black-billed magpies. Soon as I see those black-billed magpies, I know it's Doom and Gloom.

Those birds sit behind us up on the roof of the café, *caw caw caw*, sound of crushed souls, yeah I hear the troubles. Doom tells me for sure the troubles come, and Gloom adds that not only for sure the troubles come, but I'll never forget the fucked-up shit I'm gonna do.

And the *Sister Morphine* slide guitar, I hear it, that slide guitar means nothing good, and the *caw caw caw*, yeah the scene has turned so wrong, and the troubles are not just on their way, the troubles have arrived.

And I hear something else. I hear that 13th Floor Elevators' song. "You're Gonna Miss Me." Maybe it was coming from a radio, or maybe it was in my head. The maniac scream of Roky Erickson, back before the damage. Before he dropped all the acid, before the acid corrodes his mind, back when there was nothing but wide open sky and a shot at reaching the stars, back when "You're Gonna Miss Me" wasn't yet resigned to being what it would become, what it is today, a minor hit, the group's only hit, major or minor, and the end of what at first seemed to be a great beginning. Only it was really the beginning of the end. And by the time "You're Gonna Miss Me" showed up on that *Nuggets* collection of garage rock that Lenny Kaye put together, it was too late. The 13th Floor Elevators were done, a minor footnote in the history of rock 'n' roll, and Roky Erickson was done too, and the acid damage a finality as certain as death.

In my head I hear that song, hear the lyric, sung by a guy to a girl about how one morning she's gonna get up to find her lover is gone.

I didn't know it in 1966, when I first heard it on the radio. AM radio. Top 40. KEWB. Yeah I didn't know that was Sweet Sarah. What Sweet Sarah would sing to me, if she were to sing to me. How could I know. I was 13, and I didn't know Sweet Sarah existed first time I heard the song.

1966. When I bought the single and played it over and over I thought it was me singing to some chick that done me wrong.

And that day I'm there with Polanski, and I hear that song again, clueless, man. I don't understand. Don't know it's a message from Sweet Sarah to me. A warning. A warning of how bad it's gonna be. How I'm gonna wake up to the fact that she's gone. And she isn't coming home. And I'm gonna miss her. Oh yeah. And that maniac scream of Roky Erickson, that's not even close to the way I'm gonna feel, echo of an echo of an echo, man.

The hellfuck of how I'll feel.

Do you understand me? What I'm trying to clue you in to?

Things been heading south for a while, me not taking care of business, me smoking the weed I get off Polanski, letting my schoolwork slide, forgetting my chores, my room messed up and more messed up. Some of the symptoms, man. But the heavy duty symptoms are what I do to me and Sweet Sarah. Forget to call her when I say I'll call, show up late and I'm distracted and nothing she's doing and wants to talk talk talk about interests me. In fact it bores me, and meanwhile everything I do is super groovy overwhelming important, that kind of trip. Talk talk talk, and Sweet Sarah looks at me funny.

Something gone terrible wrong.

Yeah, Doom and Gloom up there, and that day I hear the message, troubles on the way. Only I think I got time. Well I don't got no time.

Polanski moves his chair, it's a metal chair that goes with the French Riviera table, moves so he's closer to me and he's too fucking close and he thinks he looks so cool, Jim Morrison crawling kingsnake cool. Getting ready to O.D. in a Paris bathtub.

And I shouldn't be here, this is a mistake, Polanski is nothing but trouble, only it's too late, already the stain of the troubles is on me.

Caw caw caw.

And the "Sister Morphine" slide guitar, cold metal sound vibrates my bones.

"You ever fuck your chick when you're both loaded, Writerman?" Polanski says.

Polanski thinks he looks cool as Jim Morrison after Jim Morrison exposes himself on stage down in Miami, only that would be the charitable way to say how Polanski looks. Me, I'm gonna tell you authentic real. He looks more same as Charles Manson than Jim Morrison, way I see it.

We sit there at that French Riviera table, him chain-smoking Chesterfields and drinking from a bottle of Coke and he thinks he looks cool as Jim Morrison, only he don't look cool at all. He looks same as some low-on-the-totem-pole sleaze-out dealer, or some mobbed-up Vegas casino manager, or Charles Manson, his dirty-blond hair unwashed for days, hangs straight and shiny, looks wet it's so greased-out, and he's got the humungous Yosemite Sam handlebar moustache, as usual hasn't shaved in maybe three days, wide-wale gold cords dirt-stained an ugly brown and scuffed-up black Beatle boots, but it was the shirt said it all. Rayon or nylon or polyester long-sleeve shirt with the wide collar, the shirt is shiny black and it has line drawings of laughing hyenas, gold laughing hyenas, all over it and he's got the top three buttons unbuttoned so I can see his curly dirty-blonde chest hair, and that plastic gold laughing hyenas shirt tells you all you need to know about Polanski.

And he does something I really don't like. His hand in a fist, he punches my shoulder, not a real punch, but a punch all the same, a punch hard enough so I feel it. I don't like him touching me. He don't got no right.

"I like to get them really stoned," Polanski says. "'cause then I do whatever I want."

I don't like what he says, and I don't like the way he says it. And what he says seeps into me, so I feel the dirty of "do whatever I want," so I understand he's not talking about giving the chick a kiss or holding their hand or a sweet hug. And he opens his mouth, lets it form an exaggerated psycho-clown smile and I see the hole between his teeth, there on the left, yeah Polanski is missing a fucking tooth, and I see this big-ass fucking pimple on his chin, and he's been picking at it, popped it I guess, and there's some pus coming out and some blood.

"Know what I *mean,* Writerman?"

And his fist into my shoulder again, goddamn Polanski.

I don't like the turn this conversation takes, and I look up from my mug of coffee, 'cause along with weed I drink coffee serious now, too much coffee, give-you-the-jitters too too much coffee, and Polanski looks right at me, exchanges the psycho-clown smile for his devil's business smile, and it's even uglier that smile, cross between a sneer and the sarcastic. It's a real up-to-no-good grifter smile.

Devil's business smile.

You know those kinda smiles. Sure you do.

Wipes his hand across his face, rubs the open pimple, gets pus and blood on his hand, wipes it on the dirty gold cords.

And I should get out of here, man, that was *un moment decisif* for sure, only I'm way to stoned to know it.

Don't have to know it.

In, or out.

And if you're too stoned to know it, and you go with the flow, well you made the decision anyway. Same as those dopes who don't vote, who claim they're too fucking good to participate in our political system, want to partake of whatever you get being a citizen, only no commitment. Too above it all to commit. Well they commit. And if Richard Nixon gets elected, well them not voting for Humphrey is a vote for Nixon, and the blood is on their hands. You think you don't commit. You always commit.

Always.

Yeah, too stoned to know it, but I commit.

"The best is fucking them up the ass," Polanski says. "You ever do that, Writerman?"

His fucking fist into my shoulder, and my shoulder hurts, dammit and even if it didn't hurt this sucks, and why do I let him do this?

"Hey man, don't do that," I say.

"You ever get a bunch of vaseline on your dick and squeeze some into their butthole and go for it," he says. "Fuck your chick hard up the ass?"

Devil's business smile, and it's as if I haven't said a word to him.

Oh I really really don't like the turn this conversation takes, not at all. Don't like him touching me. But I sit there. No I don't like it. I never talk anything personal about me and Sweet Sarah. Not to *anyone*. And I sure don't talk about fucking, and I sure as sure as sure-can-be don't want to listen to Polanski talk about squeezing vaseline in a chick's butt and whatever ugly shit he does after that, and I'm so fucked-up stoned on Polanski's weed, and I especially don't want any talk same as that to come anywhere near me or how I think about me and Sweet Sarah.

Caw caw caw.

Sweet Sarah is the innocence. Even after all that's happened, Sweet Sarah is the innocence. So bad I want Sweet Sarah to be the innocence.

And my mind gonna explode.

12. ANOTHER CHICK

THERE'S RATTLESNAKE VENOM IN Polanski's punch, he angles his knuckles so they dig into my shoulder, dares me to stop him.

"Cat got your tongue?" Polanski says. "Demon eye got you in its sway, Writerman?"

Maybe three, could be four car lengths out front of us, there in the plaza front of the old train depot, this guy is swaying under the bright bright sun, and he's barefoot. He's facing away from us, got stringy brown hair and a Mexican poncho and what's with the ponchos on a burning hot day, do all the losers wear ponchos? Some kind of loser style that's in vogue?

He got what I guess is a cigarette between his fingers 'cause I see smoke rising from his right hand. Seeing him in the poncho and I feel the heat worse than it is, and yeah that's where drugs can take you, to a place where you're a fucked-up loser wearing a wool poncho out in what gotta be 80-plus degree heat.

I look down into the chocolate brown muck of my coffee, the coffee that's cooled to that temperature where coffee don't taste good no more as I've sat in the sway of Polanski, wishing the coffee wasn't coffee at all, wishing it was the sparkling blue water of a mountain lake, wishing I was lying on a towel with Sweet Sarah after we'd gone for a swim, looking at that lake and the pines and firs surrounding it, a million miles from this dirty café patio and the dirtier plaza out front of us and the loser creep in a dirty wool poncho trying to keep his balance. What the hell am I doing here?

Polanski's waiting for my answer, waiting to hear if I ever got a chick stoned and did her up the ass, and why do I gotta answer?

"I've never been stonered with any chick," I say.

I look up into Polanski's face, and his expression changes, he gets the you're-putting-me-on deal all over his casino manager low-life dealer sleaze-ass mug.

He's too close to me and I smell his sweat, the shiny sweat on his bare skin down below his neck that's showing where he got the black polyester hyena shirt unbuttoned. Got that rotten eggs sulphur smell, the stink of Polanski.

"What's wrong with you, Mike?" he says.

It's either Writerman or Mike, dude never calls me by my name.

And I don't like it, I mean I tell him 10,000 times it's Michael, not Mike, but he don't care what I tell him, and anyways it's Writerman, or Mike. He knows how much I hate that Mike deal, and he knows I never do any writing, except when I have to for school, and he thinks it's funny, getting me mad about my name, getting me uncomfortable and flustered talking about fucking chicks up the ass.

"No chick I ever been with into weed, man," I say.

Now the authentic real of it, I only been with one chick, Sweet Sarah, but same as I said before, I never talk anything personal that goes on between me and her with anybody, not Frankie, not Bobby, and for sure not Polanski, so I say that kinda general deal, as if I been with loads of chicks, dozens and dozens of chicks, and it just happens none of the numerous and many and plentiful chicks I been with smoked weed.

"Sounds like the chicks you've been with are pretty uptight, Writerman," Polanski says. "The chicks you been with frigid, you got that problem?"

"No man," I say. "Never been with no frigid chicks. Total satisfaction guaranteed, man. And I don't have any problem, except for you. You're the problem, man."

And he's laughing, this is what he wants, get a rise out of me.

"Glad to hear it, Writerman," he says. "Sounds like you're a real Casanova. I didn't know that about you. Real Casanova, man. I'm impressed. Maybe I should start calling you Casanova, keeping your chicks satisfied the way you say you do."

He takes what's left of his Chesterfield, and it's violent the way he rams the end hard against the glass bottom of the ashtray, kills the glowing tobacco, and the force rips the paper around the tobacco, and when he takes his hand away all I see is a small pile of brown tobacco and a ripped piece of white paper in the ashtray, and I wouldn't want him angry at me, wouldn't want those hands of his pushing into me the way he did what he did to that cigarette butt.

"Ever think about being a sex therapist, Casanova?" Polanski says.

"No, man," I say.

"I'm talking about a hands on physical sex therapist, Casanova," Polanski says.

Out there in the middle of the plaza the dude with a wool poncho is sitting on the cement, got his back to us so I can't see his face but there's something wrong about how he's sitting.

"No, man," I say. "I'm gonna be a writer. I tell you that a million times."

"I'm telling you, you oughta get yourself into the sex therapy business," Polanski says.

"I'm tired of sitting, man," I say.

I stand up, do this exaggerated stretch, lift my arms up toward the sky.

"Lot of easy money to be made," Polanski says. "Best kind, easy money. Money you don't work for. That's why my dad got his fingers in publishing."

And I know about publishing.

Sort of.

Entertainment biz dudes same as Polanski's dad and Albert Grossman and Allen Klein who managed the Stones for a while, they buy up the song publishing rights. Lot of times they hardly pay anything, sometimes they pay nothing up front. Unknown artists they agree to manage, or even a famous one who's too fucked up or just plain stupid to know. Every time someone buys a record with the song on it, or one of the songs gets played on the radio, whoever owns the publishing gets a piece.

I move the chair, my chair, so it's not so close to Polanski, and settle back into it.

"You wouldn't believe it, Casanova," Polanski says. "Checks keep showing up. My dad never has to work. Work-a-day job is for saps. Publishing. Ca-ching. Easy money."

And he's got another Chesterfield lit, holding it to his chapped lips, and I see the pus where he picks at the pimple, and I see where he had other pimples he picked at, the scars left to mark 'em..

"Mike Stein, sex therapist," Polanski says. "I like the sound of it."

"I don't think so, man," I say.

"Ca-ching. Easy money," Polanski says.

He moves in closer, got himself right next to me again, the motherfucker.

"You just told me about how good you are at giving the chicks satisfaction. Were you making that up?"

"No man," I say.

"Valuable service, Casanova," Polanski says.

Fucking fist in my shoulder and I know I'll have a bruise.

"Most dudes can't do it," Polanski says. "They can give themselves satisfaction, but leave their chick high and dry. You're the goose that laid the golden eggs, Casanova. Sex therapist for all the horny Marin housewives who don't get off when their husbands bone 'em. Don't even need an office. You can be like those doctors who make house calls. Casanova Mobile Sex Therapy Clinic. Easy money. Ca-ching."

Oh boy does he have that devil's business smile going now, sucking in the smoke and exhaling it out his nose, looks at me and he laughs. Oh does he laugh hard, and it's a coughing jag deal and he stands up, his fist against his chest, hits his chest two, three times, coughs up some green phlegm gook. And I'm still thinking about what he said regards Sweet Sarah being uptight and frigid, 'cause in a way she is. I mean she never comes when I fuck her. And she only wants to do the missionary position.

So that's pretty uptight, right?

A glob of green phlegm stains the cement right near where we sit.

"You got any new songs, man?" I say.

Polanski looks at me with the devil's business smile, don't say anything, watches me, checking my react, one beat, two, three, and then he speaks.

"Maybe you're with the wrong chick, Writerman."

And his left eye, he blinks it, holds it closed too long, opens it wide, lowers his forehead, got his head leaning a little to his left, and a different sleaze of a smile.

"Maybe you need a stoned-out-of-her-mind old lady," he says. "You're missing out, Writerman. Yeah, you need a different chick. Chick who's game for anything."

And I say nothing to that, and I hate Polanski 'cause he got shit out of me about Sweet Sarah, and he's judging what me and Sweet Sarah have, and already I feel bad about the sex deal with me and her, so much guilt, and I worry we're what they call sexually incompatible, or dysfunctional, one of those, you know, where the sex part of the relationship don't come together in a groovy way. Only I never say any of that aloud, not to Sweet Sarah, not to anyone, only now it's out there in the air 'cause of what Polanski said.

He tells me Faithfull is coming by soon. There's something else Polanski tells me. Faithfull is bringing a chick friend of hers along, a chick who wants to be in the band.

"She's a doll," Polanski says.

"A doll you want to strip the threads off so she's naked," he says. "And get her sucking on your knob."

From between those chapped red lips comes his tongue, and it slowly moves along his upper lip, a pink slug crawling his lip, and I hate his gross slug of a tongue, hate him licking his lip, and I hate myself. I need to get out of here. Now. Only all I do is pick up my coffee cup and set it back down on the French Riviera table.

"She got a sexy little chick's tongue, Casanova, perfect for a rim-job."

I don't know what a rim-job is, but I don't say nothing.

I mean last thing I want Polanski to know is I'm naive about anything.

"She's a singer?" I say.

"Listen up, Casanova," Polanski says. "I'm doing you a real solid, man. Don't matter if the chick can't tap her foot in time. You get her stoned and she'll be game for anything."

And I figure he's full of shit. Or pulling my leg. Thinks he can get my expectations up for when Faithfull gets there and it'll turn out there's no chick or if there is, she don't have anything to do with me, or some such. And anyway, I mean Sweet Sarah's my old lady. So none of it matters.

Only it does. Matter. And I start to wonder about this chick he brought up. Wonder what she looks like and if she's into sex the way Polanski makes it out. And that's a bad idea, thinking about another chick. Chick I don't even know.

Hellfuck of a bad idea.

"Yeah I got a new song," Polanski says. "I'm putting the finishing touches on it."

Gives me the devil's business smile all over again.

"It's called 'Casanova's Sex Therapy Clinic,'" he says.

And I shake my head, I mean the dude is impossible, and why do I hang out with him, and why am I in a band with him. Yeah, that's something new, something you don't know.

And I hear that "Sister Morphine" slide guitar.

Me and Polanski got a rock 'n' roll band.

Polanski says what he says about his new song, and soon enough after he says it, his chick Faithfull shows up. Faithfull's got hair all Betty Boop-style, dyed black and the bangs, tight black velvet dress so you really see her ass and tits, and it stops 8 or 9 inches above her knees, black suede knee-high boots, that chick a knock-out punch for sure, only I don't spend my time scoping her scene out 'cause of this other chick.

Yeah, and Polanski is more than right about the new chick.

She's more of a babe even than Faithfull. What he don't tell me, and what I don't think about, that chick is trouble right away. Only I don't know it. Yet.

Chick is gonna be total trouble.

And what I just said, how I don't know it.

That's a lie.

I knew it, I mean had to know it, but I guess I hid the knowing of it from myself, or tried to. I mean Sweet Sarah was still my old lady that day, and I looked at this new chick in a way I hadn't looked at any chick except Sweet Sarah for years.

I still try to understand why it happened, why I let myself drift away from Sweet Sarah, why I let a discontent grow and grow.

Maybe it was 'cause of my mom.

Ghost of 'lectricity. Early 1970, about a year into me and Sweet Sarah being together. Everything was still perfect, well I mean except Sweet Sarah wasn't ready for sex, but aside from that, it was the total heavy traffic perfect trip, and I'm in the living room. Sitting on the couch my mom has been wanting to get re-upholstered since forever, when she walks into the room and starts in.

"I was looking through your sophomore yearbook, Mike," she says.

"So," I say.

I'm reading the latest issue of *Creem*, an article about The Stooges, last thing I wanna talk about is the high school yearbook.

"Lot of *really* cute girls in your class," she says.

"So," I say.

"How come you don't ask some of those girls out on dates?"

"Come on, man," I say. "I have an old lady, mom."

"I hate it when you talk like that," Mom says. "Can't you call her your girlfriend. Or your steady."

"She's my chick, Mom," I say. "I'm not interested in other chicks."

"You two are too serious," Mom says. "You act like you're married."

"No, Mom," I say. "I don't act same as me and Sarah are married. If I acted same as we were married I'd take her for granted. I'd be cheating on her. All the stuff people who are married do. Marriage is a drag. We're never gonna get married. We're gonna live together. Keep it pure."

"Well I think you're making a mistake," she says. "Not dating other girls. You might find out you're more compatible with another girl. And even if you stay with Sarah, at least you'll know she's best for you."

And I don't say nothing to that, read about Iggy and the Stooges. Read about how Iggy jumps right into the audience, how he crawls on the stage and grinds his chest into broken glass from a broken beer bottle, how he smears peanut butter all over himself and sings "I Wanna Be Your Dog."

Yeah I read about Iggy and the Stooges. They have a song called "No Fun." And another called "1969" about how boring life is, and how they got nothing to do.

Sit there with Polanski, and through my Wayfarer cool-as-Dylan shades I stare at the new chick. And I let a discontent grow.

I let a discontent grow and grow and grow.

I see this beautiful young chick and I fool myself. All the reasons why I'm scoping out this new chick, wondering what she looks like under what she got on, wonder what it be like to fuck her. And I tell myself, all the mystery is gone, man, I know everything about Sweet Sarah, well think I do, and I'm listing what's wrong about me and Sweet Sarah, the predictability of it all, everything once new and fresh and the first time, well none of it's that way anymore.

I let a discontent grow and I tell myself that with this chick it's all new and fresh and the first time. And she's impressed by all that Sweet Sarah takes for granted. And what would it feel like to touch the body of this chick, and her hands on me, and maybe she'd come when I fucked her. And there she is, she's friends with Polanski's chick Faithfull, and she wants to sing in our band. Yeah man, there she is, and in a minute she'll be sitting at our table.

"Groovy dress, don't you think, Rod," Faithfull says. "It's just like the one Marianne wears in that photo of her and Mick I showed you."

I'm gonna get up, introduce myself, maybe shake the chick's hand only before I make my move, Polanski's fist into my shoulder and something about the way he punches me. *Don't get up. Don't act like you give a shit about the chick. Don't act like she's even there.*

Faithfull stands behind Polanski, rubs the back of his neck, and it's so natural, second nature, how she touches him.

"What's groovy is when you take the dress *off*, luv," he says.

He says it with an affected Brit accent, thinks he's Jim Morrison with a Brit accent. Only he's not Jim Morrison, and no one would ever think he was a Brit based on that accent, and authentic real he's a sleaze-bag and why do I sit here?

Polanski's laughing and the chick with Faithfull can't help herself, she's laughing too, a dark laugh, and I wouldn't want her laughing at me, not with that laugh, man.

"Don't be vulgar, Rod," Faithfull says.

Only she likes it, I know she does.

With my shades on I look at the chick and she don't know I'm lookin' at her. Stands next to Faithfull and she's overwhelming beautiful, man. She's 15, I find out later, and her name's Samantha and she wears groovy Victorian groupie gear.

What I mean is she's all dressed up, looks same as those groupie chicks in the *Rolling Stone* groupie issue, you know, chick with the frizzy hair on the cover. Same kind of super groovy antiquated clothes as the groupie chicks. White lace almost-see-through blouse, kinda tight.

Already she got tits. I could see the outline of 'em, maybe even see some of 'em through the tight thin almost-see-through cotton, and a dark burgundy velvet skirt, black platform boots and dangling antique brass earrings and her blonde hair done up all curly with curls coming down in front of her ears, and did I tell you she was beautiful?

Did I tell you?

Well it's worth repeating so you understand. You need to understand the pull of the chick. She's a dark relentless undertow pulling me down down down.

And what would it feel like to touch the body of this new chick, this friend of Faithfull, what would it feel like?

Well I'M THE MAN, I'm the *fucking* man, I'm the crazy-wildest freakster bro, guns ablaze, and I got it all wired down tight. Fuck what Sweet Sarah thinks 'cause I gotta right.

Samantha stands there, 15 years old, stands in the bright bright sun, and her young perfect skin glows, and her lips the palest palest pink, and her arms so thin and her fingers so thin and her legs so thin, and her perfect skin glows.

Faithfull is excited 'cause Samantha is into singing backup in our band. By then, that day, day me and Polanski sit there, him with his Coke and his Chesterfields, me with my cold black muck, and Faithfull and this chick Samantha, yeah by then me and Polanski have a band.

The Mighty Quinn. That's our band. You know, from that "Basement Tapes" song that was a hit for Manfred Mann.

Yeah, that's funny. Not the name but the fact we got a band.

Maybe the name too.

You can laugh. It's OK, really, I don't mind. I'm laughing about it too. I mean it really was funny, even though it's a joke I only get now. Back then I was total serious regards the band. I could blame it on the weed, but that's a lie, a story that was very convenient, but never true. No, what was true was I was in a state of destabilization. I was beginning to fall apart. I was beginning to freak-out. A horrific force inside me, a battle raging. The me who wants Sweet Sarah, and the me who wants a new chick. The me who wants to be Bob Dylan, and the me who knows that's ridiculous. The me that wants to get a million miles away from my folks, and the me that knows I'm 17 and I need to bide my time.

Anyway.

Me and Polanski both sing in the band, and can you imagine

that? Me, a rock singer? I can't sing. You should know that
about me. Can't sing at all.

Me and Polanski sing, and both of us bang away at electric
guitars, and a couple losers on bass and drums just 'cause they
have a bass and a drum set and you got to have a rhythm
section if it's gonna be a rock band. So we got two losers on
bass and drums, only we already plan it out, soon as we find
some better rhythm section, we'll replace the losers.

We need chick backup singers, I mean we have Faithfull, but
if you want it to sound right, you need at least two, and three is
better, only it turns out we have two because of this Samantha
chick.

Soon as I see her, beautiful in her antique Victorian groupie
clothes, yeah she's our new back-up singer. Of course she is.

So I sit there, keep the shades on, look out at the plaza, and you
know the barefoot loser with the wool poncho, well now he's
lying on the ground, and someone, maybe one of his loser
buddies, kneeling there, yelling.

"Angel, wake up, man."

Only Angel isn't waking up. He's lying there. Isn't moving.

"Fuckin' A!"

And the loser buddy, or whoever he is, he stands up and he's
screaming, yelling his head off, screaming bloody murder.

"One less shithead we gonna worry about," Polanski says.
"They oughta load all these bums onto a bus and ship 'em out
to Ohio so we don't gotta smell 'em."

Faithfull's still kneading Polanski's shoulders, and he's
reached his hands back so each one is holding onto one of
Faithfull's bare legs.

"So Rod, I talked to Samantha about the band," she says.
"She's really into it. She wants to be a rock 'n' roll singer real
bad."

"So what else is new," Polanski says. "A couple of other
chicks came by earlier. They really wanna be in the band too. I
mean *really*, said they'd do anything to be in The Mighty Quinn,
if you get my drift. What do you think Writerman? Those other

chicks would burn up the stage."

I'm watching Samantha through the shades and Polanski's thrown her off balance. This was supposed to be in the bag but now she's not sure at all. Desperation, I see it, and you never want to let anyone know you're desperate. Act out of desperation, and be doomed.

"I don't know, man," I say. "Maybe we should do an audition, try her out."

Devil's business smile, and his tongue wets his upper lip.

"That's a great idea you got there, Writerman. Yeah I think you oughta try her out, see what she got."

I got the whole deal wired down tight.

I got the plan.

The plan goes this way. Polanski's dad being a big shot, I figure all we gotta do is get some songs together, play a few gigs and Polanski's dad can hook us up with some music biz management types and *voilà*, a record deal.

Soon enough we'll be rock stars.

I figure how hard can any of it be, after all, none of the big famous rock stars had formal rock star training. Mick studying business and Pete Townshend going to art school and John and Paul and George fucking around playing guitars and listening to American rock 'n' roll records. Dylan hitching around, sleeping on couches, stealing right left from any singer he ran into.

I got the whole deal wired down tight, man.

So now I spend hours after school with Polanski and the loser rhythm section and Faithfull and Samantha, and I can tell that chick kinda likes me, and pretty soon I'm thinking about her at night when I lay in bed, you know, before I crash. She's more beautiful each time she comes around.

Sweet Sarah, on the other hand, seems immature with her jeans and her hiking boots even though Sweet Sarah is two years older than Samantha and smarter too. I mean authentic real of it, no way Samantha compares to Sweet Sarah. That Samantha chick, only 15 but far as I can tell, she never had the innocence. Some chicks are like that, and she's one of them.

Samantha no way compared to Sweet Sarah, only I don't see it that way back then, back when she sang backup along with Faithfull, the two of them working out groovy white-chick dance routines. No man, those days, that Samantha chick, I thought about her, and she dressed so fine, she looked so good, a real rock star's chick kinda trip, and so that was the first time I started to think about fucking some chick other than Sweet Sarah.

Caw caw caw.

That first day when she tagged along with Faithfull, came to talk about singing in our band.

"Sister Morphine" slide guitar, I heard it.

First time.

13. SECOND TIME AROUND

THE SECOND TIME I looked at another chick was during the senior class exchange when a bunch of us spent a week in Fresno attending the high school there. By then I had cut my hair, and that was a big mistake.

Cut my hair 'cause John and Yoko cut their hair.

That was a stupid reason to cut my hair, only nobody could tell me nothing back then, I mean if John and Yoko got naked in a bag for peace, I would argue 'til the end of time the grooviness of getting naked in a bag for peace.

We were both gonna cut our hair, me and Sweet Sarah.

You know that chick with the black hair, Trendy Wendy, Sweet Sarah's good friend, yeah well she was there. Outside in the back yard at Sweet Sarah's house. We lay an old rag sheet on the ground and set a chair in the middle of it and I sit on the chair, Sweet Sarah gets behind me, and first Sweet Sarah cuts as much of mine off as she can with a scissors, and then she gets this old electric razor her Dad used on her brother Seymour when he was little, and she goes at my hair serious.

Oh man, she gets carried away, you know, trying to get it even and all and pretty quick there isn't much left.

Pretty quick the only thing to do is shave it all off.

I hadn't planned on a crew cut.

"What do you think?" I say.

"Well," Sweet Sarah says. "It's different. You're a total freak now."

Trendy Wendy thinks it's a serious mistake, I can tell she don't dig the new me, and she sure as fuck don't think Sweet

Sarah should cut her beautiful crazy-wild auburn hair.

Sarah sits in the chair and Trendy Wendy, who is supposed to know something about cutting hair, takes the scissors.

"You sure, Sarah?" she says.

"Maybe you should reconsider," I say.

I mean I'm wondering if Sweet Sarah would look groovy with no hair.

Sweet Sarah was looking at me kinda funny, I mean she didn't dig the new me at all. And that's when she changed her mind.

So now I've got this straight-ass straight crew cut deal, but she don't. She's still got her groovy Freak Scene Dream hair.

Oh man, that had something to do with the end of our trip for sure.

After I did it, cut off my hair, I knew it was a mistake.

'Cause I start to forget who I am.

I know that's an odd thing to say, but I look in the mirror and what I see is this straight-ass straight dude with a crew cut who looks like a narc, or one of the dudes just home from Nam, kinda guy who tries to dress hip and cool but the hair is too short, that's what I see, that's how I feel, and it throws me off balance, and maybe smoking all that pot fucks me up too.

And if all I got to do is cut my hair to forget who I am, well that's an overwhelming serious fucked-up problem I got.

So I'm gonna be in Fresno for a week with a bunch of other kids from the senior class. The idea is to experience a different school in a different place.

Seven days away from Sweet Sarah.

Bummer.

The bus is gonna take us out to Fresno on a Sunday afternoon, so we'll get there around 5 in the evening, crash Sunday night, and go to classes at the high school in Fresno on Monday.

Me and Sweet Sarah say our goodbyes Saturday night.

We go see a movie first, and you won't believe it but it's true, authentic real the movie we see is sapped-out "Love Story," and I guess that's when I first realized Sweet Sarah looked kinda like Ali MacGraw.

Oh man.

I start to make my usual sarcastic put-down critique, me being the know-it-all film critic but Sweet Sarah asks me to stop it. She tells me it was beautiful. She knows it's melodramatic and all that, but still.

She's got the blues 'cause I'll be away.

I take her back to her place and we go up to her room, fool around on her bed for a while and then I fuck her, and I can tell she don't come.

I can always tell.

And it bums me out, seems it bums me more than Sweet Sarah.

Yeah, and I think about what Polanski said, you know, about my chick being frigid and uptight, and it don't seem like it's ever gonna change.

I want to spend the night but Sweet Sarah wants me to go, she says I need to get home and get a good night's sleep 'cause of my trip to Fresno. And her parents still don't like me stayin' over.

Even with this tension between us, still we're both sad about being apart for a week, and I'm thinking I shouldn't even go but Sweet Sarah does that stiff-upper-lip routine. I can tell it's not authentic real, just Sweet Sarah doing what she can to be positive, says it'll be good for us, you know, do some things on our own.

Only if Sweet Sarah knew the things in my head I think about doing on my own, yeah, if she knew I think about finding a crazy-wild out-of-control chick who digs to get stonered so she's game for anything, if she knew I think about getting that chick on her stomach and doing all the things Polanski talked about, well, yeah, Sweet Sarah would have a different idea about more than just me heading off to Fresno.

I hug Sweet Sarah there in her room. She's got a flannel bathrobe on, nothing else. I've got my clothes back on, and she pushes up against me, and I can't help it, I mean I came less than an hour ago but I'm hard all over again. And after we get done hugging, Sweet Sarah gives me a quickie hand job.

She was like that after we started having sex. She understood how horny I was, and sometimes she'd get me off, just to be nice.

After I come I tell her I'll call her Sunday night when I get to Fresno, and I split out of there.

My hair short as it is, that's when I start up with the black top hat. You know how Dylan wears that gray top hat on the back cover of *Bringing It All Back Home?* Well I find a black one at this used clothing store and a black tuxedo jacket with shiny lapels, and I wear that over the paisley cowboy shirt and my bell-bottoms and the shitkickers.

Yeah I look crazy-wild, only when I look in the mirror it's not the cool-ass cool crazy-wild from when my hair was long. There's something wrong about it, and I think of those straights in Kansas or Idaho or Wisconsin, all those wannabes who don't have a clue what the real Freak Scene Dream was all about, and try to look weird just to look weird, don't understand that it's gotta come from your soul, that it's part of a whole trip, not a costume you put on before smoking a joint.

I look same as those losers, only I don't know what to do to change it, other than grow my hair back, which is already underway.

Fresno, man, the wrong of that deal.

I never should have gone, and I knew it soon as I got on the bus, knew it was gonna be trouble. Those black birds might as well been riding on the roof.

Caw caw caw.

Fresno is a godforsaken place about 3½ hours southeast of the Bay Area. It's where old farts go to die in ticky-tacky cardboard ranch houses. I could tell everything in Fresno was straighter than straight.

The student families in Fresno put us up at their homes for

six nights. I'm staying at some lame-ass math whiz's house. I stash my overnight bag in the guest bedroom and ditch that kid quick-like, get a ride to the senior class party this long blonde hair perky personality cheerleader-type Fresno chick Lucinda whose parents are divorced is having at her mom's place. Well it was actually both of Lucinda's parents' place but the mom kicked the dad out after the mom found the dad fucking the mom's best friend.

That's what Lucinda's best friend tells Marie.

Yeah, this cool chick Marie, only you don't know her yet. Soon enough you'll know her. Well, you won't know her, but you'll know what you need to know.

Soon enough.

Marie is one of the other Tam High seniors who come along to Fresno, she's the one told me the deal about the dad fucking the mom's best friend. I guess that shit goes down all the time, but I never knew anyone it actually happened to before Marie told me about Lucinda's mom and dad. I mean my mom and dad never thought of shit same as that, and same for Sweet Sarah's folks. Made me think Fresno was some Peyton Place deal. Ticky-tacky cardboard ranch houses, and nearly dead old folks and dads sneaking around fucking their wives' best friends.

Fresno, man, Kinky Town.

Lucinda's folk's ticky-tacky ranch house has this big downstairs rec room with the wood paneling and an OK stereo and a linoleum floor you could dance on and a wet bar.

For real wet bar, baby.

We're not supposed to have any booze but Lucinda's mom is depressed, and who wouldn't be, living out in the middle of nowhere in some cardboard ranch house and her husband goes and gets down and dirty with her very best friend, and you really gotta wonder about the "best friend."

You know that old slogan, if you can't trust your friends, who can you trust?

Well guess what? You can't trust anyone.

Get a goddamn clue.

Night of the party Lucinda's mom watches TV the whole time in her bedroom with the door closed, and the rest of the house free and clear including a couple of guest bedrooms where some action goes on for sure. Some Fresno guys chip in for a bunch of six-packs, a fifth of Jack Daniel's, a fifth of gin and a bunch of wine, and I have an ounce I bought off Polanski.

I end up hangin' with Marie. She's this super cute blonde, Marie, not my type at all usually, straight blond hair that ends above her shoulders. You can see all of her neck, and she's got one of those real normal white girl grown-up-in-the-suburbs pretty faces, and she's always wearing a solid blue or dark green short skirt and a white blouse or sometimes a blouse with flowers on it, never jeans or overalls or Victorian groupie gear, no Marie's the kinda chick ends up married to the quarterback.

Marie has a couple beers, and I share a doobie with her in the back yard, and we're having this great time, smoking the joint, talking about *Sticky Fingers,* talking about the Fresno lameness factor but how cool it is to be away from home, and I ask if she wants to go for a walk.

Man, Marie didn't have to think about it or act shy or anything.

Sure she does, and I remember Polanski that day—day he thinks he looks same as Jim Morrison only he looks a whole lot more same as Charles Manson—and what he said.

"Maybe you're with the wrong chick, Writerman," Polanski says.

That day in Mill Valley sitting at the French Riviera table.

And the birds, the black-billed magpies.

Caw caw caw.

"Yeah, I think you need a different chick," Polanski says "Chick who's stoned and game for anything."

And me and Marie both wanna split that lame-ass lame Fresno ranch house.

And Marie's blitzed for sure and she wants to go for a walk, yeah she's had two, maybe three beers and smoked a number of the good stuff I got from Polanski, yeah she's good and blitzed, and is she game for anything, is she one of those chicks who get real stoned and let a dude do what he wants with them?

Is she one of those chicks?

"Sister Morphine" slide guitar, I hear it, I hear the warnings, trouble everywhere, man, yeah I hear it.

We split the house and walk down the road and the lameness factor is 10 outta 10, 'cause it's a straight-ass suburb, one driveway after another, one cookie-cutter ranch house after another, one neatly-mowed lawn after another.

We walk over a mile and nothing but these cookie-cutter ranch houses and Marie starts to shiver, there's a chill Fresno wind, dead cold wind, straight-ass suburb-style dead-ass cold wind and Marie is shaking.

I take off my black tuxedo jacket, the one I wear along with the top hat.

"Marie, put this on," I say.

"I can't take your coat," Marie says. "You'll freeze."

"You wear it," I say.

I get my voice as serious and responsible as it ever sounds.

"Put it on," I say.

She holds her arm out and I pull the sleeve over her hand and her arm, wrap the coat around her back and I'm behind her, and I get my fingers around her other wrist, and she relaxes, and even though her wrist is cold, I mean I haven't touched any chick since Sweet Sarah, *and to touch a chick, man,* just my fingers around her wrist and I got a hard-on, and is Marie the kind of chick get stoned and let a dude do what he wants, is she that kinda chick, and I help her get her hand in the entry of the other sleeve.

"You're quite the gentleman," she says. "None of the guys I hang with ever did anything like that. Coat off your back."

She puts her hand on my arm, squeezes with her fingers.

"Thanks," she says.

Oh man I figure I got this nailed down tight, gonna do Marie on one of those guest bedroom beds at Lucinda's.

We keep on walking, but it's the same, the suburb just goes and goes and goes, we might as well be walking back and forth in front of Lucinda's house, and finally Marie stops and she wants to go back to the party, only I wanna keep walking, so we stand there, and I get out another joint, but Marie only wants to smoke it if we walk back to the party, she's already too high and she don't want to pass out.

Caw caw caw.

And I hear it, man, demon eye got you in its sway.

Yeah I hear it, but I don't care, fuck the messenger who tries to bring me more bad news, fuck it, fuck it, *fuck it,* and then I put my arms around Marie, pull her against me, and I'm gonna put my lips on hers, gonna kiss her, Casanova in action on the streets of Fresno.

Chick pulls her head away, and it's not happening at all, man.

"Sister Morphine" slide guitar.

"Let go," she says. "Michael!"

She pushes too hard, gets free of my arms and this isn't how it's supposed to go, not at all.

Marie stands, the quarter moon behind her so I can't see her face.

"Bug off!" she says.

And she's unbuttoning the coat.

"I thought you were a nice guy," she says.

"Sorry Marie," I say. "I thought you wanted to party. We're having a groovy time, you know."

She turns so the moonlight's on her and her face is sucking lemons.

"*Guys,*" Marie says.

"No, man," I say.

"Every guy thinks if I smile at 'em I wanna fuck," she says.

"Right," I say. "I mean, wrong, I mean I get it. I understand completely."

I don't understand at all. I mean how come guys are crazy to fuck chicks all the time and chicks mostly aren't interested. I guess 'cause I back off and don't push things she cools out. Or could be the weed. Her emotions flipping from A to Z.

"It's OK," she says. "Just, well I don't know you hardly at all."

"I'm freaked being out here," she says. "I don't like Fresno."

"Me neither," I say. "Fresno sucks."

Some chicks you get 'em stoned, you do what you want to them, that's what Polanski said. Other chicks you get 'em stoned, they don't want nothing to do with a guy. Gotta know how to read the tea leaves, man.

We make it back to the party, and Marie splits from me, hangs with a couple girlfriends and she's not paying me any attention, and I think of Sweet Sarah and feel like shit, feel guilty as one of those guys who cheat on their wife. I smoke another number, this one by myself outside in the back yard and the rest of that week is shit and I never should have gone to fucking Fresno.

What's the worst thing is even though me and Marie didn't do anything, I knew that if she had let me I'd have fucked her hard up the ass, fucked her all night, stuck it in her mouth, made her swallow my cum, the whole deal. Yeah, man, I knew if she let me, all of that would have happened.

None of it happened, but it don't matter. I'm as guilty and dirty and low class and a sleaze-bag as if I fucked her. I know I betrayed Sweet Sarah, don't matter nothing happened.

Demon eye got you in its sway.

And now I'm one of those backdoor man kinda dudes. And the wall is thick, a brick wall, rising up so high, separating me from Sweet Sarah.

And I didn't do shit.

14. CRAZY DAYS

HERE'S HOW CRAZY I got during my meltdown.

I get this idea I'm gonna split the scene outta my folks place and move into the abandoned Ebson's Furniture building. That place is down at the very start of our street, opposite where Lowland runs into North Eucalyptus Road, the street that if you take a left, brings you down to Tiburon Blvd.

Abandoned Ebson's Furniture building, my new home.

Get the idea, and it don't just remain a floater.

Floater, man, that's a crazy-ass weed-dream that never goes away, but you never act on.

I don't tell my folks what I'm gonna do, and they're gone baby gone anyway. Dad at work in the city, and Mom at the doctor's office where she works part-time in Mill Valley. Smoke a number, and I get to work.

If anyone been paying attention, watch out their window as I make my way slow along Lowland, this is what they see: a nut in a black top hat rolling a double bed that's a mattress on a box-spring on a metal frame deal with wheels, rolling that sucker along the road. Got it piled high with clothes and books and records, got my guitar case on there, some other shit. Roll it on the road up the hill and down the hill to Ebson's, this worn-out building built in 1922 or some such.

Abandoned in the late Fifties deal.

Go back home, load the white Rambler, make a trip to Ebson's, and another, move in most of my shit.

Empty, dirty building. Broken windows. Door that don't lock which is how I get in.

And in my fucked-up stonered state I think it's cool.

It's not cool. I guarantee you, not cool at all.

For electricity I run an extension cord out a window and plug into an outdoor plug back of the Allstate Insurance building. Figure if I gotta use the crapper, walk the half block to the Chevron on the corner.

Afternoon of the day I move into that mess of a place I drive to Sweet Sarah's house and pick her up. I'm hyped to show her my new pad.

Sweet Sarah don't dig it, don't like nothing about it, in fact she's creeped out. She gives me that serious look of hers, lips closed, jaw out. Maybe that was the first time the way she looks at me, I'm suspect. Always before when she looked, she was looking up to me. She trusted me, even with all we'd been through. Her eyes are the way a person's eyes are when they think something is wrong with the picture. Her looking at me how she is, I want to smoke a number bad. Real bad.

"What's this about?" Sweet Sarah says.

And why did I think Sweet Sarah would understand?

My bed and everything is in the corner of this big room where they once made furniture. It's empty now, but you can see on the wood floor where some machines been. Long ago.

Every few feet an area of the floor that isn't as fucked up as the rest, some kind of desk/cabinet or saw or some such been on that spot. The floor is wide wood planks, really old, worn in a lot of spots, and soft in places. I don't want to walk on the soft spots, and I tell Sweet Sarah to be careful 'cause it feels like a human could go right through the floor and whatever is under that floor, well it's not a place either of us wanna go.

I have my bed against a wall, floor lamp plugged into a multi-plug deal that's plugged into the extension cord. My Zenith stereo set up and plugged into the multi-plug deal, and when me and Sweet Sarah get there I put *Sticky Fingers* on, "Brown Sugar" starts in and I'm dancing around on that wide plank floor. I've swept my corner of the place but it's pretty dusty in there. I might as well be camping in a dirty-ass dirty warehouse.

Sweet Sarah gives me the you've-blown-it-so-bad look. Only it's an overwhelming heavy traffic worse look than the normal you've-blown-it-so-bad look 'cause there's a hopeless deal too. You ever known a person who's seriously depressed? Nothing matters to them. Nothing. They can't get out of bed and they tell you their arms and legs and everything weigh a thousand pounds.

I start to see that in Sweet Sarah. And it scares me. I start to see how Sweet Sarah must have been before I came along. Only now I'm the reason. And I don't do nothing to change. And why is that? Why do I keep going down down down?

Why, man, you tell me.

I see that nothing matters anymore deal in her, but I've got amnesia about it, and I start my rapid-fire talk, talk, talk. 'Cause I'M THE MAN, last dude standing, crazy-wildest freakster bro, and I got *everything* wired down tight.

I'm still doing that freeform Freak Scene Dream in Golden Gate Park dance trip, and I should be watching out for soft spots, but I'm not.

"I've moved out," I say. "I'm gonna live here for the rest of the school year and for the summer. 'Til we go to college."

To me it makes sense.

"You can stay here with me sometimes, it's cool."

"Somebody owns this place," she says.

Sweet Sarah has a real practical side, but I'm over the line, out of my head, yeah I'm on another planet, and she's gone straight. I'm too hip for Sweet Sarah.

"You can't live here."

She don't smoke weed, and I'm stonered all the time.

"What do you think they're gonna do when they find you here?" she says.

And I'm thinking Samantha would dig it, Polanski would dig it, Faithfull would dig it. Probably even that Marie chick.

"There's no bathroom, no running water."

Sweet Sarah's not in the groove anymore. Sweet Sarah's losing it. She's gone straight and soon enough she's gonna turn right into her mom.

"No one pays any attention to this dump," I say.

I do what I think is a slick dance move, a 360 spin with my arms in the air, spin right to where she stands, bring my arms down and wrap them around her, pull her into me so I feel her tits against my chest, and she's limp, a body without bones or muscles. Turns her face away when I try to kiss her.

And I hear 'em.

Caw caw caw.

The black-billed magpies, Doom and Gloom, must be up on the roof. Doom laying out in detail all the ways I blow it with Sweet Sarah, only I can't understand what he says, I mean I don't know the language, and Gloom adds the deal about how all the ways I blow it gonna hurt Sweet Sarah in ways she'll never recover, and when it ends I'll have to live with what I do to her. Only I don't know anything Gloom *caw caw caws* about either.

All I know is when I hear those birds, means nothing but trouble.

I do another spin, raise a foot and land it on the wood floor only the floor don't stop it, my foot goes through the wood and quick as a flash Sweet Sarah grabs my arm and I'm on the floor, one leg dangling below the floor, the rest of me lying there.

There's sadness-meets-resignation in her young girl's voice.

"Oh Michael," she says.

The funny thing, in my stoned state, I could stay where I am, let the soft cocoon inside my head protect me, only Sweet Sarah is helping me get my leg out of the hole, get back on my feet. I didn't feel anything wrong right then but later I had a big bruise on my leg where it made contact.

She asks me to take her home, I mean she's hardly been here and now she wants to split. All I can think is something's gone wrong with us. We're not on the same wavelength no more.

You know what it was? I mean this is with some years to ponder what the fuck I was doing that year. I think I was scared to death of the future, of what it would mean to live away from home for the first time, 'cause me and Sweet Sarah, the way we planned it, we were gonna live together when we went off to college that fall. That was gonna be a big step towards growing up, and I guess I didn't want to grow up.

Or maybe I just drove off the tracks, blinded by my own eye-blinding, self-generated light, man.

I didn't stay there even one night.

My parents had the major freak out.

I guess what happened, my mom knocked on my bedroom door, you know, in my folk's house. No answer. So she opened the door.

And she freaked.

Saw the place ransacked. Hardly any shit left in the room.

She called my dad and he was screaming through the phone for her to calm down. He left work early, tried to cool my mom out. They didn't know if they oughta call the cops, or what.

They called Bobby, but he didn't know. Called Frankie, and he didn't know either. So they called Sweet Sarah, and she knew.

My dad showed up down there around 9 p.m., but I wasn't there. Still, my dad saw all my stuff, so he decided to wait. I was out buying a burger and fries and a Coke at Burger King, the one on the way into Mill Valley.

I got back, and fuck, I'm in trouble now 'cause there's the green Rambler parked in front of the building. After my dad got done yelling at me, I mean he can't do nothing to me anymore, nothing physical 'cause I'm stronger than him, he tells me I need to get my stuff out of there pronto, or he's gonna call the cops. Hard to argue that scenario away.

The final deal with me and Sweet Sarah was the party.

High school graduation party at Greg's house. Not the formal dance, but one of the parties on Friday night of the last day of school. Greg, man. He looked the perfect Mr. Straight with his shortish black hair parted to the side, preppy plaid shirt and straight leg jeans. You'd never think it about Greg back then, I mean to look at him, but he was a major overwhelming pothead.

Greg lived in this big house on Mt. Tam with his 41-year-old lawyer dad. Night of the party, his dad stayed in the City where he worked at some fancy law firm. His dad was out for the night sleeping over at his 22-year-old model girlfriend's pad. So there on Mt. Tam, for the graduation party, anything goes, total party house, three floors, 4,000 square feet. Yeah, baby!

You know the trip, of course you do.

Greg invited all the hipsters, all the dopers, all the boozers, all the greasers, and a lot of groovy chicks from I don't where. The house was crazy with people. *Sticky Fingers* on the stereo and that first Led Zeppelin album and *Everybody Knows This Is Nowhere*.

You been there, you know the drill.

But I'm getting ahead of myself 'cause before I get to the party, first I have to go get Sweet Sarah, and before that, week before at least, I have to call her up and invite her to go with me, which she didn't want to do 'cause she said she wouldn't know anyone, which was true.

We argued about it on the phone, and back then I could still get her to do what I wanted sometimes when she felt insecure.

Night of the party I went to get Sweet Sarah, and that's when it began.

The end.

I drive the white Rambler, drive too fast along Sir Francis Drake, running stop lights, and I got a big problem. I got a mess of problems. Only I don't know it. Just think I have one.

Problem.

The mess of problems are dominoes if dominoes line up on a time line into the future. All I see is the one domino right in the moment of me driving to get Sweet Sarah, and all the rest extending out into the future are invisible.

I can't see the other dominoes.

Can't see all the problems that go on and on and on.

The whole 30 minute drive from my place to Sweet Sarah's I try to figure out how I'm gonna tell Sweet Sarah there will be chicks at the party I want to spend time with, no big deal, just got to let her know.

What am I gonna say?

"Hey, Sarah, I'm feeling the need to be with some other chicks, you don't mind do you?"

Or:

"You know how we've been together, just me and you, for nearly three years and I never had a girlfriend before you and you never had a boyfriend before me? Well maybe uh, you know, just to make sure that you and I are really totally the ones for each other, we oughta, you know, check out some other people, just to see, you know?"

Or maybe:

"Sarah, I was reading this article in *Psychology Today* about open marriages and I was thinking maybe it would be groovy and hip if you and I had an open relationship, that could be cool, right?"

Man, I sweat it out on the drive to her house.

Up on the roof of Sweet Sarah's folks' place, those black-billed magpies.

Caw caw caw.

Yeah I got a problem. I told Samantha and these two friends of hers, the Ferrante sisters, Rosa and Mercedes, I'd be at the party, and you don't know them, the Ferrante sisters, not yet, but you will, and each of those sisters is a domino, and Samantha too.

Soon enough you'll know all about it.

Right then, 'cause of me telling Samantha and the Ferrante sisters I was gonna be at the party, gonna hang with them, yeah I gotta to say something to Sweet Sarah.

Caw caw caw.

Sweet Sarah is in the car and I'm driving too fast, and she don't dig it.

"Are you stoned, Michael?"

"No," I say.

The car was a fucking mess. Ashtray overflowing stubbed-out cigarettes from Polanski and Faithfull and Samantha. Crushed Coke and beer cans on the floor along with candy wrappers and those yellow sheets of paper they wrap around burgers and old containers that used to hold French fries, yeah the car's trashed.

"It smells like pot in here," Sweet Sarah says.

"Just a couple tokes," I say.

Goddamn lie, but so what, man. Sweet Sarah don't understand my trip, or me, or nothing no more. Smoke a joint if I want before I pick her up, and what's it to her or you or anyone. Fuck, I'm sick of her goody-goody.

"So when we're at this party," I say. "I might spend a little time hanging with some other people. Some of my Tam friends gonna be there."

She moves over far away from me as she can get in her seat, looks out her window even though it's dark and there's nothing to see.

There's a tremble in her voice I've never heard before, and the sound of it, I mean I've never heard anything as sad as her voice.

"Are you breaking up with me?" she says.

Oh man, this is so fucked. I love her, but I mean I got a right.

"No Sarah, it's not that," I say. "I mean I just wanna have a little space but we're cool."

She gets kinda quiet and I know she's serious bummered. Probably thinking about how I got her pregnant two times, and the two abortions, and everything she's gone through, and the times she let me fuck her when she wasn't into it.

And all those hand jobs.

I turn at the 2 A.M. Club, you know, in Mill Valley, and head up Mt. Tam a couple miles to the house, park along the side of the road. I don't know why she comes in with me, but she does and right quick-like, soon as I find a couch and she sits I go off to get us some Cokes.

Damn if I don't run into that chick Marie I told you about

and it's as if she been dying to see me again. She's fucked-up, drinking from a half-pint of Southern Comfort, Janis Joplin's favorite drink. *Hey man, why don't you sit down* and I sit down and she's talking away about what a nice guy I was up in Fresno, letting her wear my coat and all, passing the bottle.

She's got a new haircut, really shows off what a cute face she got, reminds me of Twiggy how she looks this night, only she's got those serious tits. I sit there take slugs of Southern Comfort, take slugs of Coke, and talk talk talk. Too much time passes and I remember I'm supposed to be getting right back to Sweet Sarah. Oh fuck.

It's dark and smoky, everyone smoking cigarettes or doobies, only candles to light the place, lots of people, and lots of them are older, in their 20s I guess, and where the fuck did Greg find these people, push past this biker guy and his chick and a mess of 'em dancing to "Brown Sugar." Sweet Sarah's not sitting on the couch no more. She's nowhere, and after I case the whole inside I go out onto the deck, this wrap-around deck that starts at the front of the house, wraps around the right side and all along the back, got a view of the Bay off in the distance, and that's where I find her. At the very back. In the black. She's alone, sitting on a bench shivering, her face blank same as all the emotion been sucked out of her. I hold out the Coke but she don't want it, her voice a cold dry whisper.

"Please take me home. *Please.*"

"It's early," I say. "Hey, I'm sorry I –."

She reaches into a pocket of her Great Depression coat and she got something in her hand.

"Here, give it to some other girl."

She's trying to show me nothing of how she's feeling, but she can't help it, and oh fuck, she's crying, man. Thinking about it now, I don't know how her crying right then didn't bust me to pieces. It was so sad, Sweet Sarah shivering in the cold, in the blackness, a mess of tears and her voice the lonesome cry of a mourning dove.

She drops what's in her hand on the bench, and it's the

silver necklace, you know, the one I gave her seems so long ago, our initials carved in back of the silver heart.

"Take me home, and come back by yourself," she says. "You can be with whoever you want."

The black seeping in, and Sweet Sarah all given-up. Her blue eyes lost-soul-tired how they were the first time I seen her, and I've done this, betrayed what was beautiful and sacred and true. I stole Sweet Sarah's innocence, and now her trust in me, and in love, and in the possibility that two people can be pure and true and authentic real been beat to shit.

I drive her home and we go to her room and I fuck her. I don't know why she let me do it. She lay there, and I did it, and when I'm done I pull out of her, out of breath, look at her face and she don't look at me, and I feel everything is hopeless and empty—a lifeless chill freezing me. I wanted the fucking to fix what I done, but it changes nothing. Don't bring her back from the lost souls, don't bring the wild nature to her eyes, don't bring back what she's lost, what I've lost.

There are things that once they happen, you can never take them back. They're in the universe forever. That was one of the Days of the Crazy-Wild days I never wanted to live through. I lay on Sweet Sarah's bed, and I'd never felt so far from her, an emptiness in me worse than before she was my chick 'cause I'd had the conspiracy of two with Sweet Sarah, and I knew what it was to escape the lonesome, and now going forward I'd never have that again.

15. GOIN' DOWN AT THE HOUSEBOAT

THE SLUGGISH NOD-OUT groove of the Stones' "Sister Morphine."

The Ferrante sisters, friends of Samantha, fuck yeah, and we're on their mom's houseboat. And me and Samantha and Polanski and Faithfull.

All of us flake-out stoned in the room.

Smoke, man, the air dirty with it.

Sausalito houseboat. Ferrante sisters. Slow, so slow, slow nod-out groove.

On Richardson Bay, the inlet of water that opens out into San Francisco Bay, and further out joins the Forever Infinite Pacific. And that's a whole fuck-up freak-out scene down there among the houseboats. Hellfuck hippies and dead-gone drifters and ass-tired artists. Junk-sick junkies and wrote-out writers and all the ruined wrong-turn lost-their-way rockers. Time holds still down there. Down among the houseboats, man, place to get lost and gone and fucked-up bad.

Place to get lost and gone and fucked-up, man, and that's where I am, and it's who I'm gonna be. Gonna get gone baby gone, baby. And fucked-up for sure. Only I can't get lost, can't split from myself.

I'm always here.

I can't forget Sweet Sarah, last time I saw her, when she's all-given-up, her eyes lost-soul-tired. And the sad in her voice.

Can't forget.

Later I'll understand. Much later. Years later. After I live out at Susan Simone's place with Harper. Or maybe later still. Well, all in good time.

Well, all in bad time, to be authentic real about it.

No rush to get to the end when we're still so close to the beginning.

And this is a Days of the Crazy-Wild day. Fuck, man, Summer of the Crazy-Wild, a summer I wish never happened.

The blinds all drawn keep out the bright bright Sausalito sun, and the room has that wrong feel. Same kinda wrong as when you got the curtains closed and sit and watch TV at 11 a.m. when you know you should be out breathing the fresh air or going for a hike or some kinda healthy deal.

Nothing I did those days was healthy. Nothing, man.

Smoke, air dirty with it in the room, and the harsh harsh smell of Polanski's hash.

The all of us inside the houseboat with the blinds drawn and that kinda wrong-ass wrong deal.

The mom not there so it's anything goes.

The all of us.

Polanski, Faithfull, Samantha, me, and the sisters.

Rosa, 15, and Mercedes, 14. Yeah I told you about them before, you remember. Of course you do.

I was supposed to hang with the sisters and Samantha that night at the graduation party, you remember, at Greg the pothead's house. The graduation party. Sweet Sarah all-given-up.

Yeah, and I don't want to remember.

Total jailbait deal, the sisters. Rosa and Mercedes.

And the mom not there.

The mom maybe mid-30s, couldn't say, really. Maybe early 30s. Maybe late 30s. I mean what do I know back then.

Everyone older than 25 or some-such looks old to me.

Hardly ever see the mom.

The all of us all flake-out stoned. Laughing at this and that, that and this, I mean flake-out stoned and everything funny as hell, man.

The mom still totally embraces the Freak Scene Dream scene. She smokes pot with the sisters, and she got the bellbottoms and the sandals and the tie-dye. The mom. One time I see her, she even got a small rose pinned somehow into her hair. The mom.

The mom was into the free love trip, only she don't give it away for free, at least that's what Samantha told me. The mom got three or four boyfriends, and each one pitches in to pay the rent and stuff. I mean I guess if you want to be authentic real, you could say the mom's a whore only not exactly 'cause random johns don't pay her for sex. It's these boyfriends. And maybe she likes them. I mean I wouldn't know.

Pretty much everything I know about the mom, Samantha told me, or later, Mercedes told me. I might not have known the deal with the boyfriends that day all of us were there on the houseboat, but then again maybe I knew.

I only see the mom a few times, but that's other days. Not this nod-out Sister Morphine day.

Air dirty with smoke, man. Room dirty with the smoke of Polanski's Chesterfields and Faithfull's Winstons, and Samantha's clove cigarettes, and whatever the Ferrante sisters smoke. And the hash. And incense burning, always incense burning at the houseboat.

So there's all that.

And the smoke from Polanski's hash pipe. He keeps filling and lighting and passing around the room.

And the sisters over across the room on the futon giggle. Giggle and giggle.

Sluggish nod-out groove of "Sister Morphine."

Dark dark smoke from Polanski's hash pipe.

Harsh harsh hash smell fills the room.

Nod-out groove of the Stones, and side one plays over and over and over.

And the way it feels wrong in here, blinds-drawn-watch-TV-middle-of-the-day wrong. Everyone except Faithfull flake-out stoned lay 'round the room. Faithfull stoned too, maybe more stoned than anyone, for certain that's up for debate, only no one cares who's the more stoned trip 'cause all of us overwhelming heavy traffic stoned, authentic real, man.

Faithfull stands middle of the room, sways slow and sexy to

the Stones. She got a short black skirt, and a black velvet vest and no shoes.

She got no bra. No chick wore a bra in the summer of '71.

Those were the days, man. All the groovy chicks didn't wear a bra. I mean I guess it could sound sexist or some such, but I still don't get it. You stare at Manet's "Le Déjeuner Sur l'herbe," or Picasso's "Les Demoiselles d'Avignon" or Rodin's "Francesca da Rimini." Appreciate the beauty, and no one has a problem, only stare at a chick's tight t-shirt, dig to see the nipples press against the cotton, and you got a problem. Everyone thinks you're a sexist pig.

I don't get it.

Chick's body is a beautiful scene, man, and a guy is programmed to appreciate that scene.

Chick's tits a beautiful scene too.

Everyone thinks you're a sexist pig.

Way of the world.

Well not everyone. Not that day anyway. Not there in the houseboat, all of us stonered, and the chicks in their short dresses and too much makeup, and Faithfull in her short skirt and black velvet vest stands there sways to the Stones.

Not everyone, man.

And we all laugh and laugh and laugh. Everything is so funny.

I guess the room all us flake-out in except Faithfull who dances barefoot is the living room.

Big bean-bag chairs and a futon up against a wall and a big-ass Cost Plus rug.

Polanski and me sit in two of the bean-bags, he's over by the windows got the blinds drawn, I'm over by the Japanese fucking screen, only you don't know about the Japanese fucking screen yet. Soon enough I tell you about it.

Jailbait sisters sit on the futon side by side, Mercedes' dress pulled up high, and she don't care what any of us see. And Rosa's hand on Mercedes' bare thigh.

Rosa feels Mercedes' thigh and they giggle and she feels it some more.

Samantha sits cross-legged on the Cost Plus rug. The hem of her short beige dress only needs to creep up another inch or two to show me her white panties.

And I shouldn't be here.

Faithfull stands in the middle of the room slow sway to the Stones' nod-out sound.

The six-panel Japanese fucking screen, and it's so groovy. Probably a copy, but still groovy. Painting of this Geisha chick floating down a river on a bamboo raft, Mt. Fuji rising up behind her. The Japanese fucking screen separates the living room area where we all are from where there's a king-size futon.

King-size futon.

Where the mom sleeps, when the mom's there.

And where the fucking happens. Where the mom fucks the boyfriends. And when the mom's not there, that's where you go if you want to do some fucking. You know, someone and someone want to fuck in private, they use the king-size futon behind the Japanese fucking screen.

The mom is out.

The mom is out at one of her boyfriend's pads.

The mom is out and not back 'til morning.

The futon behind the Japanese fucking screen is free and clear, man.

The mom is gone.

So the oldest person in the room is Polanski, and he's 17, same as me.

I sit on one of the bean-bag chairs, and feel the beans or whatever they got inside. Feel them move around as I shift my weight. Feel the houseboat rock in the water. Subtle, the way it rocks, constant back forth, back forth, back forth.

You could fuck a chick on one of the bean-bag chairs. Well you couldn't, 'cause *you're* not here. I could. I could fuck a chick on the bean-bag chair I sit in, if one of the chicks wants to be fucked. And if we didn't want it to be private.

And the laughter. We smoke the hash and we laugh some more.

The water slaps against the side of the boat.

Gulls out somewhere nearby make their gull sounds, and it scares me this scene.

No, what scares me is I'm here and I got no backbone, not anymore. Anything any of the chicks want to do, I would do. Anything I could get any of the chicks to do, I would do. I want to get lost in the hash smoke, want to blow it all away, forget everything, man, lost in a stoned fog so thick I never find my way out.

Mercedes, across the room, sits next to her sister, man, 14, and Faithfull brings her the hash pipe. And Rosa runs her hand through Mercedes' hair and Mercedes rests her head on Rosa's shoulder.

Two sisters, and you want it to be innocent, but it's not innocent. The hand on the thigh, not innocent. The hand through the hair, nothing innocent about the way Rosa wants Mercedes.

Chick is 14 years old.

And they giggle and touch and giggle.

Mercedes looks same as Bianca Jagger's little sister. Same dark skin, same dark brown hair, same over-size lips and the same dark red lipstick.

Mercedes straightens up, sucks in the harsh hash smoke, and I should wonder what a 14-year-old chick is doing smoking Polanski's hash, but I just think about what it would be like to fuck one of the chicks on the bean-bag, or do her on the futon back behind the Japanese fucking screen, and if Polanski's right about it being total heavy traffic intense to do a chick stoned.

Somehow, after her sister sucks the harsh, Mercedes gets herself up, brings the pipe over to me. She reaches out with the pipe, and I get my hand on the stem. Mercedes' delicate little Bianca Jagger hand on the stem too, and she lets go of the pipe puts her Bianca Jagger slight fingers on my arm.

"Strong arm," she says.

And she rubs her fingers along my arm, and a chick touching me, man, that's the best, and her fingers feel my muscles.

And she giggles and I laugh. I got nothing to laugh about.

Only everything is funny and I don't care if she's 14. She got a cunt.

And I suck in the harsh, and Mercedes behind me rubs my neck, massages my neck, and the waves, not the water slap against the side of the houseboat, no man, the stonered shock waves, the dope kicks in, and I sink deeper into the bean-bag and now Mercedes reaches down, both hands on my cowboy shirt and she starts to unsnap the pearl buttons. She starts with the top buttons, and I help, I unsnap the bottom buttons.

And I look over to where Polanski sits in the other bean bag and he watches Mercedes and me, and he laughs, and across the room Rosa watches and Samantha watches and even Faithfull stands there, slow-sway dancing, and she watches.

All the buttons unsnapped and Mercedes pulls the shirt off me, and my t-shirt too, she grabs it and pulls it up and I raise my arms, and it comes off my head and off my arms, and her hands on my shoulders, delicate little Bianca Jagger little sister fingers dig into the muscles, and then her hands over my shoulders, her fingers feel my chest.

Faithfull dances over, reaches down and takes the pipe, and she sucks up the harsh, spinning around, dances slow to the Stones, sucks up the harsh.

And the whole room is laughter.

I hear that Stones' song, "Dead Flowers," the line about someone bringing the guy who sings the song wilted flowers.

The Stones into their druggy country groove, and the room is dark and so wrong blinds-closed-watch-TV-in-the-late-morning deal, and the smoke, so fucking much smoke, and the air is hot with it.

Faithfull dances slow, hardly moves at all.

"I'm Marianne," Faithfull says. "Her spirit in me."

"You want to be Marianne," Polanski says. "You get naked."

Yeah, man, 'cause when the English cops do that drug bust at Keith Richards' place in '67 the real Marianne is naked except for a fur rug wrapped around her.

"Well I will then," Faithfull says.

Faithfull sways to the Stones groove, sways slow, and she

unbuttons her black velvet vest, lets it slide off her arms and fall to the rug, and she's bare from the waist up, and her body is beautiful, man, her body is perfect, 16 years old and so perfect, and she's got firm tits, oh fuck yeah, and she sways slow, and we all watch.

We all watch and we're all laughing and Faithfull digs us watching, and brings her right hand up to her right tit and touches herself, caresses herself and she's laughing. Samantha watches and Rosa watches and Mercedes still behind me, still her hands on me, so I don't know if she watches, but I bet she does. And Polanski, he's watching and laughing and he takes his shirt off, and everyone sees the dirty-blonde hair curling on his chest. And he got a naked chick tattooed on his arm. A sailor's tattoo. And I watch Faithfull, and I stare at her tits.

Beautiful scene, man, Faithfull's tits. Beautiful as any Picasso or Manet or Rodin.

Beautiful scene.

Only right then I don't think about art. No, I think about fucking, I think about what it would be like to tit fuck Faithfull. And I'm turned on, yeah of course I am.

No guy could sit there and watch Faithfull and not be horny.

Polanski shouts out the line about the 15-year-old chick who's gonna scratch his back, you know, from "Stray Cat Blues."

I see Faithful smile, and turn to face Polanski there on the bean-bag and she shakes 'em, and we all see and she don't care what we see.

Mercedes' fingers are gentle on my skin as she works my shoulder muscles.

"I bet you'd like to suck them," Mercedes says.

"If we were betting you'd win the bet," I say.

And I'm not embarrassed, it's fine for Mercedes to know. I mean right then I don't care, nothing wrong with a freakster bro turned on by a topless chick and why shouldn't she know? What guy wouldn't want his mouth on one of Faithfull's tits?

And the pipe makes its rounds, and Polanski gets a bottle of red wine open and he takes a big-ass hit, and he passes the bottle, and first it goes to Faithfull, then Samantha, then Rosa, and Samantha stands up, she takes the bottle from Rosa, brings it over to me and Mercedes.

"Aren't you a little young for Writerman?" Samantha says.

And Samantha looks down on me, and she got the trouble smile, and she sees my hard dick against my jeans, she sees it, and she got ideas.

"Room down there?" she says.

I move over on the bean-bag, and Samantha drops down onto it, right next to me, and I feel her warm bare leg press against mine, and her beige skirt creeps up, I see her white panties and she don't care, she leaves her skirt the way it is.

Samantha brings the bottle to her mouth, drinks the red, passes the bottle to me, and I see her lips red with wine, and she's laughing, man, she feels alright, and I take the bottle. I mean I never drink, I told you that already. Well that day I take a slug. That day I don't care what I think about booze, or what Sweet Sarah thinks about it.

I don't care, not at all.

Take a slug and it tastes sour, not heavy traffic sour, but still. And I could get used to this, yeah, I could. And I will.

I'm high on Polanski's hash and the high of the red, man, so fucked-up wasted.

And fuck you, Sweet Sarah. You could forgive me, all I done for you. And it's about time I fuck another chick, about time.

Samantha takes the bottle, and brings it to her mouth and takes a good solid slug of the red, and when she's done she holds it up and Mercedes grabs hold. I look up and watch Mercedes stick the long neck in her mouth, head back, bottle up. When she's done she sets the bottle there on the rug.

Rosa across the room stretches out on the futon, she watches us, she sees Samantha's white panties, she sees Mercedes drink the wine. She sees Mercedes' hands on me.

And the pipe makes the rounds. Rosa brings the pipe over to me, and Rosa reaches for the bottle, fingers grip the neck and what I see next, she's floating back to the futon. I suck the harsh, Samantha sucks the harsh, Mercedes sucks the harsh and the room gets weird-ass weird.

Everything dreamy, and I got no troubles, man. No troubles. In the moment and this moment is the groovy moment. I flash on Sweet Sarah, and I'm not angry no more. I'm so far beyond anger. And when what Sweet Sarah would think flashes by I wrap it up in a white cloud and let it float away, and it floats same as how Rosa floats back to the futon.

Mercedes brings the pipe to Faithfull, and Mercedes walks back to the futon where Rosa lies, and Mercedes lies next to Rosa, and Rosa's arms around Mercedes, and she's kissing Mercedes, and kissing her, and kissing her.

Polanski gets up, walks to the stereo, flips the record over, and now "Brown Sugar" starts up. Faithfull sways to the fuck-me groove, undoes the button on her skirt, and unzips the zipper, her short black skirt drops to the floor, she steps out of it, kicks it away and all she wears is skimpy black lace panties.

Shakes her tits and all she wears is the skimpy black lace panties and I wanna see all of her.

Beautiful scene, man.

And Faithfull dances, and Polanski dances, and Faithfull's got her hands on Polanski's bare chest, and we all see the stomach, and Polanski got an old man's stomach, a too much beer and wine and Jack Daniel's stomach. Polanski's old man's stomach bulges out over his waist, over his jeans, and Polanski dances and he sweats, the sweat runs down his face, the sweat makes the hair on his chest shine, even in the so wrong late morning blinds drawn TV on semidarkness, and Faithfull's hands slip down along his sweaty chest, down past his sweaty stomach, and she undoes his belt, undoes his black wide-wale cords and he's dancing, wears only his black Jockey shorts. And I wonder if he dyes them black, I mean I never seen black Jockey shorts before.

Samantha's hands on my chest and I reach over, I'm gonna unbutton her dress, but she whispers *no, lie back, Michael,* and she says Michael, she don't say Writerman, she says Michael, *just relax, Michael,* and I sink back into the bean-bag, and her smooth fingers on my stomach, she slips her hands down to my waist.

And the pipe makes the rounds, this time Polanski brings it over, and the tight black Jockey shorts, and his old man's stomach sticks out and I don't want to see any of it, and I don't want Samantha to see it, and he leers down at me and Samantha, shows us that devil's business smile, and he sees her white panties.

His face all distorted ugly Manson evil devil's business smile.

"Remember what I tell you, Casanova," Polanski says. "Stoned and game for anything."

And he dances away, and he leads Faithfull over to the Japanese fucking screen, they disappear behind it, where the mom's king-size futon waits.

And Mick is singing and the demon eye got you in its sway.

Samantha undoes my belt, she undoes the metal button of my Levi's and she pulls the zipper down.

And through the loud sleazy groove of the Stones I hear Polanski and Faithfull behind the Japanese fucking screen.

"Get your ass up," Polanski says.

And they both laugh and Samantha laughs and I laugh too.

"You think Mick and Bianca do it this way, Rod?" Faithfull says.

"Fuck Mick and Bianca," Polanski says.

Rosa and Mercedes on the futon, Mercedes on her back, legs spread, and Rosa lies on her and she pulls Mercedes' dress down and Rosa's mouth on her sisters' tit.

Samantha slips her hand under the waistband of my shorts, and I'm not watching Rosa do Mercedes anymore. Hold my breath, and Samantha's fingers on me.

"Damn," I say.

Samantha's voice quiet, a whisper.

"Don't say a word," she says. "Close your eyes, Michael."

I hear bodies rocking on the futon, behind the Japanese fucking screen.

And I'm not gonna think about Sweet Sarah. If she only would forgive me. No, man, not gonna think about her.

And I let go, let myself feel what I feel.

My eyes, I close them, and Samantha pulls her hand out and

she gets a grip on my jeans and I raise up my ass and she pulls my jeans and my shorts down to just above my knees, and there for anyone to see nearly all of me naked. And she got her hand around it again, moves her fingers slow up and down, and her touch is gentle, there are moments it's the light breath of a feather, and I try so hard to enjoy her touch, and not to come, 'cause if I come it'll be over. And I don't want this over. I want it to go on and on.

Samantha's breathing hard, I can hear her, her breath fast, and her hand tight on me now, and she starts to jerk me off, up and down, her breath hard and fast. And she pumps it harder, harder, harder. I open my eyes, and she got her dress pulled up, and her other hand inside her panties, her other hand rubbing herself, and she pumps my cock but now it's more mechanical, she's lost in her own reverie, and her face, her eyes shut tight, a grim determination, her hand rubbing herself, her entire being focused on. Focused on. Focused on what? Not me.

She stops pumping, as if she's forgot about me, she just holds it, and she's all about herself, and her breathing gets faster and I watch, and she pushes her panties down and she don't care who sees, her fingers in herself, a fast rhythm, and right then I have this kind of revelation, this is all about Samantha masturbating, and my cock is a prop, no different than some dildo she holds to get turned on or some erotica she reads, yeah this got nothing to do with me, and she don't care about me. No love and not even lust. She might as well be alone in her bedroom. No connection, nothing man. Zero.

Only that wasn't the important revelation.

The important revelation was about me and Sweet Sarah. 'Cause same as how Samantha was using me, well I'd been using Sweet Sarah. Sure I'd wanted the sex with me and Sweet Sarah to be mutual and soulful and take us both up to the divine, but what I wanted wasn't what it was, and what it was, man, it was me getting off at her expense.

I should split out of here but I'm not goin' nowhere and a muffled cry and Samantha's moaning, and her face relaxes into a savage animal bliss. When a chick comes, right in that moment, all their pretense, all their pose, all their attempts at distance and remove gone baby gone. It's a flash of a moment when you see the hungry animal nature, a raw body thing a chick can't control. And she turns her body toward me, lets go of my cock, arms around me, holds onto me, presses her pussy hard against the side of my thigh, pushes against my thigh and pushes and pushes, and she's moaning, and I feel her wetness and I'm so hard and I want it in her.

I start to turn my body but she holds herself tight against me, her mouth on my face, her tongue licking my mouth, her lips on my lips and I feel her convulsions. She pushes against me, and pushes against me, and she falls back into the bean-bag, lies there, and I'm so fucking stonered, can't even lift my head, just lay there. I want to fuck her, but I don't even know how to get my body up and onto her.

Before I can do anything, I mean if I could do anything, the fingers that were in her pussy, she gets 'em around my cock and she starts to pump me again, and I try not to come, I try and try and try and her hand, pumping me, relentless, and I think about when her fingers were in her pussy and her hand on me, how horny she was, holding me, rubbing herself, and the savage animal bliss, and I can't stop it, and I feel that moment of exquisite pain, I feel it, that jerking feeling when I start to come, and her pumping me and it's all over her hand, and on my pubic hair, and she keeps pumping, pumping it hard, and I must have passed out, 'cause time is passed, time is gone and she's stopped, she's wiping her hand on my jeans. And we lay there, sperm dripping onto myself.

I don't care if Polanski sees me, don't care if Faithfull sees me, don't care if the sisters see me. I lie there naked and I take my cock and pump it some myself. Samantha watches and she laughs, pulls up her panties and pulls down her dress. I jerk whatever sperm hasn't come out yet out onto me. And I let go. Lie there naked. Yeah, don't fucking care.

And that's when I saw Sweet Sarah's face, Sweet Sarah looking all-given-up. And my cock went limp. I mean it always goes semi after I come, but seeing Sweet Sarah's lost-soul tired eyes my dick shrunk to nothing.

Samantha there next to me, she rubs herself some more, I guess she wants another orgasm, Polanski grunt sounds from behind the Japanese fucking screen and Rosa got her head between Mercedes' legs, and now Mercedes is naked on the futon, her dress on the rug, and this is all so wrong, this isn't the way it should be, and I remember lying on Sweet Sarah's bed, the wind blowing the leaves of the oak outside Sweet Sarah's window, she lay in my arms, the both of us 15, my mouth on her mouth, and the crazy-wild beauty of our love.

For a flash of a moment that scene of me and Sweet Sarah is what I see, and it's gone. Look down and my jeans and shorts down past my knees, and Samantha sighs, Samantha gets herself off all over again, and over by the Japanese fucking screen Polanski naked, stands and he watches Samantha do herself, and he sees me naked and wet with my own sperm and the wetness of Samantha, yeah he watches and he laughs a vulgar sick laugh.

"See what I told you Casanova," Polanski says. "Get 'em stoned and they'll do anything."

"Shut the fuck up, man," I say.

Even in my stoned state I felt the embarrassment taking over all of me, and I was sure Samantha was mad, certain she would think I worked her, and the whole scene was me getting her to do me, but I was wrong about that and I was wrong 'cause I didn't know who Samantha was. I thought all chicks were like Sweet Sarah, stand-up idealistic, but I learned that every chick is different, and Samantha it turned out was anything goes. A chick who's going down down down to the bottom of Hades and any guy she can get her hands on is going down with her.

And who am I and what have I become? I don't know, I just don't know.

But that's not the end, no man, 'cause it goes on and on.

The mom calls and tells the sisters she's in New York, one of the boyfriends and her gone there on a whim, so the sisters are on their own, but they're not on their own 'cause they got

Polanski and Faithfull and Samantha and me.

I mean we all end up hanging out stonered fucked-up on that houseboat all week. But you don't need to hear any more about that scene. You get the idea, I'm sure you do. Yeah nothing good happened that week. Nothing.

16. BAD CHECKS

HERE'S HOW CRAZY I got.

Week after I'm out at the houseboat I start up with the bad checks.

The bad checks.

Demon eye got me in its sway.

Only in the stoned state of mixed-up confusion, blinded by my own eye-blinding, self-generated light, I write the bad checks.

Another symptom. Symptom of losing who I am. Of my need to forget what I've done, escape where I am, and not only the literal of where-I-am, but the where-I'm-at state of where-I-am. And the where-I-am too, time and space, and I want to get the hell out of Dodge, gone baby gone. Dead-on bull's-eye.

The plan is simple, and now, looking back on it all, it makes no sense. The plan of a crazy man. That's not right. The plan of a crazy immature 17-year-old. That's more on the money. The plan of a crazy freakster bro. Dead-on bull's-eye.

The plan has no escape hatch. The plan has no tomorrow. The plan is so in-the-moment that soon as the moment is over, everything gonna fall apart. And everything does fall apart.

I have a checking account at Wells Fargo and I open a second checking account at Bank of America. Two checking accounts, but there's almost no money in either.

Deposit a check I write on my Wells Fargo account into the Bank of America account and withdraw some cash, and then I write a check on the Bank of America account and deposit it at Wells Fargo and get more cash, and somehow, don't ask me how, I really don't understand it at all, I end up with a couple hundred that way.

I decided to fly to Hollywood with Rosa's little jailbait sister Mercedes, me being 17, nearly 18, and Mercedes being 14, but closer to 13 than 15. I keep thinking of Rosa's mouth on Mercedes' tit. I am going down down down, man. Got that one right, brother.

Dead-on bull's-eye.

First I ask Samantha to go, but her parents are due back from a week in the Bahamas and she needs to be home when they return, and anyway I don't think she wants to go even if they weren't coming back. She don't like me all that much. It's just less of a bore fooling around with me, than not.

Anyway, don't matter.

Authentic real, I don't know what I thought I was gonna do with a 14-year-old chick in Hollywood.

I don't blame anything on the weed and the hash, but you do start to go squirrelly if you smoke enough of it. I have nothing to do in Hollywood.

But hey, little sister, let's go.

I write a bad check to cover two plane tickets. And this is easy. You want something, you write a check. And don't think about tomorrow. Don't think about what happens when they bounce. The checks. All the bad checks.

Mercedes got nothing to do and she likes me well enough, I mean that deal with her taking my cowboy shirt off, massaging my shoulders, yeah she likes me OK. So she comes with me. She never been to Hollywood, never been nowhere, man, so who knows where she thinks we're going.

Land of the movie stars. Maybe that's what she thinks.

We fly down to LAX and waste the day on Sunset, trying to find groovy boutiques. It's sleazier than I remember. I was there with Polanski a few months back. Well that's not exactly right. I hitchhiked down and showed up at the recording studio where this producer friend of Polanski's dad was recording this band, and I knew some of the band 'cause me and Polanski hung around where they rehearsed. Polanski sold dope to some of 'em.

But anyway.

Some real lowlifes on Sunset. A lot of greasy guys give Mercedes the twice over once. Look at her, and look at her again, and both looks are the same, look at her in a way that makes me want to take care of her, makes me want to send her off to Catholic school or a nunnery or a Buddhist temple. Makes me want to beat the shit out of those guys. The way they look at her, man, makes me feel the fuck guilty. Makes me think what am I doing in Hollywood with a 14-year-old chick?

And every answer I got is a bring-me-down answer. Every answer makes me know I've become as much of a sleaze as the Sunset lowlifes.

Dead-on bull's eye.

I know it's wrong, yeah I do.

On Sunset I buy Mercedes a dress. And a necklace. Two pairs of earrings. Some kind of bath soap she wants. Some kind of perfume. I write more bad checks to pay for all of it.

More bad checks.

And now I don't even think about it, don't think about no money in the accounts. There are times when in-the-moment is a bad idea. A very bad idea.

I get us a room at the Gold Digger Motel on Sunset.

I know about the Gold Digger 'cause of that time I told you about when I hitchhiked down to L.A. and ended up crashed-out on the floor of Polanski's motel room, lay there and listened to Polanski fuck Faithfull on the bed. And I wondered if Polanski pushed a glob of Vaseline up Faithfull's butt and fucked her hard up the ass. Or if he fucked her normal. I was crashed on the floor and it was dark, so I don't know.

Anyway.

Somehow I had this idea the Gold Digger was cool, 'cause all the members of the band stayed there, and Polanski and Faithfull. I remembered it as, well, groovy.

But the way I see it that other time is so wrong, and I didn't get it at all then, but now I know. Man, the crowd you hang with in a place can make the place, or disguise the place, perform a kind of sleight of hand.

Only it was a sleight of eye, or a sleight of view, a sleight of perspective, where I didn't even see how mundane the scene was, how stained the carpet, how the curtains were torn and the bed sagged and the bedspread had what I figure was dried cum on it.

Polanski and Faithfull's Gold Digger room where I crashed that time is the room I get for me and Mercedes.

Same room.

And this time, no sleight of hand going on when I see that motel, when I see that room.

Gold Digger is a dump, man.

Only it's worse.

It's one of those motels where the hookers bring their johns.

You can rent rooms by the hour at the Gold Digger.

Sunset Boulevard, down there where the Gold Digger is, that's where those chicks hang out, wait for some dude to stop the car and pick them up and drive around the corner for a quickie blow-job, or pull around the back, get a room for an hour or two. All these hooker chicks with short shorts and tits out to here walk up and down Sunset, and they give me and Mercedes the twice over once.

We walk by one of those chicks who stands outside the motel lobby and as me and Mercedes are about to go in so I can buy us a room, hooker chick wants me to pay her so we can have a party. Hooker chick says for Ulysses S. Grant she'll get us both off any way we want it.

And I flash on the Vaseline and hard-up-the-ass deal.

"Or if you want," hooker chick says. "You can watch while me and your little friend have some fun."

That scares Mercedes, and I hustle to reassure her everything's cool, babe, no sweat, don't worry about that chick, just forget about her, that kinda deal.

I get us the room in the Gold Digger same as I already told you, same room Polanski and Faithfull had where I listened in the dark to those two go at it, and the guy behind the counter won't take a check, cash only. I gotta pay him 30 bucks up front.

We take the outside stairs up to our room on the second floor, and I'm ready to fuck Mercedes, man, yeah I am.

And that's what this is all about. This trip to Hollywood.

Authentic real of it.

So I can fuck Mercedes on the bed in the Gold Digger.

Same bed where Polanski fucked Faithfull.

Same room, same bed.

Only I don't know it. That I've come to Hollywood to fuck Mercedes.

I mean I know it, but I won't let myself know it. Not back then. Later I know it. Of course I do.

And I don't even want Mercedes that bad. I sure don't love her. Don't hardly know her. And I'm so fucked-up crazy, man, don't know what I'm doing or why I'm doing it.

Down, down, down, that's where I go.

And I hear that Mothers of Invention song, the one about the chick who's 13 and already she knows how to nasty.

The room is barebones. A bed and a dresser and black and white TV on it, and a chair that Mercedes lays her dress on, only that's later. We haven't got to that part yet. And a door that opens into the bathroom. For sure kinda room where you bring a hooker, get it on and split.

Nowhere to sit in that room except on the bed.

The bed is this queen-size deal.

OK that's wrong, about nowhere to sit only the bed.

One person could sit on the chair, but later that's where Mercedes lays her new dress, and then for sure nowhere but the bed.

Don't matter.

We both sit on the bed.

Well Mercedes sits on the bed.

Before I sit on the bed, I got to get us dinner.

First I find out if Mercedes digs pepperoni pizza with mushrooms and green peppers and onions, and she wants a Coke too, and a Mars bar and maybe some Jujubes. I tell her I'll be right back, make sure she locks the door and I go down the block, get us an extra-large pizza and at the liquor store next door I get the Cokes and the candy.

That should have stopped me in my tracks. Chick I'm ready to fuck is 14 and she asked me to get her candy—a Mars bar and maybe some Jujubes.

Wrong man, my trip so fucking wrong.

Back in the room, we sit on the bed, smoke a joint, eat pizza, sit on the bed, add a tomato sauce and greasy cheese stain to the bedspread. We smoke another number, and we drink Cokes and another, got the munchies so we eat more pizza and Mercedes eats her Mars bar and some Jujubes. More reefer, and we watch that movie on the tube staring Gloria Swanson and William Holden, this old black and white, "Sunset Boulevard."

Man that movie creeps Mercedes out.

Past midnight when we're gonna get some action going.

I mean that's the way I think it. I figure Mercedes gonna let me do her, she's come all the way to L.A. with me and we're sharing a bed. And she's so fucking stoned.

What else would a dude think?

Mercedes turns off the lights and then she goes off to the bathroom.

Some of the Gold Digger red and yellow neon glow gets past the curtains, onto part of a wall, gives the room an eerie vibe.

She's in there forever, you know, the bathroom.

When she comes out she lays her dress on the chair. The one chair in the room. The chair neither of us sit on. Quick-like she gets under the covers, but before she does, some of that red and yellow neon gets past the curtains, shines on Mercedes and I see she got on pink panties and a white sleeveless t-shirt.

And it's me and Mercedes in a sleazy motel room where hookers bring their johns. And when it's me and her, she acts different than when her sister is around, and Samantha and Faithfull and Polanski. Alone with me, she's scared or nervous deal, I mean she don't know me. Not at all.

Pink panties and a white sleeveless t-shirt and she don't have much in the way of tits yet, I mean she's only 14.

I got nothing on but a pair of boxers.

And a raging hard-on.

She's under the covers, and I sit cross-legged on the bedspread.

"Hey, Mercedes," I say. "That was groovy that time you rubbed my shoulders, you know."

She gives me this small smile. Bianca Jagger's little sister smile.

She gets out from under the covers, stoned smile on her face, adjusts the thin straps of her sleeveless t-shirt and she gets behind me, starts to dig her fingers into my shoulder muscles. Soon enough I lay face down, and she's sitting next to me, rubbing my back. I think maybe she'll work her way down my body, get her hands on my ass, maybe reach between my legs and touch my balls.

She don't do any of that, only my shoulders and back.

So I roll over on my back, look up at her.

She sits there, got that stoned smile, and some of the Gold Digger red and yellow neon on her, man she looks psychedelic, and I tell her and she laughs, she digs it.

"I'm the light show girl," she says.

And she raises her arms, moves her body the way she'd move it if *Sticky Fingers* played on the stereo, even though the only sound we hear is some guy and chick in the next room yelling at each other and one of 'em throws something that hits the wall.

Mercedes lays down next to me, on top of the bedspread, lays there on her back, her eyes open, I can see them, and she's stoned and even fucked-up she's a scared little sister, but I got one thing and one thing only on my mind, so I tell myself she's scared 'cause it's Hollywood and 'cause of that hooker who said what she said when we came into the lobby to register.

I roll onto my side facing Mercedes and put my arm across her chest, my hand around her far shoulder and pull her to me, and lean over her, bring my mouth down on her mouth, start to kiss her. Start to kiss her Bianca Jagger's little sister lips, only she don't respond, and she twists her face away, and the distaste, her mouth looks same as she tastes some bitter food and she tries to get away only I got my hand still holding onto her shoulder, so she struggles her little body, and I'm stonered, man, and I think she's gonna get into it. I think Mercedes is playing hard to get or one of those deals where a chick wants it, but pretends she don't. I might have thought that. Oh I don't know what I thought. I was so fucking stonered. I was so fucking horny.

I bring my hand down, feel her little 14-year-old tit through the t-shirt.

That's when she says *don't, don't do that,* and she don't want me to touch her, she don't want any of this, and the way her face looks, I can tell that sooner than later she's gonna cry.

Fuck man, it's same as a little girl in bed next to me gonna start to cry.

And I could have gone ahead and fucked her, who was gonna stop me. I was the Man, stopped my dad in his tracks that time. No one gonna stop me.

Un moment decisif.

In, out.

One of those moments, man, where you pull the trigger, or don't. Where you commit the crime, or you walk away. Where you do something so wrong you can never make it right.

Out.

Out, man.

And the part of me that knows what's right and good and true takes over, and I take my hand off her. I back way off, say I'm sorry a million times, tell her not to worry, tell her I won't touch her or anything, we'll fly home in the morning and everything will be cool.

I tell her all that.

There's nothing sadder than a 14-year-old girl gonna cry, man, especially if you're the reason. You meaning me. It broke my heart to see her that way.

And I see Sweet Sarah's face, only nothing sweet about the way she looks at me. Yeah, for sure the you've-blown-it-so-bad look. The what's-happened-to-you-Michael? look. See Sweet Sarah give me the cold eye. How she looked at me when I

showed her my scene at the Ebson's Furniture building, and I
see her how she looked at me when I told her I wanted to hang
out with some other friends at Greg's party. And I know this is
wrong, and I feel the shame. I feel same as one of those dudes
on a TV crime drama who flips out and does some horrible
crime, stands there, knife in his hand, blood all over the floor,
body and blood on the floor. And what have I done? What have
I done, man?

Fourteen-year-old chick gonna cry. Got her here in the Gold
Digger, dried sperm on the bed cover, where the whores take
the johns.

What have I done, man?

Mercedes sees how freaked I am, and how I keep my hands
off her, how sorry I say I am and she calms herself down and
we get under the covers, and now I'm her older brother, now
I'm looking out for her and we watch some more TV and after
some time passes, she falls asleep with the TV still on. I look at
her face, and it's a little girl face, and her face all relaxed, that
stonered smile, and what the fuck am I doing in a bed where the
hookers do the johns, what am I doing here with this 14-year-
old chick.

I go into the bathroom and jack off.

I don't think about Mercedes. I don't think about Sweet
Sarah. I think about Samantha with one hand pumping my cock
and the other rubbing her pussy.

After I'm done I get back in bed, and Mercedes still asleep,
still that stonered smile, and soon enough I drift away, sleep,
baby, sleep.

We sleep late, don't get up 'til nearly noon, and then we rush
'cause check-out is supposed to be noon. Before we head out to
the airport, I insist we go to the big Tower Records on Sunset
and actually, Mercedes is cool with that, I mean she never seen a
store with that many records. It's early evening when we cab out
to the airport.

I pay cash to cover the fare. You can't write a cabbie a
check. Can't write them a good check or a bad check. I don't
know what they do if you don't have the cash, hold onto your

bags maybe. Anyway, I got cash.

The airport is where I write my final bad check. Write it to get us two tickets back to San Francisco.

Sit side-by-side, middle seat and an aisle seat. Mercedes is still tired, she falls asleep there, and she's a mess. Wears the new dress I bought her for the second day and the dress is wrinkled, and she has that worn out look, the way a person looks when things have been hard for too long.

It's only been a day and a half since we left the houseboat, so in real time no big deal, but it seems like days. Seems like this trip gone on forever, and I sit in the middle seat, and that's when it begins to hit me.

The bad checks.

And how the fuck is this gonna end. No money in either checking account.

No money.

So all the checks I been writing, by now they've all bounced. Or will bounce in the next few days.

Do you go to jail for writing bad checks? I don't know but I'd think so. And by the time the plane lands, I'm freaking.

And I should be.

17. THE BIG DEAL

NOT EXACTLY A BONNIE and Clyde shoot-out, but still the high drama deal.

When the plane lands, after it goes down the runway, they don't bring it right up to those moveable hallways. You know, that normal scene where they hook the moveable hallway up to the plane and you walk along it after you exit to get into the airport. Instead they park the plane away from the terminal, and roll this metal stairs deal up to the plane's front doorway.

All of that I don't know about when it happens. For most of the flight I'm reading a new translation of "Crime and Punishment" I bought at the airport bookstore, and feel more and more hellfuck guilty.

Someone says something same as, what's going on, maybe there's a criminal type on the plane.

And that would be me.

I'm the criminal type.

And how will all this sound in the newspaper: A 17-year-old criminal type whose name has not been made public was arrested late Tuesday afternoon on American Airlines Flight 0069 shortly after the plane landed at San Francisco International Airport. According to a police source, the juvenile wrote a series of bad checks, and was accompanied on a Hollywood spending spree by a 14-year-old girl. The juvenile allegedly drugged the girl with marijuana and hashish and took advantage of her at the infamous Gold Digger Motel on Sunset Boulevard, site of numerous prostitution raids.

And so on.

And so on.

I look out the window see three cop cars. Three fucking cop cars.

Six cops run fast up the stairs and they're in the aisle, at our row, and the two in front have guns drawn, and they got the seat numbers, they want Michael Stein and Mercedes Ferrante, and *raise your hands above your heads, and step into the aisle and face the rear of the plane,* and they grab hold of my hands and I feel the cold metal and hear the click of the cuffs.

And that's when Mercedes starts to cry.

And that's when I start to yell. Scream that my dad knows F. Lee Bailey, "the most powerful fuckin' attorney in San Francisco and you're gonna pay. You better fuckin' believe me. F. Lee Bailey's gonna get me off and you're gonna really get in trouble."

Mercedes looks at me, tears on her Bianca Jagger's little sister face, mascara running, and they got her in handcuffs too.

And when I yell, man, they don't appreciate that one at all. That's when they start pushing us down the aisle, one of them tells me to keep my fucking mouth shut or else, only he says it right near my right ear, so only I hear it.

And they get us out of there, right quick-like, man.

Soon as they get us down to the ground off those metal stairs, they hustle us into the rear of one of the cars. Me and Mercedes, handcuffed, in the back of a cop car behind the bulletproof glass.

And I keep on yelling about F. Lee Bailey and how he's gonna sue their asses off, that kind of motherfucker talkin' loud, sayin' nothing bullshit.

Those pigs tell me to shut up, tell me I might trip and really hurt myself on the way into the station if I don't shut my trap. Say crude shit about Mercedes. Want to know what it's like to screw a little girl, and *what's your problem, Jesse James, too fucked-up to get a chick your own age.*

Rest of the ride the cops ignore us, talk back and forth and forth and back between each other.

"And don't you think, Rudy, gonna get this chump on more

than just the bad checks?"

"Sure I do, Sam, screwing a minor is statutory rape, even if she does look like a little Tijuana whore."

"Might book him on pimping her out, right Rudy?"

"Well sure, and if he's got any weed on him, an ounce or more, they'll book him for dealing, Sam."

Goddamn motherfucking pig-ass cops.

"We didn't do nothing, man," I say.

"Yeah well you can tell that to the judge," the cop called Sam says.

The cop called Rudy laughs, but it's a laugh that let's me know I'm a lyin' piece of garbage and I'm gonna land my ass in juvey.

Get mug shots of me and Mercedes at the Mill Valley police station and put us in separate cells. Of course they do.

What I find out later is Mercedes' mom was already at the station and soon as they got me locked up, they let Mercedes go home with the mom. I'm glad about that 'cause Mercedes didn't break any law. She didn't write the bad checks. She didn't do anything except come along for the ride.

I'm the one did something wrong.

That night they transfer me to juvey, up in Novato, which is 25 minutes, give or take, up 101 from my folks' place, and I spend the night in this cell and the next day my parents show up. My dad pulls some strings and convinces them I had a breakdown.

I'm a crazy motherfucker not responsible for my actions.

That's a good story.

I'm game for that one.

And it isn't that hard. To convince whoever needs convincing.

All anyone has to do is look at me. Crazy-wild freakster bro, man, total heavy traffic crazy-ass crazy motherfucker, way I look. Got the black top hat and the shades, cool-as Dylan Wayfarer-style shades with the dark dark dark green lenses, black tuxedo jacket over my black cowboy shirt with the white pearl snap buttons, jeans with the hole in the knee and the shitkickers. Crazy-wild as the Mad Hatter, yeah that top hat makes me look as crazy-like-Zelda as a freakster bro can look.

My dad tells whoever he tells how he's gonna cover any bad checks I wrote and unless any of the merchants press charges, and as long as they get their dough why would they, and since I didn't do anything else against the law, and this is the first time I ever been in trouble, and thank John Goddard at Village Music for not calling the cops that time he caught me stealing those albums, and since I'm a minor they drop the charges. There's some kinda deal where if I don't get in trouble for the next two years, it won't go on my record.

Man, do I owe my dad for pulling that one off, only I don't get it. It was later, much later, when I realize what my dad did for me.

He's an asshole, but I guess he does love me.

Here's how crazy I am.

And everyone knows it. Knows I've total lost it.

And the way everyone knows is 'cause I don't understand, think I done nothing wrong. Think everything's cool and no big deal and since my dad fixed things it's time to get back to business, get back to doing everything I been doing.

Get stonered-out stonered.

Hang with Samantha and Polanski and Faithfull and the sisters at the houseboat.

Only my folks got other ideas.

Right away they hook me up with this shrink my mom been going to every week since the Stone Age, and after he listens to me psyche man basically tells my mom and dad I'm nuts. After I sit with him an hour, him and them talk in private and next thing they take me to this mental hospital on Sir Francis Drake, a little north of Kentfield.

It's a closed ward, which means I can't leave and the shrink got me on downers, and that shit does a serious number, slows me down to molasses.

And still I don't get it.

How crazy I am, man.

One afternoon, after I been there, oh I don't know, could be two days, could be three, Rock 'n' Roll Frankie, Big Man Bobby and Polanski show up.

My mom drives them.

I guess she called them, told them the deal, and anyway they do what friends are supposed to do, come to see a freakster bro in trouble. The nurse brings them into my room and you'd have thought they wrote the bad checks, those dudes scared-ass scared, look at me, guess they see Jack the Ripper, that kinda deal.

I don't got a clue, not a clue, man.

Clueless, what I am.

Sit up in the hospital bed grogged-out-loaded on the downers they feed me twice a day, look same as shit, haven't shaved in two weeks probably more, not since before I'm out at the houseboat.

Rock 'n' Roll Frankie is freaked, but his freak is the freak of a concerned freakster bro. The way he comes over, hand on my shoulder, and the worry face tells me he hopes it's gonna be OK. I mean Rock 'n' Roll Frankie is the authentic real. I could tell you a bunch about him, but he's not the story. Not this story. Frankly, Rock 'n' Roll Frankie deserves a whole book of his own.

Polanski is Polanski, stoned for sure, probably here for the freak show as much as anything, check out a psycho ward. And the crazy who I'm supposed to be.

Big Man Bobby, he's a whole other deal. He sees me and after that me and him never the same.

That was it.

Big Man Bobby writes me off. I see it there between the lines, yeah I see it. I don't understand that's what it is, but later I know. Later he don't want to be friends with psycho-boy, afraid it's contagious. And really, knowing Big Man Bobby, I should've expected him to write me off, not stick by me, no loyalty. Big

Man Bobby being Big Man Bobby.

I think Big Man Bobby is there 'cause he's one of my trusted freakster bros, and of course he used to be a trusted freakster bro, but I'll find out he's not no more. Not from the moment he sees me in that bed. I'll find out.

But anyway.

That day, the mess I am, I don't get it.

That day I think I'm the big man.

Talk talk talk, even on the downers, I'm racing.

"Yeah, man, I'll be out of here soon, hey Polanski we'll get the band happening, no problem, great to fuckin' see you guys, hey Bobby, what you listening to, man, I'm kinda out-of-touch with the latest cool shit you gotta hip me to it, man, Frankie what's goin' on with Sweet Sarah, you got to tell her I'm locked in here for a little while and ask her to please come visit, tell her I'm sorry about fuckin' up but I love her, you know. Tell her I'm changed now. It'll be same as it used to be. Can you tell her, man?"

Rock 'n' Roll Frankie waits while I do this whole woe is me victim deal, talk talk talk, and I can't wait to see Sweet Sarah loopy downer rant. Finally I stop and I see Rock 'n' Roll Frankie's upset. My best buddy. I mean we met in seventh grade, six years before that day there in that hospital. He knows Sweet Sarah from before I met her. Watched the whole deal go down, man, and Rock 'n' Roll Frankie is still friends with her.

Rock 'n' Roll Frankie doesn't want to say nothing. I guess he thinks he could freak me out, send me into some further psycho trip.

But finally.

Yeah he's seen Sweet Sarah, only he can't tell me what she said to him. Private deal. I mean she asked him not to say anything they talk about to me. Yeah she knows I'm in the hospital *but*.

She knows.

Me being flipped out, I think that's the excuse for everything. I can recover and put it all behind me. No consequences.

Only I forget. You know. I forget that conversation me and
Sweet Sarah had that time we got ice creams and sat on that
bench by the pond near her folks' place. Later I remember, later
when I got all the time in the world to think about everything
gone wrong.

Ghost of 'lectricity. That day in 1969 when I tell Sweet Sarah
about "Strawberry Fields Forever," and then later I ask her
about back before me and her got together.
    "What if I were crazy," Sweet Sarah says.
    "Crazy like Zelda," she says.
    "I'd take care of you," I say. "No matter what."
    But if things were reversed Sweet Sarah has a different plan.
    "If you were me and I were you," Sweet Sarah says. "And
you were crazy like Zelda, I don't know if I'd stick around. I
don't think I would."
    Yeah, if only I don't forget. But I forget.

Big Man Bobby and Polanski stand there, don't say a word, and
Rock 'n' Roll Frankie decides it's time to tell me straight.
    "Mike, listen to me for a minute," Rock 'n' Roll Frankie says.
    Rock 'n' Roll Frankie is the only one other than my
grandfather who can call me Mike and not have it flip me out.
He's known me from before I became Michael.
    "What's the big deal," I say.
    "The big deal is this," Rock 'n' Roll Frankie says. "Sarah's
not going to be coming to see you."
    And I'm gonna say some shit, but he's not done.
    "I'm sorry to tell you this, bro," Rock 'n' Roll Frankie says.
"She's not your girlfriend anymore. I'm sorry, man."

I'm not going to waste your time with the three lousy weeks I
spent in a psycho ward in San Francisco. That's where they
moved me after another day in the other crazies ward. If
anything worth telling happened there, you'd be the first to
know. It's not as crazy insane as "One Flew Over the Cuckoo's
Nest," that's for sure, so if you want to read about a psycho

hospital and all that, the Kesey book is the one for you. My trip, I pal around with this crazy guy they give shock therapy to, and meet once a day with the psyche dude doctor, and sit at this upright piano, imagine what it would be like to be Bob Dylan, and write songs for the band I think Polanski and I still lead. Mostly though, I can't wait to get out.

After what Rock 'n' Roll Frankie said, well I don't believe it. He don't know Sweet Sarah, not the way I know her. He don't know how even after a fight or her pissed at something I did, if I said the right words it always worked out. He don't know. He wasn't there. He don't know that just because Sweet Sarah said some words with a firm voice don't mean that's the way it is. He don't know.

Still.

And as the days pass, I feel the overwhelming heavy traffic bummered-out bummerosity deal, about everything. About trying to make all those chicks. About smoking weed all the time. About hanging with Polanski. About Hollywood and Mercedes and the bad checks. So bummered-out, man, by what I do to myself and everyone who knows me.

Mostly, though, I think about Sweet Sarah. Miss her so bad, and figure for sure she's gonna understand. All that time we been together. Sure she'll forgive me. I mean me and her, same as one person for so long. She won't throw that away. She can't do that. No, man, she won't do that to me. She's gotta understand shit just fell apart with me, but that I got it back together.

Yeah I really do. I'm back, man, I really am.

And I'm never gonna make those mistakes I made again.

Authentic real.

And for sure.

Just because I figured out during those three weeks on the 9th floor ward with the bars on the windows and the locked doors and these people who were really nuts that I made the *big* mistake of my life, that don't mean Sweet Sarah can forgive.

And in fact, Sweet Sarah has moved on. Three years of us

old man-old lady deal, but what was once innocent and beautiful, all gone wrong.

It's over, man.

Over.

I mean what 17-year-old chick gonna hang out with psycho-boy, only that isn't it, or maybe that's some of it. Yeah, that's a lot of it. Not all of it.

For sure not all of it.

And you know why. Blow-by-blow you know.

Man, I fucked Sweet Sarah over bad.

Betrayed her.

Betrayed our true love vows.

Palm against palm.

Forever true.

Get out of the loony bin, call Sweet Sarah.

Her parents, the activist lawyer dad who drives the black Jaguar, and goody-goody mom, and her brother, Seymour, and her little sister Esmé all run interference.

Hang up on me or get lost or fuck off, 'cause their sister don't wanna talk, and by then they all hate me, they forget all the good I do for Sweet Sarah. I've become the devil who fed their sweet Sweet Sarah the Eden apple, the big bad boyfriend who turned her against them, and turned her on to sex and rock and stay out all night.

No good boyfriend.

For a while I convince myself this is all her parents' fault, poisoning how she feels about me. Feeding her lies. Twisting the story until the story they tell about me got nothing to do with me or Sweet Sarah. Yeah, I think they keep her away from me and if only I can be face-to-face with my chick everything will get back to the way it was, you know, before it all went hellfuck wrong.

But authentic real, in my heart I know it's Sweet Sarah, she uses them as a screen, and she don't want any more of me.

A couple times I drive to her house, but her family won't let me see her.

Say they'll call the cops if I don't split.

There were other times I parked on the road and sat there, didn't go onto their property, sat there and hoped she'd come out but she never did. One night when I can't stand it, brain gonna explode, I drive there don't know what the fuck I'll do. Park out on the road. Sit in the car write this letter expressing my love and beg forgiveness and a second chance and some such, only I don't got a pen or even a pencil so I use a red lipstick my mom left in the glove compartment and the letter looks same as something a psycho or kidnapper or 6-year-old leaves.

I walk down the gravel driveway and a bunch of cars are parked in front of the house. I don't know how many, I mean I don't count them. Wonder who all the people are, some kind of party. I fold the letter, step onto the front porch and there's a small mail box on the outside wall, right of the door, and that's not the real mailbox, that's where friends leave notes, and that's where I'm gonna put the letter, only I don't. Stuff the fucking letter into my back pocket.

I turn and look around the yard, try to ignore the cars, see that oak tree and the swing we sat on, swung together, so in love, man, her just looking at me and so happy, and I lost all that, look over to the garage with the open door and her dad's black Jaguar that we drove to a movie, her in the driver's seat 'cause her dad wouldn't let me drive his prize possession, and I wish we'd crashed the damn car.

I turn and stand before the front door.

I ring the doorbell and this time it's not the mom who answers, not Seymour or Esmé. No man, it's her. Sweet Sarah.

She looks same as she's been dragged through Hades, I mean she's crazy beautiful as ever, but she got a bad case of *the sad*. She stands inside the doorway, I'm still on the porch, and she don't ask me in. I say some shit but she don't wanna talk.

So that's when I say, "How can you not love me, Sarah?"

The tragic of her face. Flash of a moment, man, face of an old lady, lines and wrinkles, and her eyes shriveled. Oh man, it's a death mask.

"How is it possible," I say. "I mean if you really *ever* loved me, to stop."

And she's gonna fade to dust.

"If you love a human," I say. "You love them forever. You can't stop loving."

What I say is the authentic real, and we both know it. We both *fucking* know it, and there's nothing for her to say. Only it changes nothing because she's already had her *un moment decisif*, and there's no going back. She closes the door, and she's behind it, must have been standing there going nowhere, nothing but the solid wood door between us, and I hear her cry, hear *the sad*. Oh fuck, and what have I done. Forever after she goes inside, I hear her cry. And in her cry, this sad southern sound, barely there, but it was there. Sometimes even now, when I get thinking about Sweet Sarah, I hear her cry, I hear *the sad*.

So now you know a whole lot about me and what I been through.

Some of it, not all of it, and even what you know, well it's an echo of an echo of an echo.

But still.

Remember that day I first met my freakster bro buddy Lord Jim, and how unsure of myself and self-conscious and some such. Remember? Sure you do. Indelible. Etched in your brain, right?

So now you know.

Where I come from, and what happened. Yeah, well, when I first told you about meeting Lord Jim, you didn't know me the way you know me now.

Didn't know me at all.

Only now you maybe get it, the why of how fucked up I was, the mixed-up confusion. The hellfuck of how I felt all that year, sophomore year at The University.

And I wasn't the Man, not the crazy-wild freakster bro, all that gone from me the day I stood in the quad, and met Lord Jim for the first time.

THREE

1. A HARPER STORY

THE DAY I MEET Harper starts in the Arts College dining hall two days after I meet Lord Jim. Kate sits there with her dealer boyfriend Nate. Kate's this pushy chick who went to Tam High, this chick I saw around campus. Kate's a freshman at The University. Remember when I said I didn't know no one at the Arts College? That wasn't true. One chick I know, only that's still not right. Don't actual *know* Kate. I never talked to her at Tam. She knows me 'cause I was a happening guy, I mean among the freaks, and I know her 'cause I saw her there. So I don't really know her, but now we're both at a place where we don't know no one, so when I see Kate and boyfriend Nate I head over. Something else. Right off I think of her as Sappho 'cause her outfit makes her look same as a dyke off the island of Lesbos.

First thing I find out about Sappho is she's a vegan. A my-way-or-the-highway vegan. I set my tray down. Got a plate with sausage and scrambled eggs and pancakes soaked in syrup and toast slathered with butter.

Sappho's one of those chicks, you barely say hello and she's in your life.

Tidal wave coming at me, this Kate chick.

"Stop!" she says. "Don't eat that shit."

Her face is the chick in Modigliani's "Seated Nude." Squint a little and what I see is that Modigliani face. Only Sappho got a pointed chin, and her nose is long and thin and it comes to a point, blunt point but still a point. Yeah, Sappho's all about making her point, damn blunt about it too.

She got her shiny brown hair pulled back in a braided ponytail. Always she wears a denim work shirt, a guy's shirt over some worn t-shirt and faded blue jeans and the black engineer boots. She don't got a clue about what it is to be a chick. And that isn't sexist, that's the facts.

The dining hall is a huge gray room with a bare cement floor, bare cement walls, steel-frame windows, mile high ceiling. Same as a modern art museum. We sit at a long vinyl-topped table. Me across from Sappho and fat shaggy Nate, who I find out later, drove her up from L.A. where she's been living with her dad and stepmom ever since she graduated this past June, and who's got a bruise on his left cheek.

"Hey man," I say. "What happened?"

"This is Nate, my boyfriend," Sappho says. "He tripped over my boots."

"Yeah, that's it," Nate says. "I tripped."

The dining hall is full of us jabbering too loud and smoking too much and the clack clack clack of silverware against plastic plates. Sappho points her skinny index finger with the chewed-off nail, all her nails chewed-off, my direction and shakes it.

"Do you know," she says. "What that disgusting greasy devil is made of?"

Nate sits there spaced out flyin' high. Nate caught the early flight. Nate being Nate. Everyone knows a guy same as Nate, the kind of fat pudge loser with a homely mug no one cool gonna have nothing to do with except for one thing. Dealer, man. Everyone wants to know the Dealer.

"Pig," I say. "I'm not an idiot, Sappho."

Sappho always got her green nylon backpack. Libber pack I call it 'cause she glued a women's lib patch on the back, the fist surrounded by a circle with a cross descending. Feminist freak, Sappho is. Vegan freak. She gets a pack of Kool Lites out, looks at that sausage same as it's a live critter wiggling at the end of my fork.

"And what part of the pig, Mr. Smarty Pants."

I don't even know the chick.

"It's made from all the grossest parts," she says.

She's got an evil smile. If that Modigliani chick were possessed by the Devil, and you squint, that's Sappho. Nate picks at a plate of raw veggies.

Sappho has the cig pack in her hand, fooling with it, putting off the inevitable.

"You ever see that painting?" I say. "Modigliani—."

"Don't you flip the subject on me, Michael Stein," Sappho said.

I take a bite, taste the burnt and the fat and the dead pig as one burnt greasy shit taste—can't eat no more, and I put what's left on the plate.

"You're not my mom, Kate."

Her face changes, and for a flash of a moment all the smart-ass gone, and all the chutzpah in her voice takes a hike.

"Don't you want to stay alive?" she says. "And the animals. Don't you care about them?"

She shakes a cig out, drops the pack on the table, and lights up. Long drag, head back and she exhales. Nate looks up and watches the smoke vanish, and I figure Nate spends a lot of time watching smoke vanish. One day he's gonna wake up realize his whole life has vanished.

"Heavy, man," Nate says.

"You're sure rapping a lot," I say.

I don't know why, but that day I didn't want Sappho to know I'd started smoking so I didn't say nothin' about it.

"Enjoyin' that Earth Day approved Kool?" I say.

"It's a goddamn habit," Sappho says. "I'm gonna quit."

Nate goes for the Kools, "Me too," only Sappho beats him to the pack.

"What are you up to now, Nate, three packs?" she says.

There's one more sausage on my plate, but what I see is pig guts. Pool of syrup and soggy pancakes and the eggs are ill too. Breakfast gone to shit, thank you Sappho.

"Gonna see if they got something a tad more healthy," I say. "Like a donut."

Through the swinging stainless doors fluorescent lights hang from the ceiling. Across the room the stainless food counter. A glass window separates the tray track from the hot stuff. Above it are glass shelves with small white plastic plates of food. You been in a cafeteria, you seen it. Well there amid the sea of salt, sugar and grease, an oasis of fat-free sugar-free grease-free oatmeal. There's a bearded guy behind the counter, and I aim a finger at the pot.

"Can't be anything wrong with fucking oatmeal."

And I swear I heard it, *caw caw caw,* a sound I never wanna hear again.

He ladles some into a bowl. *Caw caw caw.* Last I see of that oatmeal.

'Cause this chick been standing quiet looking at me.

Harper.

And I tell you, that day, even with what happened, don't got a clue Harper's my own private Altamont.

Harper's voice, dark smoke of Nico, and I know *the wanting.* You know Nico, right? "All Tomorrow's Parties" and "Venus in Furs." And the solo albums: *Chelsea Girl* and *The Marble Index* and *Desertshore.* A cool monotone, only Nico got a German accent, and Harper don't. The power a chick got over a guy. Her voice is the black Portolano leather gloves, and the black leather mini-skirt and the Wanda von Dunajew spike heel boots.

First time I see Harper, and she's fooling with her silver necklace, and there's a silver skull, only it's not silver, none of it, stainless steel—turns out she mailed away to get it. Harper was beautiful that day, and I'm not going nowhere, man. Later she was beautiful, but it's different, it's the beautiful dying. You'll understand when I get to that part. But I can tell you now, Harper was never as sweet beautiful again.

Harper's eyes on me, black as night, black as coal, and it might as well been Anita Pallenberg stood there—I mean if Anita Pallenberg were 18 and still the innocence.

First time I saw Anita Pallenberg it was the bath scene in

"Performance," the druggy *ménage à trois*. Mick and Anita and 16-year-old Michèle Breton. Naked in the bath. So right there, mixed-up confusion. Groovy freakster chick Harper in front of me, and a memory of Anita with Mick and Michèle.

Harper's hair cut so Anita she coulda copied it from photos. Mod London groovy with the bangs beginning to touch her eyelashes and the rest of it spin-in-the-sunlight golden yellow with a hint of a wave dropping to her shoulders. Don't get me wrong. She didn't look so much same as Anita—less than I've made out. You had to see her to know what I mean. 'Cause her nose, well that's Lee Miller, you know, Man Ray's chick.

I look and look. Harper's wearing faded bell-bottom jeans with paisley cuffs, and a peace symbol patch on the left knee, and a short-sleeve white peasant blouse that's so white this might be the first time she ever wore it. She has on a backpack and the straps pull the blouse tight across her chest. And no bra. Of course no bra. College chicks for sure don't wear bras in 1972. The top two buttons of her blouse undone; her nipples press against the thin cotton; I can almost see them. I look and I look. Eighteen-year-old chick same as Harper, her tits are the sweetest fruit, and to taste the sweetest fruit, oh for a taste, to know the taste of the sweetest fruit. It's too much, man. I'm a freakster bro, no different than any freakster bro who sees a beautiful chick, and I got the wanting, *bad*.

"Tu n'as jamais vu de fille?" she says.

No chick ever spoke French to me before Harper. Bearded guy who works behind the counter is back in the kitchen—so it's me and her alone.

"You've lost me," I say.

"You never seen *a girl* before?"

Caught, man. Probably never been a time it was cool to stare at the tits of a chick you don't already sleep with, but since the feminism deal, a guy can't be too careful.

Harper's black Keane eyes drop to my crotch. I adjust my jeans but it's too late. For sure she gonna tear me down.

"I'm trying to salvage breakfast," I say. "Most of this shit could kill ya."

"Really?" she says, and her eyes flash to the oatmeal, and back to my crotch. "Well if you eat all your oatmeal, should keep you healthy young man."

Black as night, black as coal.

"And fit," and she laughs, and Harper has this laugh that only Harper got—same as she knows something she's not telling. She hums a song, leans back against the counter, an old Stones' song, "Ruby Tuesday." You know that one, right? About a wild and free chick who's not ever gonna be tied down.

I don't know why she did what she did next. Maybe she thought it was sexy. She don't need to act sexy. All Harper got to do is nothing and it's more than plenty. Her right hand on the stainless counter to steady herself and she shifts her weight onto her right leg. Rests her other hand on her hip and I see her long fingernails are painted black. I never seen a chick with black fingernails.

She raises and extends her other leg out front of her dancer graceful. It's what they call Grand Battlement in ballet, her left leg, foot and toes a straight line, pointed forward, and she's barefoot. She got delicate small feet and if only I could see her legs, but what got me more than if I seen her bare legs and bare thighs and everything else, well there's a way her slender ankle comes out of her paisley cuff, slays me, man. It's art, her ankle emerging. It's a Katsushika Hokusai ukiyo-e wood print.

Harper's toenails are painted black, and I never seen a chick with black toenails either. Chicks didn't paint their toenails black in 1972. Chicks didn't paint any of their nails black that year. Not in California.

Harper drops her leg and moves closer, reaches toward a bowl of apples. Her thin fingers same as blown-glass birds and small fish and violet wildflowers. First she holds one apple, but no, then another, the apples shiny under the fluorescent light, and she takes one. Hesiod had a name for Harper. *The beautiful evil.* I don't know about Hesiod that day. It's something Harper told me.

Later.

"Want a bite?"

Her laugh—she gets the joke and I don't got a clue.

"Didn't that cause all kinds of trouble?"

"I dig trouble," she says. "You're not one of those guys who's always trying to be *good*, are you? Not some Mr. Rogers kind of guy."

Oh man, no, *no way*. I'm not one of those guys. No, Harper, really. I'm one of Peckinpah's Wild Bunch, Brando's Wild One, Ray's Rebel Without a Cause. I'M THE MAN, last freakster bro standing, guns ablaze. Really, Harper. I swear, isn't me at all.

"And if I take your apple?"

"Je vais te pervertir."

Un moment decisif.

In, or out? Always, a choice. Always. And the moment's gonna pass, almost gone, there it goes. *In.* I reach out but she pulls it away.

"You sure you want a bite, Mr. Rogers?"

I step forward, and I still don't know how it happened. Maybe it was nerves, or grease on the floor, but I don't think so. I fall into Harper, pressing her against the stainless counter, and for sure she gonna scream. Harper doesn't scream, and her arms around me and I feel her warmth, all of her curvy chick's body against me.

"I think you're rushing things," she says.

"Fuckin' sorry," I say, stepping back. "I didn't—."

Her face got a pink blush, and freckles on her nose, a handful, brown freckles. Sex dust, man, it's the innocence hiding the darkness, only I don't know about the darkness. I got some clues of course from Polanski and Samantha and the houseboat scene, but Harper's gonna teach me what I still don't wanna believe, gonna teach me a chick isn't the innocence, yeah from Harper I'll learn that for me at least, every chick I feel the wanting for can be toxic.

Again she holds out the apple. "Well?"

I get my fingers around it, and my fingers touch her fingers, and her fingers are beautiful blown-glass birds and small fish and violet wildflowers, and the charge of touching a chick again.

A Harper story, that was Harper that day. She's not who I
thought she was, but it don't become clear 'til so much later. At
Simone's place on Morning Glory Way. Don't worry about the
deal with Simone. I'll tell you about it when I tell you about it.
Thing is, it was when it was only me and Harper out at Simone's
when Harper told me who she'd been the day we met—and by
then it was too late.

Harper grew up in a San Diego suburb, Harper said, and her
parents were way too protective. I never saw her San Diego
scene, never met her parents, so I gotta take her word for it. Her
word's not so good.

So many Harper stories.

Harper had a list of what she'd do after her parents dropped
her off at The University. First item: she got out the black nail
polish she bought mail order from a theatrical supply house in
New York and painted her nails black. So it was black Sunday,
the day she got to The University. Black Sunday, the first Harper
ever been on her own.

First time I look at Harper I see *the beautiful evil*. The trouble
girl with the black nails, and the blacker heart. Only turns out
the trouble girl is who Harper wants to be. Day I meet Harper
she's still one of those chicks from the suburbs where nothing
ever happens, where all roads lead to the shopping center.

"I would know the black of the abyss," Harper said.

This was so much later, Harper telling me all of this. At
Simone's place. Harper said she wanted so much more from life
when she got to The University. She wanted everything she
dreamed back when she lived in the suburbs. Harper told me
she wanted life to be symbolic as Rimbaud's "Illuminations,"
and harsh as Henry Miller ordering a chick to shut her mouth
and get on her hands and knees so he could fuck her same as a
dog. She says she wanted some old married man to lust for her,
to want his gnarled fingers on her pale flesh, and promise her
everything and she'd scorn him and walk away just 'cause she
could.

More of Harper's list: she wanted to stay up all night,
wander the streets of some city she never seen, drink 'til she

blacked out. Snort coke, pop pills, shoot junk. Gotta know what it was to swim far far out into the ocean 'til she was exhausted and nothing left. Harper wanted to burn bright and burn fast and burn out.

Harper said when she got to The University she was ready to feel something, even if it took her down. Later she'd want it to take her down. Yeah, Harper had her list. But it's hellfuck easier to lie on your bed in a San Diego suburb and make a list of what you're gonna do *someday*, than to go do it. Black nail polish, that was easy.

She taps hurried eighth notes on the metal counter with her index finger.

"So my ceramics class is cancelled," she says. "Wanna do something?"

In, or out? If I don't say something fast, I'm out.

"We could hang in my room," I say. "Dig some sounds, smoke a number."

It was easy as that. Easy action, she stops tapping, and I put the apple in my jacket pocket. "Guess I'll eat this later."

"La douceur qui empoisonne l'âme."

She hadn't figured on picking a guy who don't know French.

"Baudelaire," she says.

We split the cafeteria, and as we come into the dining hall Sappho and Nate are bussing their trays.

"You wait for me?" I say to Harper. "Over by the stairs? I need to say bye to my friends."

Harper raises her arm as if to look at her watch, only she's not wearing a watch.

"Give you 10 seconds."

I guess Nate been watching me and Harper come out of the cafeteria 'cause when I come up to him and Sappho he says, "Wow. Some chick you're hanging with, man. What a fox!"

"Nate!" Sappho says.

"We're just talkin', man," Nate says. "No harm done."

Sappho crosses her arms. "Goyim. I bet your parents gonna

love *her*."

"My lucky break," I say. "I think she's an exchange student."

"I don't like the look of that girl," Sappho says.

"She's French," I say. "Very sophisticated. Paints her nails black."

"You know, Michael," Sappho says. "The French were Nazi sympathizers."

And this is taking way too long, and I'm gonna blow it. "We bonded in the cafeteria. She loves sausage."

"I bet," Nate says.

Sappho slaps the palm of her hand fast against Nate's cheek, the one that don't got the bruise.

"Fuck!" Nate says.

"Hate to leave you love birds," I say. "Gonna miss my ride."

Nate, man, total mixed-up confusion. *Fuckin'* chicks.

"Have a safe drive, Nate," I say. "See you around, Kate. Been a pleasure. Maybe we can talk omelets next time."

Harper's up the steps and onto the mezzanine, and she coulda been out through the glass doors, but she looks back.

"Wait up," I say.

"Thought you lost interest," she says.

"No you didn't."

"Yeah," she says. "I didn't."

We get outside and onto the path leads up to the Arts College quad.

"So you're from France," I say. "I really want to visit the south of France, that town where Toulouse-Lautrec is from. You been there?"

"Try just north of L.A.," she says, and that's when she tells me her name's Harper, and she's a freshman. That was true — well true enough. Harper was the name she used all the time I knew her, and she really was a freshman.

Everything else she tells me as we walk to my dorm is a Harper story.

Said she grew up near Santa Barbara, some beach town, parents divorced when she was 9. That's a lie. Said her mom supported them working two jobs so her and her sister pretty much raised themselves. Major lie. Well the part about her mom supporting them. Harper did have a younger sister, that was true. Said she'd done some dope, dropped acid and snorted coke, but she really dug pot. Lies, all of it, except for the pot.

Said she had boyfriends through high school, and fucked them all. Overwhelming lie. About the boyfriends, about fucking them. I mean she did tell me, at Simone's place, how she let this one boy fuck her after the prom. That was true. One boy. One fuck. At least I think it's true 'cause she wouldn't say any more about it.

2. HARPER'S WEIRD HIGH MOAN

BEFORE I TELL YOU what happened that afternoon, I gotta explain something. I'd never fucked any chick the same day I met her. The first chick I ever kissed was Sweet Sarah after she became my old lady, and that kiss happened weeks after we started hanging out. Sure I knew about the whole free love deal, but I thought sex was something you did with a chick you were head-over-heels in love with, not someone you picked up that same day. So Harper coming back to my room so soon after we met, that was uncharted territory for me—and as it turned out, for her too.

Harper's in my room, her feet in the soft pile of the rug, and she's checking my scene. I flip on the overhead and my room isn't a blank canvas. Got my mark everywhere.

"Groovy bed," Harper says.

Fuck yeah.

"I hate those singles. How'd you manage a double?"

Talk, talk, talk, we talk to fill the air, to keep away the silence of what now?

"Got my ways," I say.

Oh man, oh God-who-for-sure-don't-exist, what the fuck now? Harper's eyes on my eyes, and we know why we're here, but how does it start when it's two strangers?

"Groovy view," she says.

Harper looks past my bed out the windows, and she moves *shodō* graceful. You know *shodō*, right? It's Zen calligraphy, and to do it Zen monks achieve *mu-shin*, "no mind state." *Shodō* turn of her head, her pack slides down her arms, down to her hands, as if she has nothing to do with it, and in one motion, her left arm free, her right hand holds the strap, drops it to the rug.

"Oh wow," Harper says. "You can look right into the rooms across there. If you have binoculars."

"I got binoculars," I say, but no way am I gonna tell her they're from when I'm in the Scouts. Nothing cool about being a Boy Scout.

Spins around to watch me. "See anything you shouldn't, *Mr. Rogers?* You watch guys fuck their girlfriends? Leave the curtains open so they can watch *you?*"

Harper sees the Jewish guilt over something I haven't done. I got so much guilt, man.

Guilt for being alive.

Un moment decisif.

"Yeah, I been watching this one room."

"Oh wow," Harper says. "What have you seen?"

"I feel kinda awkward about it," I say. "You being a nice girl and all."

"If I were nice I wouldn't be here," Harper says. "You better tell me Mr. Rogers."

"OK, OK," I say. "There's a guy and a chick."

"*And?*"

So then I go into this stalling her routine, same as I got a dirty secret.

"Come *on*," Harper says.

"They strip, do some kinda black magic sex ritual in front of *that* window."

"Oh wow," Harper says. "Maybe a sex cult."

"You think so? They light all these candles."

"Oh *wow!* Give me the binoculars.*"*

So I get them for her, and of course she wants to know which room.

"See that Black Sabbath poster," I say.

"The tombstone?"

Harper gets onto my bed, she's on her knees, ass up, *oh man*, and she knee-walks to the window.

"You better get down," I say. "If it's a sex cult, they'll come after us. Same as Manson. And I don't want anyone to think *I'm* a peeping tom."

"Some girls are turned on by it," Harper says. "A guy watching."

She gets down, Mata Hari spy chick looking for the taboo scene.

"I don't see them," she says.

And I can't help it, I'm laughin', man.

"Motherfucker."

She rolls onto her back. Her white cotton blouse has come up some, and her stomach so pale, same as the sun's never shone on it.

"I should have known," she says, and she sits up. "You're *too* good. Need to do something *bad* Mr. Rogers. For once in your life."

Harper's off the bed, looking in the full-length mirror glued to the closet door. Pulls at her blouse, gets her jeans lower on her hips, fingers touch the stainless steel skull, and her slender ankles come out of those paisley cuffs, *oh man oh man*.

"It's rude to stare."

"I'm taking your advice," I say. "You know, do something bad."

Harper laughs her laugh, and I don't got a clue. She runs a lipstick along her lips.

"You *do* like to watch."

She's on my bed again, gets over to the window, closes the thick curtains.

"I like the darkness," she says. "Turn the light off why don't you."

She sits cross-legged, and watches me, and waits. It's a game for Harper, she knows what she wants but she wants me to feel the awkward, to fumble towards the fucking. There's something else she wants, but I'll have to wait for her to tell me. I take the apple from my pocket, the apple that'll ruin me, and put it on the desk. The room is quiet, and a tension blows onto us and maybe this isn't gonna work.

I turn off the overhead but it's too dark. I get out The Dylan and light the candle.

"Dylan's lighter," I say.

I hold it up and the candlelight reflects off it onto the *Blonde on Blonde* poster, a blotch of light on Dylan's face.

Either she don't hear me, or she don't care and what the fuck.

So I pocket the lighter.

"You into The Doors?" I say.

The flickering candlelight on her, and she laughs a different laugh – the conspiracy of two laugh. "I got stoned for the first time to 'Light My Fire,'" she says, and with a *shodō* turn of her head the tension splits. Gone baby gone.

"You know he died in Paris," she says. *"Une overdose d'héroïne."*

I get *The Doors* playing, and away we go, the throbbing sex sound, and Morrison's cemetery voice.

"It's so romantic," she says, her thin fingers on the third button of her blouse. "An overdose."

I unzip my snakeskin boots.

"Same boots as Keith Richards wears," I say.

"Too bad the rest of you isn't Keith Richards, then you'd have it made."

She waits a beat.

"And I'd get to fuck Keith Richards."

I get out the doobies I got off Lord Jim, light one with the candle and take a mouthful of the harsh. Harper pulls my arm to her, and if how Harper's fingers feel against my fingers were a sound, the sound is Nico when she sings "Femme Fatale." Harper licks the end of the joint, and that joint, seconds earlier in my mouth, between Harper's lipstick pink lips, and she sucks at it, holds the smoke. Yeah, she's smoked weed before, that's not a Harper story. Already I feel it, and I'm trippin' on Harper's face. She has black eyeliner, not a lot, but enough to make her Keane eyes extra spooky, and those eyes got hooks, hooks she'll hook into me, hooks same as indelible ink, once you're hooked, indelible, and good luck unhooking 'em.

Some of the glowing ash falls on the paisley bedspread. Harper presses her palm down hard on the ash.

"Don't burn yourself," I say.

"Why not?" Harper says.

It's hot in the room and I want to open a window, but Harper says I should take off my t-shirt, and her cool fingers help me pull it off, my long hair curling onto my bare shoulders.

Beaux nichons," she says. *"Je te montrerai les miens dans un moment."*

Somewhere I find some words from high school French.

Je ne sais pas ce que tu, uh, just said."

"Tres bien," she says. *"Bon garçon.* I said you have nice tits."

Hooked, man.

She takes the apple, takes a bite, holds it out so I see the side she's bitten into—pink lipstick smeared. "Dare!"

I reach for it but I'm too late—it's behind her.

"There's no going back, you know."

She gives me a hard look. One beat. Two. She bites off a big chunk of the apple with her teeth, and holds out the apple chunk.

"If I don't?"

"I don't like chicken shits, Mr. Rogers."

And that was the beginning. Harper starting to fuck with me different than before, and she turns away, gives me the freeze-out.

Un moment decisif.

In, or out? I'm not Mr. Rogers; not gonna let Harper slip away. *In.* Reach out, my thumb and index grip the apple chunk. She lets go, and before I pull away her fingers stroke my hand, only it's not "Femme Fatale," it's "Sister Morphine."

"Ça, c'est sérieux," she says.

Yeah, this is for real. She got that right.

"You taste it," she says. "No telling what'll happen."

"You *already* tasted it," I say.

"Yeah, but I *know* I'm going to hell," she says.

"La douceur qui empoisonne l'âme."
The sweetness that poisons the soul.

The room is dark save for light from the one candle making shadows of me and Harper against the curtains. How a hummingbird darts—at the flower, and it's gone—yeah, that's Harper, and she's off the bed. She dances a free-form Freak Scene Dream dance, face relaxed, eyes closed, thin arms high in the air, shakes her head so her hair falls across her face.

The music is danger whirling in the darkness. And his voice. Jim Morrison, man. Harper dances as if she's danced to "Light My Fire" a lot, her ass moving, jiggle of her tits beneath the white cotton blouse. I'm still sitting on the bed. There's a picture I seen of Jim Morrison shirtless at Venice beach, and I shake my head and fluff out my hair with my fingers, and hope I look cool as he did. Yeah there's times when looking cool matters. I feel the rhythm, do a slow stoned sway.

I watch Harper, and her eyes are open watching me.

Harper's hummingbird deal, flits here, flits there, and she's at my bookcase. There's a pile of magazines on one shelf, Creem and *Phonograph Record Magazine* along with some copies of *Penthouse*. Harper's not interested in the rock mags. She sings along to "Light My Fire" and flips through *Penthouse*. She unfolds the "Pet of the Month," and holds the magazine out so we both see the naked chick lying on a zebra skin rug. Silicone tits the size of bowling balls and nipples big as grapes, legs spread, soft brown hair curling around her pussy. I never looked at porn with a chick.

Me and those *Penthouse* chicks, that's my secret world only now Harper's walked in on it. Yeah she sees the guilt, and she rips out the "Pet of the Month" centerfold. She lets the magazine hit the floor, and she's hovering near me, holds the picture so the bowling ball tits are in my face, the candle light glaring off the slick paper.

"Why don't you tack *this* on your wall instead of that peace symbol," she says. "Or would that turn off the hippie chicks you bring up here?"

I figure Harper's a libber chick turning the tables, but she blows that theory to bits.

"I bet you don't know many girls into porn," she says.

I'm still sitting on the bed and she's standing right front of me, sways her hips to the snake rhythm of "Light My Fire."

"When I was little my dad kept *Playboy* in a cabinet in his office," she says. "I wanted so bad to know what was in those magazines with the pretty girls on the covers."

And is this another Harper story? "I guess I was 11 when I took one to my room," she says. "I was like 'Wow, these girls don't have any clothes on!' I was mesmerized, and I *had* to look. There was a girl who looked like me, only much older."

Harper's watching, and I got the self-conscious deal. All she gotta do is talk and it gets me hard. "She had a great ass, and big boobs. I'd lock the door to my room and lie in bed naked and look at this one picture. She was sitting up all perky, and I'd pretend I was her and I'd been picked 'Playmate of the Month.' That picture scared me. I couldn't keep from looking. *'Cela m'a rendue honteuse et salie.'"

She translates 'cause she wants me to know.

"It made me feel ashamed and dirty."

She's closer now, dancing as she talks, her pale face in profile, her substantial Lee Miller nose and she's got a cruel mouth. "It excited me," she says. "To feel dirty. That's the biggest turn on—when you've done something you're not supposed to do."

"No Harper," I say. "Being with someone you love is the biggest turn on."

"Love!" Harper says. "You're hopeless."

She flits here and there, alights a few feet away still holding the centerfold. "I bet she's the love of your life. Am I right Mr. Rogers? All the time you two spend together. *Se Palucher.* You jack off looking at her, right? Or is it jerk off? Makes me think of some jerk who can't get laid. That's not you, is it?"

I should have told her to fuck off, but if you'd been there, if you were me, you'd understand. Authentic real, her saying what

she said turned me on. But what did it mean, me, the freakster
bro who believes in love, wanting to fuck a chick I just met?
Harper couldn't be more than a sex object to me that day. You
can't love someone you don't know. And if I'd known Harper,
but I didn't know her, not that day.

Her hard stare, and she stands close again, too close. I smell
her sweat, but there's something else, some kind of perfume,
she smells how the rose color of rose-colored granny glasses
would smell, if you could smell a color. And her cruel smile,
yeah it's more than she gets the joke.

"Jerk off now!" Harper says. "Let me watch."

I didn't know chicks could talk how Harper talks. Chicks
don't talk about jerking off. Sweet Sarah never did.

I dig trouble, what Harper told me.

Un moment decisif.

In or out? *In.* Oh man, I'm *in,* and I'm not Mr. Rogers.
Gonna talk the authentic real to Harper. And what happens will
happen.

"No," I say. "I don't wanna jack off. Isn't why I brought you
here."

"You didn't bring me here. But if you think you did, what
do you have in mind?" and she's looking at me, her eyes red and
her pupils huge, the hook penetrating my flesh, and she's gonna
get everything she wants, that's what I saw in those fucked-up
eyes.

"Guys are *dogs,*" she says. "They'll fuck anything with a
cunt."

Laughing her high stoned laugh. And again she changes,
she's not laughing, and a huge silence sucks all the sound from
the room. I mean even with The Doors carrying on. Harper's
voice is solemn and what she says next isn't a Harper story.

"Girls masturbate too, you know. We have our fantasies."

She sits next to me on the bed, drops the centerfold and her
hand on my thigh, and it trembles. I don't think she knows what
she wants, but it's more than just to fuck a guy. You don't make
yourself vulnerable if you don't want some heart-to-heart.

"Sometimes I read porn to get myself off," Harper says. "It

turns me on too. So do the *Penthouse* girls. Does that make me a
dyke?"

"God," I say.

"There is no God," she says.

The candlelight flickers on Harper. The fingers of her hands
work the third button of her blouse, and there's an urgency,
pushing the ivory button through the hole, the blouse parting
and her pale skin, more pale than her arms, fingers on the
fourth button, straining the fabric in her rush to get it off, and
the blouse separates, pink-brown nipples and the dark brown
areolas, the final button, undone, and as she gets her left arm
out of the sleeve she pushes her chest towards me and the
candle makes a huge shadow of her tits on the curtain.

Her hard nipples, smaller than Sweet Sarah's, smaller than
the *Penthouse* tits, but the way Harper sticks her chest out they're
the dirty magazine tits I've jacked off to, only these are real,
these are in my room, a chick's flesh and blood dirty tits there in
the warm glow, that stainless steel skull hanging above them.
She gets her blouse off, lets it fall onto the bed. So young, man,
and is that fear?

"You know I told you class was cancelled," she says. "It's
not cancelled."

We kiss, my tongue between her lips, feeling her tongue,
rough and wet and alive, her tongue hard into mine, her nipples
against my bare chest, it's too much, and finally, *finally.*

"Not yet," she says. "You like to watch, and I want you to
watch."

Harper up on her knees, a hand on my shoulder, her fingers
grabbing my skin to steady herself. She's acting out the role of a
pin-up chick same as I seen on auto repair shop walls, each
hand cups a tit, she licks her lips, pink lipstick smeared. Acting
the role of a sex object as if this is what she's supposed to do. I
lean in to take her nipple in my mouth. She grabs my hair close
to the scalp and pulls my head away.

"How bad?"

"What?" but I know what she means.

"How fucking bad, motherfucker?"

Her face inches from mine. "You really are Mr. Rogers," she says. "Tell me something real, like you want to fuck me doggy-style or you want me to blow you. Tell me what the fuck you want. I'm not here to listen to music, or get stoned."

I can't say those things but I want them.

"You know what tarantulas do, *Mr. Rogers?*" Harper says. "When they *fuck?*"

"I bet they don't have a big conversation about it," I say.

"You got a cigarette, man?"

I get her a smoke, and my fingers shake, and Harper's fingers shake, the cigarette in her mouth, and I bring the candle over and fuck, she got a small scar, maybe from a knife cut, on the side of her right tit and something about that scar marring her perfect skin – oh man oh man.

"The female tarantula bites the head off her mate," she says.

A hit of the Pall Mall, and another, and she crushes it out on my desk.

"Et si tu devais mourir pour pouvoir baiser?"

She reaches over, both hands around the back of my head.

"I'll tell you. What if you have to *die* to have sex?"

I feel the chill, you know, that creepy deal, and what the fuck have I got myself into?

Her hands move down the side of my head, and her fingers around my neck, her face in my face, too close and it's a dark blur. "If we fuck, I'll kill you."

Her fingers tighten and she tries for a tough sound.

"That's the price."

"Let go of me Harper," I say. "You're talking crazy."

Her fingers relax and I pull back. She laughs, you know, she gets the joke and I don't got a clue. *That* laugh. Well I haven't fucked anyone in two years. Finally I got a chick half naked in my room. On my bed. I've *got* to make this work.

"I'm not crazy, Mr. Rogers," she says. "I'm trying to break through your goody-goody programming. Life isn't a game show. It's not mom knitting a sweater and dad smoking his corncob pipe. There's always something at stake."

She pushes her ass up off the bed, works her jeans down past her ass and she sits on the bed, pushes the jeans down her thighs. Oh man, the warm light on her black panties, and they've come down in the back so half her ass is bare and her thighs bare, her skin smooth and so pale it's as if she's got white makeup rubbed on her.

I put my arm around her back and get my hand so I'm touching her stomach how I used to touch Sweet Sarah, real gentle.

"Look, Harper," I say. "I really truly want you."

Oh fuck, she don't dig that sweet lovers touch at all. She's mad, reaches for her blouse and she's standing. "I took a risk coming up here with you," she says. "Some guy I don't know from Adam. What have you risked?"

Black eyes burn me up. "You risked *nothing!*"

Got the jeans and the blouse, and I'm gonna lose her.

"OK, Harper. I'll risk. *What the fuck do you want?*"

She turns, whole body that *shodō* deal. "You better fuck me like it's the last thing you'll ever get to do on this godforsaken earth."

Man, that's when Harper tells me about the beautiful dying.

"It's so beautiful," she says. "Right in the moment of coming, comes death."

She looks at me, and laughs again. Yeah it's that laugh. "You still don't get it."

"Get what?" I say.

"Never mind my sweet, innocent Mr. Rogers."

She let her clothes fall to the floor, her thumbs under the elastic waistband, her fingers touching her darkness through the thin nylon, and she's back on the bed.

"I wanna get fucked-up," she says. "And then you'll fuck me like you're the *man.*"

She picks up the second joint same as it's hers, Harper's joint, gets it between her lips, leans into the candle, and she's more beautiful, more dangerous, girl as weapon, sucking me in, a mouthful of smoke, and she blows the smoke into my mouth, and I take a hit, my mouth on hers, and I blow it in and she holds it and we smoke the whole joint that way.

"You got 'Stray Cat Blues'?" she says.

Harper sits on the bed so close her knee into mine as she rocks to the Stones swampy voodoo, her arms in the air again, smell of pot and sweat, the light brown hair curling under her arms, and I could die to kiss the sweet curve of her neck.

Her tits are wet with sweat, and there's sweat on my chest. I try to let the anxiety go, but it won't go 'cause I don't know what this chick gonna do next. One way it could go, it'll be all groovy. Another way, one false move and she'll be all over my case again. Hard to get into the moment when the moment is ready to explode.

Her and Mick sing that her mama don't know she can scream how she's screaming, don't know she can spit how she's spitting.

"Nothing's worth shit if you're not putting it on the line," Harper says. "Take your jeans off, *Mr. Rogers*."

Harper lays back on the bed, her eyes checking me out, and she pulls her panties down, kicks 'em off and she spreads her legs, feet on the rug and finally, finally, her golden brown snatch in the flickering light.

"What about birth control?" I say.

"What the fuck about it?" and she brings her legs together, covers her breasts with her arms, sits up.

"What if I'm not on the pill? What if you don't have a condom?"

She's got that goddamn stainless skull between her fingers as if it's some kinda voodoo charm and she's gonna hex me.

"Go look at your *Penthouse* and jerk off," she says. "This is your life, buddy, and it's about to pass you by."

And that was fucking it. I push Harper back down on the bed, and I'm on her, hold her arms tight, my chest against hers, the cold metal of that skull, my lips into hers and she bites my lip, slimy taste of blood, my blood, and I push her legs apart and she's so wet and she digs her black nails into my ass, nails ripping the skin, and I push into her and she's tight, I push in more, her black nails dig hard into my ass and I shove it in, I'm deep in her and she makes this weird high moan of a sound. I don't give a fuck about Harper, don't care if it hurts or she comes, don't care, and I fuck her same as it's my one and only chance ever to fuck a chick. Ram it into her again and again, and her weird high moan, the room gone baby gone, nothing but tits and snatch and pussy, her face contorting, eyes closed and a fuse lit at the base of my cock, red hot burning, and Harper cries out, *jouir*, and her waist bucks and bucks, and she grinds into me.

Days of the Crazy-Wild day for sure, man.

Thanks to Lord Jim and Harper, I start to find my way, which is funny 'cause in the end it's those two, as much as anyone other than me, who set me up for my demise. Lord Jim I'd been hanging with, and in those first days of knowing him I thought he was a heavy traffic freakster bro for sure. Hadn't seen Harper again, but whatever, my first fuck since losing Sweet Sarah. Nothing same as fucking a chick to amp up the self-confidence quotient.

I fuck therefore I am.

THE FREAK SCENE DREAM TRILOGY

But that was only the beginning.

Michael Stein. Writerman.

The young man. The Myth.

Michael Stein is obsessed with sex. Writerman too; only for Writerman the sex is more than sex. Sex is the door to intimacy, and transcendence. And women, especially one woman, his Visions of Johanna, is the only door he knows to escape into ecstasy, experience the Forever Infinite Ecstatic and free himself from himself.

For Michael Stein, the Sixties ended in the nut house. Where they put the crazies. His parents blamed his erratic behavior on drugs. Michael Stein just blames himself. After all, he broke his Sweet Sarah's heart.

Aware. Both Michael Stein and Writerman are aware they are living through one of the biggest social changes America has experienced. The trouble is, Michael Stein's not aware that the biggest social change has already changed, moved on down the line. Writerman, though, always The Warrior, always The Seeker, Writerman has a clue: The love is gone and all that's left is the drugs.

The Freak Scene Dream Trilogy is one long deep breath. The exhale is obsessive, transgressive. How macho meets feminism. How second chakra rises up to third. Through all the women: Sweet Sarah, Beat-Chick Elise, Jaded, Simone, Harper, Eve. A puff, a party, a tragedy—from marijuana to angel dust, teenage heartbreak to addiction, from "All You Need is Love" to the junkie garage rock of the New York Dolls.

How the dream died and what there is left after.

If you enjoyed, "True Love Scars," come along for more of the ride as Writerman struggles to escape his past and invent a brave new life. Along the way you'll meet Lord Jim's girlfriend, the seductive Jaded; Writerman's mentor, the infamous Sausalito Cowboy; and watch Writerman try out his Casanova moves on the tragically-scarred Beat-Chick Elise. Plus a second encounter with Harper. All this and much, much more in book two of the Freak Scene Dream Trilogy:

"DAYS OF THE CRAZY-WILD"
by Michael Goldberg

For more information about the Freak Scene Dream Trilogy, and "DAYS OF THE CRAZY-WILD":

www.truelovescars.com

If you want to keep up with what I'm up to as a writer and blogger, please sign up for the Days of the Crazy-Wild Communique at:

www.daysofthecrazy-wild.com/novel/email

ACKNOWLEDGEMENTS

I want to thank my wonderful family: Leslie, Joe, Anne, Norah and Sammy. You're the best!

This book could not have been written without the help of the 2008-2009 version of Dangerous Writers in Portland, OR. And I owe more than I can ever repay to Tom Spanbauer, the most dangerous of the Dangerous Writers. Thanks for listening, Tom, and for six years of support.

Thanks to the Writer's Cafe, September 2010 – November 2013, for your comments, support and advice.

My best buddy David Monterey is one of a kind for sure. They don't make friends like you anymore, Dave.

Thanks to Jolie Holland, Emme Stone, Brittany Flynn, James Cushing and Mark Mordue — you five were the first to read the Freak Scene Dream Trilogy, and your enthusiasm was and is appreciated.

Thanks to my wife Leslie Goldberg for the amazing cover drawing, Emme Stone for the cover design and Mary Eisenhart for copyediting.

Thanks to Jeff Rosen, Lacey Chemsak, Kevin Rice and Gloria Dixon for being so gracious regarding use of song lyrics.

Thanks to Charlie Haas, Julie Smith and Robert Wallace for the meaningful conversations about writing and publishing.

And to Bob Dylan, the Rolling Stones, Captain Beefheart, Neil Young, Jack Kerouac, J.D. Salinger, Richard Meltzer, F. Scott Fitzgerald, Jean-Luc Godard, François Truffaut, Robert Frank, Diane Arbus, Andy Warhol, Picasso, Salvador Dali, and all the other musicians, visual artists, film directors and writers who have been so much more than an inspiration.

— Michael Goldberg, April 2014

ABOUT THE AUTHOR

So what do you wanna know?

When I was a kid, rock 'n' roll and literature made life worth living.

Or rather, it was literature that rocked my world—"Treasure Island," "Crime and Punishment," the Hardy Boys books, the Oz books, all those sexy 007 novels—until I turned 12, and then rock 'n' roll—The Beatles, the Stones, Dylan, The Yardbirds, John Mayall's Blues Breakers—blew my mind, with literature a strong second.

Well girls trumped both, but that's another story.

I started writing my own stories in sixth grade and by high school I was certain that writing was my vocation.

So while my friends and I promoted dance-concerts at the high school (mostly so we could project psychedelic lights behind the bands), I was also writing for the school paper. And I did have one of those "Almost Famous" moments, writing *Creem* editor Lester Bangs and getting an encouraging letter back asking me to send him some record reviews (which he didn't end up using).

Fast-forward to 1975, the eve of the punk rock revolution, and I was in the thick of it, interviewing Patti Smith and The Ramones and the Talking Heads and Crime and so many more for stories that ran in the *Berkeley Barb* and the *San Francisco Bay Guardian.*

I had some close calls. The Clash nearly threw me out of the San Francisco recording studio where they were recording their second album, the Sex Pistols tried to break my tape recorder and Frank Zappa said if I was one of his fans he was in big trouble.

The life of a rock journalist.

Things did work out, and I spent 10 crazy years talking to everyone from George Harrison and George Clinton to Brian

Wilson and Stevie Wonder for *Rolling Stone* where I was an Associate Editor and a Senior Writer. My writing has also appeared in *Wired, Esquire, Vibe, Details, Downbeat, NME* and many more.

In 1993 I got hip to the Internet and by 1994 I'd founded *Addicted To Noise (ATN)*, the highly influential music web site. People said I was a distinguished pioneer in the online music space; *Newsweek* magazine called me an "Internet visionary."

I joined forces with SonicNet in 1997. I was a senior vice-president and editor in chief at *SonicNet* from March 1997 through May 2000. While running SonicNet editorial I interviewed Neil Young, Patti Smith, Lou Reed, Prince, Tom Waits, Metallica, the Smashing Pumpkins, Sonic Youth, Pavement, Sleater-Kinney and, and, and...

In 1997, *Addicted To Noise* won a Webby award for best music site, and a Yahoo Internet Life! award. While I was at *SonicNet* the site won Webby awards for best music site in 1998 and 1999, and also won Yahoo Internet Life! awards for three years running as best music site in 1998, 1999 and 2000.

I started writing the book that became the Freak Scene Dream Trilogy in the mid-2000s. You can expect the second book, "Days of the Crazy-Wild," to be available by August 2015. I currently write a monthly column, The Drama You've Been Craving, for the Australian version of *Addicted To Noise*.

And I publish the video-and-audio-intense culture blog, *Days of the Crazy-Wild* at www.daysofthecrazy-wild.com.

Any other questions?

PERMISSIONS

Lyrics for the following songs are by Bob Dylan:

Made in the USA
San Bernardino, CA
30 August 2014